P9-DOB-614

BLACK STORM COMIN'

DEMCO

To Ken, with all my love

If you purchased this book without a cover, you should be aware that this book is stolen property. It was reported as "unsold and destroyed" to the publisher, and neither the author nor the publisher has received any payment for this "stripped book."

This book is a work of fiction. Any references to historical events, real people, or real locales are used fictitiously. Other names, characters, places, and incidents are the product of the author's imagination, and any resemblance to actual events or locales or persons, living or dead, is entirely coincidental.

ALADDIN PAPERBACKS
An imprint of Simon & Schuster Children's Publishing Division
1230 Avenue of the Americas, New York, NY 10020
Copyright © 2005 By Diane Lee Wilson
Map by Derek Grinnell
All rights reserved, including the right of reproduction in whole or in part in any form.
ALADDIN PAPERBACKS and colophon are trademarks of Simon & Schuster, Inc.

Also available in a McElderry Books for Young Readers hardcover edition.
Designed by Kristin Smith
The text of this book was set in Adobe Caslon.
Manufactured in the United States of America
First Aladdin Paperbacks edition October 2006
10 9 8 7 6 5

The Library of Congress has cataloged the hardcover edition as follows:
Wilson, Diane L.
Black storm comin' / Diane Lee Wilson.—1st ed.
p. cm.
Summary: Twelve-year-old Colton, son of a black mother and white father, takes a job with the Pony Express in 1860 after his father abandons the family on their California-bound wagon train, and risks his life to deliver an important letter that may affect the growing conflict between the North and South.
1. Pony express—Fiction. [1. Pony express—Fiction. 2. Slavery—Fiction. 3. Identity—Fiction. 4. Racially mixed people—Fiction. 5. Self-acceptance—Fiction. 6. Frontier and pioneer life—Fiction. 7. West (U.S.)—History—19th century—Fiction. 8. United States—History—1815-1861—Fiction.]
I. Title: Black storm comin'. II. Title.
PZ7.W69057BI 2005
[Fic]—dc22
2004009438
ISBN-13: 978-0-689-87137-5 — ISBN-10: 0-689-87137-6 (hc.)
ISBN-13: 978-0-689-87138-2 — ISBN-10: 0-689-87138-4 (pbk.)

ACKNOWLEDGMENTS

My thanks to Fred Campbell-Craven for guiding me along the western end of the Pony Express route and to Susan Covington at Gold Trail School for providing additional research materials.

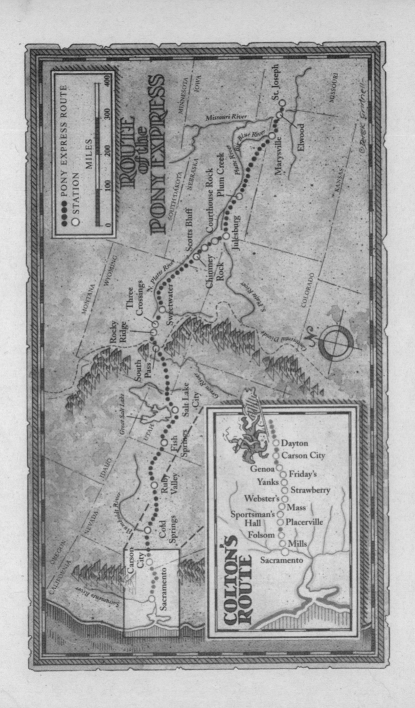

CHAPTER ONE

On the morning of September 16, 1860, my pa shot me. Maybe that's what set him to running. And, later, me to galloping.

Running, walking, galloping, plodding. Seems like one way or another we were always moving in those days, be it leaving something bad—like poor luck or general mean-spiritedness—or chasing after something good, like gold or land or any kinda job that'd keep a bowl of beans on the table.

He didn't mean to do it, of course—my pa didn't. I know that 'cause, somehow, in the blackness of that morning I caught the look on his face. When I close my eyes, I still see it. With no words at all it said, *I'd sooner shoot myself as my son.*

It was the last look I ever got from him.

We were somewhere in Utah Territory. God only knows where, 'cause we'd been chewing the same dust for days and still those mountains sitting low on the horizon looked to be no more'n knee high. But we kept moving toward 'em, one foot-achy, boot-heavy step at a time. We and about twenty other families, with all our worldly goods piled onto covered wagons that were hitched to teams that kept inching due west in one meandering line. Like the wobbly needle of a compass. Chasing hope. Or running from hurt. All of us following a dream.

The morning it happened, the sky was still dark. The night sentry—as usual—had fired his rifle straight up at 4 A.M. And that—as usual—had shot me right outta my blanket. After fifteen weeks on the trail I still wasn't accustomed to being wakened by gunfire.

Shivering, and rubbing my pimply arms to warm myself, I set about my chores. Laid some more wood on the fire. Rolled up the blankets—mine and Pa's. (He was already off gathering up our four oxen.) Pulled the bridle from its hook on the back of the wagon and set off to locate Ned, our one saddle horse.

Most mornings I liked doing that. Gave me time to think. Gave my feet time to uncurl and spread inside my boots, set for another long day. But this morning, as I stepped outside the circle of wagons, I was balancing on my toes cross the crunching sand. Word was we'd camped on the edge of Paiute territory, and I wasn't 'bout to be surprised by some painted stranger crouching behind sagebrush. Dang that Ned, anyway, for wandering off as he had a mind to.

The deep black sky, with only its onion sliver of moon, yawned over the empty land. Made me feel small, awful small. I kept walking, peering into the darkness, my heart thudding uneasily under my wool shirt. As I got beyond hollering distance of the circle of wagons I pulled up and looked over my shoulder, wondering if I should return. With their swooping canopies, the wagons seemed to slumber like pale, swaybacked horses. Here and there I saw cooking fires being coaxed to life. Tents were being struck, livestock gathered.

But it was quiet. People didn't talk much at this hour, specially worn-to-the-bone people like us.

Beyond the circle, no more'n pencil-thin shadows under the starlight, were the twin tracks we were all following. They'd been pounded into the desert by hundreds of wheels and thousands of hooves, and they shot straight west toward the mountains called the Sierra Nevada. Those tracks were like a couple of open arms, just begging us to follow 'em. *Follow to a better life,* they sang, *follow to gold and land and easy living. Others have done it,* they promised; *you could too.*

I was only twelve, but I'd spent enough of my days moving from place to place and back again to know that promises of easy living were no more'n words on the wind.

We'd started in Missouri, where I'd been born, then moved to Illinois, even though it was illegal for Ma, being colored, to cross the border into that state. Pa—who was white—had heard of work there milking cows, and so, jobs being scarce, we went anyway. He wasn't very good at it. The farmer complained that the cows got twitchy when Pa even looked at 'em, let alone laid a hand on their flanks. Didn't matter, 'cause somehow our cabin got burnt down. So we moved over to Kansas. For a while Pa worked in a dry-goods store there. But then there was some sorta trouble with "border ruffians" and lots of talk 'bout slave states and free states (you had to take a stand). Ma got a bucket of whitewash dumped on her, which wasn't an accident, and we were moving again. It was back to Missouri, where a letter was waiting for Ma. It'd come from a sister I didn't even know she had, a sister living in Sacramento, and Ma suddenly decided—as womenfolk do, and even though she was expecting a baby—that it was real important that we get there. Life would be better in California, she promised.

Huh. Promises again. Well, I had eyes, didn't I? I'd been walking this trail, hadn't I? So I knew you couldn't count on any such promises. The slapped-together crosses along its sides told me that plain enough. And all the cast-off furniture and the broke-down wagons and the bleached bones of animals that had given up pulling 'em. No, this trail was only a guide. It wasn't a promise for what would happen when we got there. It wasn't even a promise that we *would* get there.

I heaved a wearisome sigh. For close to four months we'd been trying, though. One day at a time. Fifteen miles a day. Every day the same. Except when we crossed the Platte River. That had eaten up three days. And when we stopped to bury the little German boy. He was run over one morning by his own wagon and killed flat out. We only made eight miles after stopping to bury him.

So that we could make our miles each day, we had to rise at four every morning for chores and be hitched and ready to move out at six. Then we had to be circled by four in the afternoon so we could drag ourselves through the same chores, eat, and get some sleep before the clock rolled round to four again. Numbers were what this journey was all about, it seemed. Numbers that kept rolling round like the wheels of the wagons. They could crush you, they could.

A horned toad, caught out in the morning cold and sluggish, tried to skitter away from my footfall. I managed to miss him, and he tilted his head to watch me pass, blinking solemnly. There was a sunken, leathery look to him, sorta like the one Ned had been wearing of late. We weren't even riding the ribby horse now, he'd gotten to looking so poorly. At the end of every day we turned him loose with the other livestock to graze the area inside the circled wagons. He must've thought we were funning him, 'cause there hadn't been a blade of grass to whistle on for two hundred miles. Sand and salt and scattered sagebrush were all that constituted this part of the territory. Even the jackrabbits were thin as rails, if you could spot one. So Ned had taken to sneaking out and away from the wagons, leaving me to track him down every morning. He did have a sense of humor.

The cold night wind was still blowing some, busy with its work of shifting the sands from one side of the desert to the other. A devilsome gust picked up a handful and blew it at me, and those little specks hit my cheek with the bite of broken glass. All I could do was turn my collar up and trudge on.

When I finally spotted the dark hump on the flat gray plain, I knew that Ned had heard me coming. His pointy ears said that. But that bold rascal didn't bother getting up. He stayed resting, his legs tucked under nice and neat, making me come to him. As I got closer, he nickered. *Good morning.*

I shook my head and squatted. "Good morning yourself, you sorry animal. Find anything to eat?" I scratched behind his ears while I spoke with him. The hairs there were stiff with yesterday's sweat and caked with the white dust that covered us all. There was a raised scar there too, where someone's rope had cut into him at some time. When I stopped working my fingers, he shook happily, let out a groan—like he knew the long day ahead of him, and of course he did—and climbed to his feet. I slipped the bridle on him and fastened it.

I didn't really need it. He'd have followed me anyway. Horses always did, always had. Don't know why. They just cottoned to me somehow. Made me feel special, and I liked that.

The piece of moon was lower in the sky as we headed back, tipping the sage with a frosty coat of silver. Seemed unreasonable that in just a few hours we'd be burning in a fearsome heat. Just like yesterday. Just like tomorrow.

Pa had gathered our four oxen by the time we got back to the wagon. That's 'bout all he'd managed, though. Those stubborn beasts did next to nothing for him on a good day, and this morning they were hardly budging.

"Give 'em a little inspiration, will ya, son?" Pa fought to make his voice cheery. Over the years I'd learned it took an awful lot to drown his spirits. But the waters were rising. I could see it in his face.

Flicking the ends of the reins, I stung first one ox and then the other. Ned was a no-nonsense animal, and he rushed to help, pinning his ears and raking his teeth cross the nearest flank, and if that didn't get them on their way! They came close to hurrying. While trying to get 'em yoked, Pa got himself stepped on, not once, but twice. Then one of the hickory bows that was already split opened up more. "Hang it all!" he shouted.

"You want me to finish hitching 'em?" I asked. I held some sway with oxen, too, it seemed. Leastways, more than my pa did.

"Sure," he answered. Through the morning's gloom I could see discouragement weighing him down. But Pa being Pa, he shook it off with an effort and replaced it with the confidence of a man holding all aces. "I'll take Ned and throw the saddle on him. Least he can do is carry his own pack." He forced a grin and took the reins. Ned snorted and followed.

I glared at our oxen. They rolled their eyes and licked their wide, wet noses with their wide, wet tongues. Not only were they a scrawny bunch, but if those imps of Satan had ever been broke to a hitch before Pa paid good money for 'em back in St. Joseph, then I'm a natural-born fool.

Shoving my shoulder into the near one, I whooped. "Get up!" I ordered. He wasn't convinced, so I grabbed hold of his ear, threatening to give it a good twist. Sullenly he stepped into place, his teammate moving with him. When I leaned into the second pair, they moved over before I could holler, and in no time at all I had 'em hitched. Sky wasn't even near pink. For once we wouldn't be the lone outfit everyone was waiting on.

Inside our wagon Ma was nudging my sisters through their chores. I knew what was coming and hunched my shoulders. Sure enough, there it was: little Willie's piercing wail. He was only a few days old, I understood that, but the one time he wasn't wailing, it seemed, was when he was sleeping—and that wasn't near often enough. Since our place was at the end of the line of wagons, Pa had taken to easing up on the oxen, letting 'em travel slow enough to put a little ear space between us and the others. He wasn't 'bout to provide any new excuses for them dropping us off at some two-cabin "settlement."

Folks already had their opinions 'bout our family belonging, mixed as we were and looking different from them. Some of those opinions had been expressed in passing at the creeks or while bent over collecting firewood. Others were held behind tight lips and turned shoulders. That was something I couldn't do anything 'bout. Animals I could manage. People were a whole different matter indeed.

"Here's your soda biscuit, Colton." Althea, the older of my two younger sisters, stuck her arm out over the wagon seat. "And some coffee." A tin cup followed. "It's cold," she warned. "Fire went out before the water could boil." She ruffled her feathers and disappeared back inside the canvas canopy. It was the same as her henhouse now. With Ma so worn and sickly from birthing my brother, and little Willie not giving her any sleep since, Althea had taken charge. She'd "rose to the occasion," as they say, though I don't think it'd stretched her much.

My stomach growled even before the biscuit passed my teeth. It was always growling of late, though you'd think it'd give up hope by now. The sour cake settled on my tongue and started to swell. It tasted like paste. When I twisted my neck and tried to swallow, I dang near choked. A swig of coffee was no help. It was only spit-warm, made with bitter water and more dust than beans. Too late I discovered a grasshopper trying to climb outta the cup by way of my tongue. I spat him—and the coffee—out.

"That's all you're getting, Colton," came Althea's voice outta the darkness, like it was spoke from God himself. Bossy for ten.

To my surprise, the man from the next wagon suddenly turned and headed our way. He was marching, like he'd taken orders he was none too happy 'bout having to deliver. "Your pa here?" he asked.

I didn't have to answer 'cause Pa was just coming round the wagon. "Mr. Suttles! Good mornin' to ya."

"Supposed to pass the word that there could be trouble today. Rifles to be at the ready."

Pa reached up to the wagon seat. "Got her right here." He smiled at the man.

Mr. Suttles stayed stone faced. "Try to remember what we told you 'bout using it," he said. "And for God's sake, fire at *them* and not us." He spun and stalked back to his own wagon.

Pa looked like he'd been whipped. Mr. Suttles was still making references to the first week, back in Kansas, when we'd all been a little jittery. Pa had shot off his rifle at a bear coming toward him in the night. He'd just missed hitting Mr. Suttles's brother. No one let us forget it.

Willie's crying climbed another earsplitting pitch. Pa and I exchanged helpless looks, then walked to the back of the wagon. Wedged in between a pine cupboard and boxes of breakables and three mismatched chairs and an iron kettle and quilts and pillows and Ma's precious tin buckets of rose cuttings was Ma herself. Or a shadow of Ma.

"Willie hasn't nursed all night," Althea announced, somber as a preacher. She was holding Jewel, our four-year-old sister, on her lap, braiding her hair into pigtails. "And there's no more rice and almost no cornmeal."

In a weak voice Ma scolded, "Hush now. We'll make do."

"He needs a doctor," Althea insisted.

No one scolded her for that. It was probably true. But where were you going to find a doctor way out here? Even the last settlement, if you could call a half dozen scattered shanties a settlement, was five days' ride behind us. And they probably hadn't seen a doctor themselves in the past year.

Pa started to go under then. He looked like a packhorse partway cross a river that finds itself loaded too heavy. Losing its footing, it goes tumbling and spinning, helpless against the current. Jewel started whimpering, low and gaspy, like she was going under too.

"Get on with you, now," Ma said. "Sun's coming up. All we can do is keep moving."

Pa nodded and trudged back round the wagon, and I followed. He pulled himself up into the seat. Fumbled with his rifle, a Hawkins .50 caliber. Cocked and eased the hammer, then cocked it again. Reached down to check his ammunition. His movements were jerky. Like he wasn't thinking, just acting. He kept digging for something in the bottom of the wagon, then sat up suddenly and moved the rifle cross his lap.

And that's when the gun went off.

CHAPTER TWO

What's happened?"

Ma's cry cut through my fog. In a rush that hitched my breath up short I felt the fierce burn in my leg, the throbbing ache on the side of my head. A thousand sharp stones poked into my cheek. All mixed up with that were the smells of dust and crushed sage and burnt gunpowder.

"Elbert?" Her cry held as much frustration as fear. She suspected someone—one of her own—was hurt. But she couldn't climb outta the wagon to help. "Colton?" Nothing but silence. "Althea! Go see what's happened."

And so it came to pass on that gray morning that the angels couldn't welcome me into the pearly gates 'cause of my little sister. She was shaking me so hard and yelling at me so loud that they must've looked down and decided I was deserving of a different fate.

"Colton! Colton!" In the hurricane of sensations her chicken voice kept pecking at me. She pushed at my shoulder. "Are you killed?" She pushed again, and then again, harder.

When I finally realized I wasn't—killed, that is, though I hurt something awful—her question struck me as kinda funny. Guess the angels were right in leaving me behind, 'cause something evil sprang up inside me then. I decided to see just what she'd do if she thought her big brother was dead. So, in spite of the hot pain in my leg and the dull one in my head, I held my breath and squeezed my eyes shut.

No use. She saw through me straightaway. You can't fool women, I've learned, even girls that are only practicing to be women.

"Pa!" she wailed.

Strange that he didn't come running. I opened one eye just a bit, but the wagon seat was empty. All I saw was the mean, dark barrel of his rifle pointing off into nothingness.

"Ma!"

There was a rustling inside the wagon. Willie had worn himself out with his wailing, but now Jewel was in full voice. The canvas accordioned up; Ma peeked through the opening. The worry in her eyes was sharp enough to stop my pretending, and I raised up on one elbow.

"He's not hurt at all, Ma."

"Am too!" I protested. "Look!" I pointed at the sticky stain low on my pant leg. Dang if it wasn't burning now. And my head! Ow!

"Oh, Lord!" Ma cried. "You've been shot! Where's your pa?" The answer to her question came in the sound of hoof-beats. Riding *away* from us. But that couldn't be. "Elbert?" she called. "*Elbert?*"

Time seemed to grind to a halt. To a one, we fell silent, trying to digest the situation: Pa had left us, it seemed—at least for now, but surely he'd come back—and we were stuck in Utah Territory. Sick baby, sick ma, shot kid. Somewhere the buzzards started stretching their wings.

I sat up kinda gingerly, examining my leg and trying to get my bearings. Now, in the past few months I'd noticed how people helped one another in a situation. If someone's wheel broke, why, someone else would stop and help mend it. And if someone's water ran dry, well then, there was always a full bucket hanging from another wagon and a dipper at the ready.

Only, that help didn't seem to apply to our family, and nobody had to waste their breath explaining why: It was because we were colored. Well, we were part colored. Ma's ma had been colored. She'd been a slave in Missouri and was dead now. But Ma's pa—he'd been a white man. The two of 'em never married, that much I knew, and Ma had been raised— as a free person—by a preacher and his wife.

When it came time for Ma to marry, she chose herself a white man, just like her own pa. Or more likely, he chose her. Pa's crazy in love with Ma. Or he was. Maybe he's just crazy now.

I didn't want to think 'bout that and shoved it outta my head. Lordy, how it was hurting! Everything seemed topsy-turvy of a sudden.

Surely Pa would come back. When we first headed out cross the prairies, Pa'd picked a handful of wildflowers for Ma every day. And every day Ma'd squealed like a young girl, though by my calculations she had to be 'most thirty. She kept those shaggy bouquets in a thick blue glass in the back of the wagon and didn't seem to mind at all when the life went outta 'em and the stems drooped and the petals shriveled. She didn't seem to notice the difference.

I guess Pa was the same way when he looked at Ma: He didn't see anything 'cept a flower; he didn't take notice of her color. But other folks? They look at us—Ma and me and

Althea and Jewel, and now Willie too—and they see the color first off. They don't see nothing after that.

Which, I suppose, is why they didn't want to let Pa join their wagon train. I never heard him say so directly. But every day when he came back from trying to sign us on in St. Joseph, he had a new frown and a new list of "required" supplies. In two weeks' time his little wad of bills, our "seed money," was starved right outta his pocket. Until one day, late in May, he busted in the door to announce, "We're off! We're paid up and we're leaving tomorrow morning for California. Golden hills, green valleys, and the prettiest house for the prettiest wife."

What we learned soon enough was that "paid up" meant nothing more'n they didn't actually boot us off their ol' train. "Paid up" meant they tolerated us tagging along at the tail, suffered us to join in the nightly circling of the wagons—for safety reasons, I heard the boss tell someone who'd complained. But the dipper was never extended when our bucket mysteriously turned to salt water overnight, and some mornings when the other wagons were headed toward the horizon, we were still tugging on our oxen, trying to get 'em hitched.

So now, when a gun had been shot off and Ma had hollered out, there wasn't a one of us who expected help. But someone did ride up: the wagon boss. Following on foot came some of the others.

That got me off the ground fast enough. Trouble was, I stood up so sudden that my head tried to explode and my leg all but broke underneath me. It shamed me to look weak in front of these men. I grabbed hold of the iron-rimmed wheel so tight you couldn't have pried it loose with a team of horses. I turned to face 'em.

"What's happened here?" The wagon boss, Mr. Haphorn, growled his question. He greeted any disturbance of his orderly wagon train with a curled lip.

Words wouldn't come for me. Althea slinked away like a cat to climb into the dark safety of the wagon and peek out. I was so scared; my face felt so hot. I worked my mouth but . . . still nothing.

"He's been shot, Mr. Haphorn." Ma's voice was a mix of respect and fear. I knew it was taking all her strength just to hold herself up close to the wagon's side and talk to him. "Can you help him, please? Sir?"

Mr. Haphorn's gaze swung back to me. "You need help, son?"

I moved my head from side to side. That was the manly thing to do, I knew, but it sure scrambled the images of people and wagons and animals. I blinked hard and they settled into their rightful places.

"Who was holdin' the gun?"

Now, that was a question none of us wanted to answer. We all knew Pa's standing. He didn't need the extra blame.

Mr. Haphorn heaved an impatient sigh. "Where is he?"

"We don't know . . . sir." The words came squeaking outta my mouth.

"Ma'am?"

"Like my son said, we don't rightly know, sir. He's probably just gone off for a bit to gather himself, you know. If one of you could kindly go fetch him, we'll be ready to move out. Colton's got the oxen all hitched, as you can see."

A rider appeared from the other direction. "He's busted outta here. Thought I saw him headin' north, through the sand hills, but I lost him."

"Look for him again," Mr. Haphorn said.

The man wheeled his horse and galloped off. A couple of the others ran for their horses and rode after him.

Mr. Haphorn looked down on us like we were the sorriest bunch of jugheaded nags he'd ever seen, animals not worth saving. I knew he wasn't of a mind to. The lightening sky revealed his reddened cheeks. "Your husband in the habit of runnin' off?"

"No, sir."

"He crazy or somethin'?"

Ma's humiliation showed itself in the pause. "No, sir," she answered quietly. Her fingers were gripping the wagon board so hard they were shaking.

Then the bullet: "What do you plan on doin' if we can't find him?"

"He'll be back. I'm sure of it."

"And if you're wrong?"

Ma pursed her lips. "We're paid up all the way to California, Mr. Haphorn."

His horse, a big-boned bay, shook his head and snorted, like he was expressing an opinion shared by his rider. "Ma'am, are you aware there's folks in California that don't want you and your kind in their state?"

Ma didn't answer. Just kept looking steady at him. That was rasping him some, I could tell.

"You got your free papers?" he asked with sudden heat.

Ma bristled. "No. I've never needed 'em 'cause I've never been a slave."

He shook his head. "Doesn't matter. Without your husband, anyone in California can claim you're a runaway.

You want to risk that? You want to lose your young'uns?"

Willie started his wailing again, like he understood, and that was 'bout all Ma could take. "What is it you want us to do, Mr. Haphorn?"

"I want you off my wagon train. I want you to agree to my settin' you down in the next town we come to."

"No," she said, simple as that, and loosed her grip on the wagon board and collapsed back onto her pillow inside the canopy. Willie's crying sounded muffled, and I knew she'd pressed him to her breast, trying to quiet him, trying to keep from irritating Mr. Haphorn any more than we already had.

He grunted. "Damn mongrels." Glaring down at me, he spat the words. "Look at you, with your tail between your legs, shivering like you got no backbone. You're ready to run off like your pa, ain't you?"

I was still gripping the wagon wheel, balancing on my one good leg and feeling like everything that I knew as true and dependable was spinning away from me. All I could do was shake my head.

He raised his voice, kept up his arguing. "You're sick," he hollered at Ma, "you got no menfolk—"

"We got Colton!" Althea said, popping her head over the wagon seat. She was blazing mad. Mr. Haphorn tried to stare her down, but she fastened her two dark eyes on him, as she could do, and he was the one that looked away first.

"Geez . . . ," he started to swear. He shook his head and slammed his fist onto the saddle horn. Giving up, he hollered, "Have it your way. But he's as good as dead out there by himself, and I ain't got time to play nursemaid to any of yourn." He looked over his shoulder and called to a man waiting and watching beside a team of mules. "Hank! Can you spare your brother to drive this wagon today?"

"I can drive the wagon," I spoke up. No squeaking this time. Not even a *sir.*

He whirled and pinned his narrowed eyes on me. But if Althea could stare him down, so could I. No little sister of mine was gonna outdo me. I stood tall, even though my gunshot leg was paining me something fierce, and looked directly into his scowling face.

He jerked his chin toward the oxen. "Then, let's see you get 'em in line."

The near ox, the one with the mean-looking red splotch over his eye, swung his head round and gave me a look. If an animal could sneer, he was doing it. With my heart giving rabbit kicks, I pulled the braided leather goad from under the wagon seat. It felt heavy in my hand. Pa'd let me practice with it a few times, but since he wasn't much good at using it himself, I hadn't learned a lot. I took a deep breath. Snapping my wrist, I flicked the tangled lashes. "Get up!" I ordered.

Nothing. The silence roared in my ears. In that moment of failure I was aware of a swishing tail, an impatient cough, a stamping foot. I took a step closer, raised my arm high, and yelled, "Get up!" The goad came whistling down on hide.

At that the oxen plunged forward. The wagon tongue creaked, the wheels groaned in resistance, then slowly began turning. We were moving! I snapped the goad again. "Gee!" I called, and the four oxen leaned to the right, still moving, angling now toward the twin tracks of the trail. I stepped with 'em, forcing myself to ignore the flames shooting up through my injured leg. *Just keep putting one foot in front of the other,*

I told myself. *And smile, smile to stop the scream that's rising in your throat.* But oh, Lordy Almighty! I wanted to cry out. What was I doing walking in my pa's place and taking part in leaving him out here in this wasteland?

The wagon wheels rose up over a little ridge, then dropped with a rattle and a bang onto the other side. That knocked the gun to the floorboard with a thud, and I jumped.

"Hold on there," Mr. Haphorn said.

"Whoa," I ordered.

Riding up to the motionless wagon, still looking down on me with that curled lip of his, he said, "I better take the gun. Don't want any more accidents." He reached for it.

I didn't want to let him have it. No man would. I should've spoke up and said, "No, thank you, sir. We'll keep the gun and be just fine with it." But I was scared he would leave us behind, leave us all alone in the territory with no one and no food, and soon we'd be nothing more'n another pile of bleached bones on the side of the trail. And so I let him take the gun and prayed that he'd take us along too.

The wagons lined up and began moving west. We took our place at the tail end. The morning wind rushed straight at us, trying to push us back, it seemed. It threw sand round hooves and wheels, tried covering 'em up, holding 'em down. I put my chin on my chest along with the oxen and kept plodding. To the north the hills began shifting again. A low, sad moan hummed cross the desert. That made me shiver. It was only the sands, I knew, but somehow, that morning, they sounded an awful lot like my pa, crying out for help.

CHAPTER THREE

I don't know if we got the kinda trouble that day that Mr. Haphorn was expecting, 'cause rifles were no help.

It was a storm that attacked us first. Wickeder than any I'd ever seen. 'Most as soon as the wagons started moving, in fact, the sun was snuffed out at our backs and an allover gloom kept the day from arriving. The wind that had been shifting the sands round died down to nothing, and it got awful still. Awful prickly quiet. You could hear the air rushing in and outta the animals' wet noses, and the sands crunching and collapsing under the iron-rimmed wheels, and the stiff canvas rubbing against the hickory bows. But you couldn't hardly breathe yourself 'cause the air had got so heavy. It smelled damp and earthy. Moldy, like when you lean down into a well. And it took on a peculiar watery green color that had the effect of lighting up all the desert colors. The sage came green and the sand white, and the ever present, ever distant mountains turned all shades of blue and purple. It was pretty, all right, but it gave me a mighty twitchy feeling too.

And then a white-hot crackle of lightning burned through the darkening sky straight to earth. *Boom!* That made the hairs on my head stand to and made the girls cry out and

Willie shriek to wake the dead. But Ma? She hadn't spoke a word since we left camp. Just sank back among her things and let me drive us away from her husband and my pa. Her silence scared me.

I thought for certain we'd circle up and wait it out, but we didn't. We kept moving toward the storm, and it toward us. There was some more lightning, bolts that ripped the sky cloth apart and blinded me with their white fire. There were cannon booms of thunder that rocked the ground under my feet. And then, cross the desert, came a sheet of rain so thick you couldn't see through it. It was like a great gray curtain closing off the mountains, shutting us away from our goal, setting us apart, even, from each other. One by one it began drenching the wagons ahead of us. It came on so fast that before you could gulp, it was at our first yoke of oxen, then the second. I watched it streak their coats gray with dust-turned-to-mud, then with streams of dirty water rushing down their sides. They hung their heads under the deluge and kept plodding.

I braced as it hit me 'cause it came down *hard*. I was so wet so fast I might as well've jumped in a river. Nothing I could do 'bout it. I hunched my shoulders and held steady. That's what Pa would've done. I wondered if, wherever he was, he was getting as wet.

For a miserable spell we kept working our way west, though we couldn't see where we were going. Rainwater built up round hooves and wheels just like the sand had been doing. Since we were at the back of the long line, we got the worst of the trail. What had been smooth ruts before turned to slippery troughs full of ankle-deep quicksand. The oxen struggled. They tried hard enough, but their hooves kept sliding out from underneath 'em. When the spotted one fell to his knees, our progress came to a sudden stop. I ran forward to give him some encouragement, forgetting my sore leg, and yelped in pained surprise. That put the scare into him. With a mighty effort he began clambering to his feet, moaning at the mistreatment. His efforts jostled the wagon such that even with the deafening downpour, I heard the wood snap.

Fighting the sick feeling in my stomach, I hurried round the wagon. Sure enough, one of the wheels had got stuck and twisted in a steep-sided rut. Two spokes had broken already. Wondering if the rest would hold, I hollered to the oxen, and they leaned into their work. The damaged wheel wobbled crazily. Its creaking crescendoed and exploded in popping splinters as two more spokes snapped. A shudder ran through the wagon. "Whoa!" I yelled just in time. The oxen stopped and the broken wheel stopped and the other wagons kept moving, and before you could say "God bless," we were cast adrift, on our own in the rain-soaked wilderness.

I must've stood there fifteen minutes, balancing on one leg and letting the rain beat down on me and just staring at the busted wheel. How long had I been in charge of my family? Not half a morning, and already I had us stranded.

Standing there like that, I got to thinking 'bout the little German boy who'd been crushed by his family's wagon. I guess 'cause it'd been raining that day too. We all ran ahead when his ma screamed, then stood looking at him, too helpless to move. Funny thing was, there wasn't a mark on him. Just a little line of blood trickling outta his nose, and that kept getting washed away by the rain. His mother cradled him in her arms and cried and cried. Two of the men fetched shovels and began cutting a grave right there in the wet prairie. Someone else brought a sheet and wrapped him in it. We all gathered round the grave—all except my pa— and listened to Mr. Egan recite the Lord's Prayer. Then we traveled on like it had never happened.

It was the rain that bothered me the most. I remember wondering for days if the water would trickle down to the boy's body, if the drops would soak through that thin sheet and bead up on his waxy skin. I wondered if he would feel the cold.

As I glanced down at my own hand clutching the wagon, I noticed the drops beading up on my cold skin. With a hard shiver I shook 'em off. Felt like I was shaking off death itself. It was that near.

I didn't want to tell Ma about my failure. I couldn't. So I just stood beside the broken wheel, numbly noticing the hot tears on my frozen cheeks. My boots filled up with rainwater. Didn't matter. We wouldn't be walking away from this one.

After the rain had passed, the sky shone itself a blinding blue. The sun stoked its fires and set the land to steaming. Vapors drifted round the clumps of sagebrush like captured clouds. Slapping the rain off my hat, I looked up and saw a spectacle the likes of which I'd never seen. Off to the north, and stretching clear across the sky, was a rainbow—not a single one, but a double. The yellows and oranges and greens were just as bright as store-bought ribbons, and the two bands were stacked perfectly, one on top of the other. The words *terrible majesty* came to mind, something I must've heard from a preacher at some time or nother; and I was stirred with feelings of awe and some hope.

The inside of the wagon was still awful quiet. I knew I had

to break the news to Ma that we were pretty well stuck, but while I was deciding how to say it, I saw a horse and rider coming down the trail. I couldn't see the wagons anymore. They'd disappeared beyond a muddy ridge. Or maybe they'd been swept away. The horse, dark colored, was coming slow 'cause the deep-rutted trail was sloppy wet. There was something strange about the rider, something 'bout the headgear he was wearing. As the pair got closer, I realized the rider was a woman wearing a sunbonnet. What had got me confused was she was riding her horse cross-saddle, just like a man.

She rode right up to the oxen and jumped down, never minding the mud splashing her skirt. Tossed me a motherly smile so warm it made my throat grow thick, made me wish that, just for a few minutes, I could be a boy again instead of a man. Not have so much responsibility. She walked straight past me and climbed into the wagon, to see to Ma and Willie, I suppose, 'cause she shooed Althea and Jewel out. Whispering to each other and looking scared, they came and stood by me. They stared at the broken wheel and then the endless wilderness running in all directions from us. I started to point out the rainbows, but they were gone. Like he'd been pinched, Willie took up screaming, and I felt the sun burn on my neck hotter than ever.

Althea was staring down the trail behind us. "You think Pa's comin' back?"

"Course he is," I answered brightly. With a guilty jolt I realized I sounded just like him.

"Where did he go?" Jewel asked above the wailing.

"Most likely to find a doctor," I answered. "'Cause Willie's sick. But he'll be coming back soon."

Althea gave me a sharp look, charging me with lying. I shrugged my shoulders. What'd she want me to say? That I figured we could last maybe two days out here after our water ran out and the oxen died and the buzzards started circling? *If* it was buzzards that found us first and not some worse kinda fate. There were plenty to choose from.

A terrible cracking sounded inside the wagon, wood splintering from wood. I started to go see what it was, but the woman with the bonnet climbed out carrying the spindled legs from one of Ma's favorite chairs.

"Now then," she said. "Let's get this wheel fixed so you can make it into camp before supper's through." Looking up the trail ahead, a sort of triumphant expression on her face, she snorted, "Self-minded fools!"

She bent over the busted wheel. "You got an ax somewhere?" I dug for it and handed it over, but she wouldn't take it. Just pointed at one of the broken spokes. "Think you can knock it outta there?"

Well, I was sure enough gonna try. Felt good to be doing something toward getting us outta this mess. In a couple of good bangs I had it knocked loose. I attacked the others with all the vigor my twelve-year-old arms held. The traitorous spokes must've known they weren't long for this world, 'cause it only took a few swipes apiece.

The woman measured a chair leg against the socket in the wheel, then handed it to me. "Whittle it down some, just around the ends. And not too much, mind you."

I put all my concentration into it. Took a few short stabs that missed the wood completely. Althea snickered. Focused my eyes, stabbed again, and knocked off a chunk of wood.

"Good!" the woman exclaimed, and I never felt prouder or more important in my life. Together we worked the chair legs into place. The wheels were swollen with the rain and I was grateful for her help. Once we finished, she pointed to the wood chips knocked off by the ax. "Better save those for shims," she said. "When the sun dries the wheels, our hand-fashioned spokes are liable to work loose. You can shove the chips into the gaps. Just keep a close eye on 'em."

I nodded. "Thank you, ma'am."

She looked over our oxen—two of 'em lying down and the other two standing like their hooves had grown roots into the mud. "Can you get 'em moving?"

I nodded again and showed her my goad.

"I'd like to stay and help you along, but I'm already in hot water for coming back in the first place. But I'll be keeping an eye out for you."

"Thank you," I said. "We'll make it."

She started to turn, seemed to think better of it. Laying her hands on my shoulders and speaking like she was angry, she said, "The key is sticking together. Remember that. You stand by each other and you'll do fine, no matter what happens."

After that she climbed on her horse and rode off. We set off behind her. My hurt leg hollered at the first few steps. I ignored it, and sometime later it went silent and numb. The oxen still struggled in the muddy ruts, so the going was slow. But the damaged wheel turned and the makeshift spokes held. As the sun baked the earth into a gummy mess, I got to worrying that we'd get stuck again. But I kept on the oxen and they kept moving. Hours passed. The sun slid over our heads. My very bones ached. The sky faded from blue to purple to black, and still we were plodding along. When the stars came out, the oxen started protesting with a mournful bellowing, but I kept the goad to 'em, too scared to stop and pass the night alone in the desert. And then, as we climbed over a ridge, there was the wagon train, circled, in a hollowed-out area below us. Campfires were glowing all throughout the darkness, and I don't think I'd ever seen a more welcome sight.

I didn't want to bother anybody by pushing into the circle, so I just drove the team up near to it, still keeping a little ways off. To save time in the morning, I even left the oxen yoked for the night, though I unhitched 'em. "You're gonna have to eat at the same plate tonight, boys," I told 'em, "'cause I'm not about to get left behind tomorrow from chasing you down."

I tried to talk to Ma, but she was tight lipped and not herself. I think maybe she was feverish. Even Willie wasn't making any noise, not crying or whimpering, just lying there in his blanket like a worm in a cocoon. Jewel was sound asleep atop the bureau with her mouth hanging open. Though she was beginning to look as worn out as Ma, Althea was still climbing 'bout the wagon, trying to put things right by sheer willfulness. She handed me some dried apples and another soda biscuit, already half eaten. "You want I should try and start a fire?"

I knew she would've, but truth be told, I wasn't sure I'd be awake long enough to eat anything warm. "No, I'm too tired to even set up the tent. Think I'll just crawl under the wagon and sleep."

"But it's wet!"

"So am I," I answered. Plopping onto the ground right then and there, I fought with my boots. The leather was wet and swollen so much it was glued to my skin and my squishy socks. My pants were still wet at the seams. Carefully I rolled up one pant leg past the bloodied area and felt round the wound. From what I could tell in the dark, there was some skin missing from my shin and a small hunk of meat with it, but the bone itself wasn't hurt. Now that I had time to sit and think on it, though, it started throbbing again.

Best tonic for that was sleep, and I didn't need a doctor to buy any. Just as I was crawling under the wagon, a quilt dropped onto my backside. It was the double-thick, extra-heavy one that Ma had sewn from scraps of wool and stuffed with straw. The one we affectionately called the ugly quilt. Not much to look at—none of the colors matched, and so Ma had gone crazy with fancy stitching—but it was the warmest, most comfortable one we had. "Thank you," I murmured, knowing Althea had sent it. Wrapping its warmth round me, I curled up square in the middle of the four wheels, with the dark wagon bed above making for me a starless sky. My head fell onto my arm, my eyes closed. Sleep was pulling at me. But there was another ache that I had, an ache in my heart, and just before I slipped into unconsciousness, I silently mouthed, *Where are you, Pa?*

CHAPTER FOUR

Even before the sentry's gun went off the following morning, I was outta the quilt and hurrying round in the dark to make sure we wouldn't get left behind. My leg was fairly howling, but I had the oxen hitched and waiting when the people inside the circle began stirring. No one said anything when they saw we'd made it. Even the nice lady who'd helped us yesterday stayed behind the fence of wagons. She busied herself getting breakfast for her family but kept glancing over, worried like. I made myself stand tall, as much as to say *We're still together and we're doing fine.*

My stomach wanted to argue that point, 'cause the cooking fires were sending out some mighty tantalizing smells that were pure torment to it: fried corn mush and molasses beans and bubbling coffee. I didn't know whether to pinch my nose to stop the suffering or simply let my mouth drool. Althea climbed down to stand beside me, looking over at the wagons and rubbing her arms and shivering. She handed me some more dried apples, along with a solitary piece of hard candy, sticky with dust.

"Where'd you get this?" I asked.

She shrugged. "I got it. But you can have it."

I dropped it into my pocket. Knowing it was there for later was near as good as tasting it now. I bit off a piece of apple. "How's Ma?"

Althea turned her sad and solemn face toward me. Her eyes burned in their hollows. "Something's not right with her," she whispered. "She's leaving us, I think. Just like Pa did."

The apple went sour. I got a cold, thorny feeling inside me, like winter was blowing in and planning on staying. I swept it outta there. Had to. Had to do it then and there or it'd take me down, I knew it.

"Maybe there's a doctor in the next town," I said, hearing myself sound as blue-sky hopeful as Pa again. "Been days since we passed by one. Got to be another town soon."

Althea looked at me funny, like maybe I was talking stuff and nonsense. Silent as a ghost, she began backing away, not making a sound, not moving her limbs, just sorta floating. Up and into the wagon she floated, and she and Ma and Jewel and even little Willie stayed silent. Everything stayed silent. Everything 'cept the buzzing in my head that was growing louder and louder, until I couldn't think straight.

The sentry's second gunshot blasted away the buzzing. Men hollered and wheels creaked and the big circle of wagons began unwinding. When the last one had straightened on the trail, yanked with the others toward the mountains like some giant pull toy, I nudged our oxen into line. They bawled their complaints, and my sore leg and feet echoed 'em. Didn't seem right to start off the day with an empty stomach and damp boots, but there was nothing I could do 'bout it. Had to keep going. Had to get Ma and my sisters and new brother to California. Glancing ahead at the mountaintops, just showing pink against a gray sky, then down at the ruts that ran toward 'em, I started stepping off our fifteen miles.

It was still early in the morning when I heard the hoofbeats thundering along the trail behind us. It sounded like a lone rider, coming fast and hard, and for a fleeting second I thought it might be Pa. But there was an urgency in the hoofbeats that spoke of danger. I guessed we were done for.

Ahead of me heads started turning. Men grabbed their rifles and started aiming into the dawn, which of course meant they were pointing at me. I wondered if it was gonna be bullets or arrows that punched holes through me first. I wondered if anyone would dig a grave for me, like they had for the other boy. Swallowing hard, I studied the ground and kept walking.

That's when the little hawk set himself down on my shoulder. I near jumped outta my boots, 'cause I sure as heck wasn't expecting that. With the rising sun I'd taken off my coat, so his claws, sharp as teeth, gripped right through my shirt to my skin. They pulled back and forth as he fought for balance. My heart kicked with excitement, but I turned my head real slow, so as not to scare him. The sight of him made my breath catch in my throat.

Slick as a bullet, he was, with a little round head, blue as gun smoke. His back was reddish and all covered with spots, like a cat. When he tipped his head to get a better look at *me*, my heart bucked. Something in his eye, which was round and black and near big as a nickel, was simply ablaze. He *owned* his world, he seemed to be telling me. Owned it! Soared above it and over it, came and went as he pleased. Did I want to?

I almost forgot 'bout the hoofbeats then. All of a sudden

they were upon us—and just that fast, gone. A lone rider crouched atop a powerful-looking bay, galloping flat out.

"It's the Pony mail!" someone called.

The voice broke the spell. The little hawk lifted off my shoulder. Smooth as glass, he soared up and over the next wagon, dipped, then up and over the wagon ahead, and kept going until he was no more'n a speck against the morning sky. A shrill *klee-klee-klee* sounded as he disappeared, and I never felt more earthbound.

Something changed in me that morning. When that hawk squeezed his claws into my shoulder, it filled me up with a longing to go with him. I didn't want to plod beside oxen anymore. I wanted to gallop. I wanted to lift off the earth and go somewhere, to fly over the ground like that smoke-colored hawk.

A bittersweet ache wrapped me like a cloud. Took some time to realize that Jewel was looking out the front of the swaying wagon, staring into the sky like I was. "Where'd your birdie go?" she asked.

My face flushed hot. Here I was thinking the fool-crazy thoughts of a child instead of concentrating on getting my family to where they needed to be. I packed those thoughts away tight. They weren't for me. "He went to California, I suppose," I answered her. "Maybe we'll see him when we get there." *If we get there,* I added silently.

Soon as the sun cleared the horizon, it started beating us up with its heat. Brighter and hotter it shone, reflecting off the white sands like a thousand mirrors. By mid morning it even hurt to breathe, 'cause taking in the desert air was like sucking fire into your lungs. There wasn't a speck of shade to be had. Far as the eye could see it was just sand and rocks and a scattering of brittle greasewood.

By the time the sun was overhead, the horizon had turned shimmery with heat. Lifting my chin and squinting, I couldn't begin to tell where the land ended and the sky began. There was a time when, for 'bout an hour, I even thought I saw a lake ahead. That made my aching legs step lighter 'cause they sure wanted to be rid of those boots and go wading. Though we kept walking toward it, the lake kept shifting, first showing, then disappearing, then showing itself again. I got to thinking it was just one of those dream sightings—mirages, I think they call 'em—that isn't really there. And after that I got to thinking that maybe the hawk had been a mirage too. That made me sad. Made the sun burn hotter, my blistery feet swell more. Made me want to give up like Pa had.

Those were low times. But they weren't the lowest.

Late in the afternoon the wagons circled up near a ramshackle stone building that was missing a roof. There was water nearby, I heard, though when I followed the livestock to it, I found it was no more'n a muddy hole in the ground that smelled like something had fallen in and died. I was so parched that I shouldered up to the edge with 'em anyway and cupped my hand. The thick, yellowish liquid was hot, and dang if it didn't burn my skin like a horse liniment. Crouching eyeball-to-eyeball with a weary mule, I watched as he swallowed the nasty stuff. It didn't appear to kill him— right off, anyway—so I lifted my hands to my own lips. Lordy! No home-brewed tonic ever tasted worse. My throat clamped shut, but some liquid got by, and then my stomach put up a good fight. Thinking maybe I was gonna be sick,

I quickly soaked my handkerchief and staggered back to our four bellowing oxen. As I wiped the trail dust outta their noses, I warned 'em to keep a close eye on me and not drink the water if they should see me fall over anytime soon.

Althea was waiting in the front of the wagon. She sat real still, staring at her folded hands in her lap, not talking.

"How's Ma?" I asked.

She shook her head.

"Willie?"

Same response.

"I'm gonna go see if there's a doctor anywhere," I told her. "The spring's awful bad tasting, so if there's any rainwater left, drink that. And try to get Ma to take some." She nodded, sighed, and climbed back inside the wagon.

Feeling like I was buckling under a too-heavy yoke of my own, I hurried toward the roofless stone building. It looked to've been the sorry victim of a recent fire. Its sides were blackened, and some charred remains along an outside wall showed there must've been a lean-to attached at some time. Part of the chimney had tumbled down too, leaving a broken-off stump pointing at the sky. The corral had been newly built, though, 'cause the rails were still splintery and fresh looking. It held three horses—two bays and a roan—that were awful fat and sassy for such pitiful surroundings. One of the bays turned his head to watch me, and right off I recognized him as the one that'd gone galloping by us that morning. Something in his eye, the same blazing black look that I'd seen in the hawk's eye, made my heart skip over a beat.

The building's insides—if you could call 'em that, being open to the sky, and all—appeared empty 'cept for a smelly, dirty-colored dog lying by the hearth. Too small to do anybody any good, he didn't even bother to bark at me. Just looked up, then went back to chewing the fleas near his stubby tail. Only when I stepped inside did he stop his scratching and climb to his feet. He looked scared, like he was ready to run off.

"It's okay," I soothed, and he tested the wag in his tail and decided to stay put.

"You got any tobacco?"

The gravelly voice made me jump near outta my shirt. My head whipped round, searching. Behind the rumpled curtain of blankets strung cross the room, back in a shadowy corner, was a man lying on a makeshift cot. And he was watching me close as death itself. Lifting one finger, he beckoned to me.

As if I had no control over my own feet, they started moving toward him. I measured the distance to the doorway. The man was half naked and hairy, his pale belly wrapped in a stinking bandage. It looked like he might've lain in the same spot for a month without moving. My neck prickled with warning.

"Tobacco," he repeated as I got closer and the stench got stronger. He turned a watery eye up toward me. "You got any?"

I shook my head. "No, sir."

He cussed some and made a flapping, dismissive motion with his hand. "Then, get the hell outta here and leave me alone."

But I couldn't go yet. "Pardon me," I said, "is there a doctor anywhere in the area?"

He rumbled like a bee-stung grizzly. Lifting the grimy bandage to show a fist-size hole black as night and crawling with maggots, he sneered, "You think I'd be layin' here rottin' to death if there was a doctor in the area? What kinda jackass are you? Get out, I say!"

I got out, sure enough, and gladly, too, the dog flinching as I scrambled by.

Feeling more hopeless than ever, I returned to our wagon and unhitched the oxen. Most of the other teams had drunk by now, so I led our oxen to the smelly water. They pawed at it and bawled some but eventually gave in and drank. There wasn't any choice in the matter. Then I turned 'em loose inside the wagon circle with the others. Just let someone boot us out if they dared.

I was feeling dizzy again; it was still awful hot. And downhearted and hungry and tired. It occurred to me I'd gone the whole day without actually looking in on Ma myself, so I mustered the courage to head round the back of the wagon.

Althea and Jewel were standing there side by side, looking scared. Jewel was crying, kinda low and whimpery. Althea had tears streaming down her face, but she wasn't making a sound. She was holding a wrapped bundle in her arms like she was too scared to move with it. I knew right off what it was, and I swayed on my feet.

"Willie's dead." Her voice trembled in despair. "He's already stiff! What are we gonna *do*, Colton?"

CHAPTER FIVE

A whole flood of mixed-up feelings washed over me. I felt 'em trying to carry me down, but I still had some fight in me. I wrestled my way to the surface, focused on staying strong. I had to, though it was taking its toll.

"What else can we do?" I snapped. "We gotta go bury him." Instantly I regretted the sand in my tone. It wasn't their fault we were having troubles.

To make up for being so rough, I knelt down and opened my arms for Jewel. She folded into 'em, still whimpering. I carried her off a ways and Althea followed. We climbed a sandy ridge to where there was a flat ledge of rock sticking out, and I set Jewel down. To stop her crying, I gave her the candy I still had in my pocket. She popped it into her mouth and worked on sucking it hard, staring at the horizon as serious as any old-timer. I couldn't remember the last time she'd laughed, and here she was, only four.

Althea carefully laid the bundle that was our little brother on the rock between her and me and sat down too, pulling her knees up under her chin and looking away toward the mountains. There were those twin tracks, stretching westward. Those open arms making promises. Huh.

Silent with our own thoughts, we watched the mountains turn from green to gray to black. In the dying light I couldn't help glancing down at the motionless face of my baby brother. Strange, it almost seemed like he was smiling. Something stabbed me real hard then. In a dizzying rush I thought 'bout all the things I could've taught him, all the things we could've done together. It was gonna be nice having a brother. And now he was gone too. I looked away.

Below us cooking fires began flaming in orange points throughout the circle of wagons. My stomach growled. Althea's did too. Jewel curled in my lap and fell asleep. The temperature plummeted faster than the sun, and before it was full dark, the air had turned frosty. Somewhere unseen a coyote yipped his eerie welcome to the night.

"Well?" Althea said, choosing to take charge. "Where are we gonna bury him?"

I looked through the twilight. The spot near where we were sitting seemed as good as any. We could point Willie in the direction we'd be going. That way he could kinda watch over us as we moved on. "Right here, I suppose. Beside this rock." I eased Jewel aside and stood up. "You two stay here and I'll fetch the spade."

The digging was a lot harder than I thought it'd be. The first stab sent a jolt up my arms and slid my fingers willy-nilly down the wood handle, filling me as full of splinters as a porcupine has quills. I moved over and tried again, taking a firmer grip and not stabbing quite as hard. For my efforts I got about a cupful of sand. I heaved a sigh. This was gonna take all night.

"You take Jewel back to the wagon and tend to Ma," I ordered Althea. "I'll be there as soon as I can."

"I'll bring you something to eat," she promised.

"Make it a fried steak with hash and a slice of peach pie." I answered that fast, and started chuckling right there in the middle of our misery.

"Colton!" she scolded, like I'd just turned a somersault down the church aisle. But the sides of her mouth were turning up a little, and Jewel, watching the two of us, let out a squeal of laughter that must've been pent up inside her for a month.

The two of 'em walked back to the wagon, and I kept digging, not getting far. Told myself it was like the trail. You couldn't look at the whole distance you had to go, just step off your miles each day. So I kept pulling up a cupful of sand and dirt at a time, slowly making a shallow hole here and a slippery hill there.

In between the crunches of the spade hitting the sand I heard another noise. Sounded like an animal coming, and by the way it was traveling, I figured it was most likely a coyote. I gripped the wood handle, prepared to fight off any hungry predator.

What came into sight, though, was the scruffy little dog from the stone building. He walked right up and sat beside me. Looked down at the hole, then up at me with a big question mark in his eyes.

"Sorry," I said. "No bones here. And *I* haven't had supper either."

He let out a long, mournful whine that seemed to say we *were* a pitiful pair.

I smiled and set the spade down a moment to rest beside him. Wiping my sweaty neck, I scratched his, even though his coat was greasy and rough. My fingers felt a plowed field's worth of bumps and scabs, probably from all the flies and mosquitoes. His ears were so raggedy they were 'most chewed off. The tips were crusted with dried blood. But smelly as he was, I welcomed the company, and we sat there a short spell watching the activity in camp. As people finished their eating, they congregated together to talk. Someone took out his violin and started drawing out some teary-eyed notes that suited this lonesome place.

When I'd been digging a while longer, Althea and Jewel came climbing up the ridge, Althea carrying a plate in her hand.

"We got steak!" Jewel burst out, and Althea gave her a scolding look, like she'd told a secret.

The dog immediately sat up on his hind legs, a proper beggar, which made the girls laugh.

I had a forkful in my mouth before I could manage to ask, "Where'd you get this?"

"The lady that helped us yesterday," Althea answered. "Her name's Mrs. Sheridan, and she brought us *four* steaks— one for each of us and Ma!" Wonder showed itself strong in her voice.

"Where'd *she* get it?" I asked between chewing and swallowing.

"Said they'd decided to butcher an ox. It was sickly or something and wasn't doing anybody any good." She was beaming. "Doesn't it taste wonderful? I cut 'em in half so we'd have more for breakfast."

All I could do was nod. Then, "Did Ma eat?"

"She took a bite, said she wasn't up to more." The flush of happiness left her face. "She asked where Willie was."

Giving me a glance full of guilt, she said, "I told her you were looking after him."

"Well, that's true, I suppose. We're *all* looking after him, aren't we?"

She glanced down at Jewel, who was busy petting the dog, and seeing her chance, whispered to me, "Do you think Ma's gonna die now too?"

I heaved a sigh, wrestling with being irritable again. "I don't know. Maybe not. Maybe everything—the birthing, the fever, Pa leaving—just knocked the wind outta her. If she can hold on till we can get her to a doctor, I'm sure she'll be all right."

Althea didn't look much assured. I was just a brother, after all. What did I know about living and dying?

"He's a nice doggy," Jewel said to no one in particular. She was still squatting, petting the dog's back. He wasn't paying her any mind, though. Ramrod straight, he held his balance, begging for his share of my steak.

I tossed him the bone and dug into the beans. I knew I was eating too fast. My stomach was painful full, but my teeth were so enjoying their practice. "Why do you suppose she—Mrs. Sheridan—is being so nice?"

"She's just a nice lady, Colton." Althea looked at me with disdain for even asking the question. "I gave her a card of buttons, some shell ones, in exchange for the steaks."

"Did she *ask* for 'em?"

"No." Althea frowned. "I didn't want her thinking we *needed* handouts. Ma always says if you act proper, people will treat you proper."

"Can we keep him, Colton?" All of a sudden Jewel was begging with the same desire the dog had shown.

"He isn't ours to keep," I answered.

"He says he wants to go with us."

"Did he, now?"

"Uh-huh." She smiled. "He told me."

"That's nonsense," Althea scolded. "Dogs don't talk."

"Maybe they don't talk to *you*," I teased.

She rolled her eyes. "You're both addled." Changing the subject, she asked, "You 'bout done digging?"

"I guess so. Ground's getting harder and harder. If we bury him like this and then pile rocks on the grave, I don't think he'll get dug up by anything."

We went 'bout our business in silence, and by the time the campfires below us had sunk to embers and the violin had been put to bed, we'd made a respectable grave for Willie. Althea made us hold hands and pray. She asked God to watch over Willie in heaven. She stumbled over some other thoughts 'bout Pa and his safety, before giving up and saying, "Amen." We echoed her.

As we walked back down to our wagon, I was surprised to see that Althea had pitched the tent already. She had the pillows and quilts arranged too.

"I think we'd all better sleep out here tonight," she said. "Ma needs the peace."

I didn't need any convincing and dived onto the bedding like it was a sea of feathers. Jewel curled up next to me, round as a cat, and was instantly asleep. Althea looked in on Ma, then came and stretched out on the other side of me. I could sense her worrying in the dark.

"How's your leg?" she asked.

"It fell off a few miles back. Go to sleep."

"You should've put something on it, wrapped it maybe."

"Uh-huh."

"You think we'll make it to California, Colton?"

"Not if you talk me to death first. Go to sleep!"

"Well, good night, then." She rolled over on her side, but I knew she stayed awake.

Didn't take long for her worrying to poke its fingers under my own eyelids, and then I was lying there wide awake and worrying too. Seemed like it was just the three of us now doing the pulling, three kids so small we could fit inside the same small tent and still have room to roll around. How did we figure on making it to California? We still had to get over those mountains that'd been taunting us these past weeks, and they looked steep and straight up as a wall.

That terrible loneliness started creeping over me again. I missed Pa. The tears were rising up in the corners of my eyes, threatening to spill over, when I felt a wet nose under my hand. A dog's nose. That smelly little jasper had sneaked into our tent without making so much as a sound. He was trembling something awful, and I knew it was 'cause he expected to get booted out. Pa would've. He said animals belonged outta doors. But Pa wasn't here anymore and I didn't want the dog to leave. Besides, it felt good to have him snugged up next to me. Soon as he realized he could stay, he let out the happiest sigh I ever heard come from an animal. Worming his way up between Jewel and me, he stretched out, and before either of us knew it, I think, we were asleep.

CHAPTER SIX

Same as the day before, I rolled outta my quilt in the dark of the morning and went searching for our oxen even before the sentry's gun was fired. Only this time I wasn't doing it alone. The little dirty white dog was trotting at my side—head proud, ears pricked. Taking his work seriously, you might say. He was too small, really, to be of any help, but I didn't shoo him away.

As we moved through the livestock gathered inside the circle of wagons, I saw that some other folks were awake too, gathering up their teams and getting a jump on the day. Most of the men had one or two nice riding horses to saddle. That made me miss Ned. I wondered how he and Pa were faring.

He's as good as dead out there by himself. Mr. Haphorn's remembered words punched me in the stomach. Gruesome images crowded my mind—broken bones, a bashed-in head, a gaping mouth crying for help—and I had to shake them off. There was nothing I could do to help him. Mr. Haphorn was probably right: By now both Pa and Ned were just another pair of carcasses drying in the desert. I shivered, kicked hard at a stone and sent it flying, and kept moving through the mules and oxen and horses.

Funny thing was I found our first team—the spotted one and the black one—right off, but for the life of me I couldn't locate the other two. People kept coming to gather up their animals, so the herd was getting thinner and thinner as I searched, but it was like they—the second team—had up and vanished in the night. Figuring they might've slipped outside the circle like Ned used to, I started hunting on the outskirts of the wagons. Wasn't all that easy in the dark.

The whitish-colored dog was still with me, running left and right and sniffing the ground like he understood the problem. After we'd made it most of the way round the circle, I got accustomed to picking out his pale shape in the gloom. So when he didn't return after one of his drifts, I whistled. He didn't show himself. I whistled again. Still he didn't come, but I thought I could hear him, and followed after to see what he was doing.

What he was doing was chewing on the remains of our other two oxen—the butchered remains. Strewn in the darkness on the far side of the wagon circle were two hulking carcasses, insides gutted, meat hacked off and carried away.

I dropped to my heels with a real sick feeling. We'd eaten our own animals last night. And been tricked into it by that lady Althea claimed was just being nice.

Even worse, we were stranded again. Stranded in this godforsaken graveyard of a place, 'cause there was no way only two oxen could pull a wagon as heavy as ours.

In a rush of anger I picked up a rock and hurled it into the darkness. It landed far off with a muffled thud. Picked up another one and hurled it. Then another. And another. Started hurling 'em with a fury at the mountains that loomed in the dark, hurled 'em back toward the circle of wagons, even hurled one at an empty carcass, like it was the ox's own fault.

None of it made me feel any better. Outta both breath and arm, I turned to go, whistling sharply for the dog. He followed, dragging along a piece of bone near as big as he was, with meat and red hide still attached.

The sky was coming gray as I trudged back to our wagon. I could see Willie's ridge outlined black against it. I wondered if he could see us. Before long, I reckoned, someone would be digging a few more graves beside him.

What was I gonna tell Ma?

CHAPTER SEVEN

There I was, marching along full of tears and anger and heartache and whatnot, when another figure came striding toward me through the gray morning. The skirts told me it was a woman. The man's pace told me it was Mrs. Sheridan.

Now, I'd been raised to show respect to girls and women, but my hands were shaking so right then I couldn't trust 'em. I couldn't be certain they wouldn't pick up another stone and heave it at her if I caught sight of her smirking face. Feeding us our own oxen for supper! Turning a shoulder to her, I walked off in another direction.

"Pardon me!" she called, and I thought that was a funny turn of phrase, considering the situation. Thinking it best to ignore her, I kept walking. She gathered up her skirts and started running after me, begging me to stop. "Pardon me!" she kept saying. "Pardon me! Young Mr. Wescott, *please!*"

I stopped cold in my tracks and turned, working hard on reining in my anger. To my surprise, her face was 'bout as twisted up in a fit as I imagined mine to be.

She was so outta breath she couldn't speak right off. While she was gasping and wheezing, she was digging her fingers into a small coin purse. Into the palm of her hand she counted out four twenty-dollar gold coins. "Here," she said at last.

I guess it proves I didn't have a lick of sense that I didn't just grab that amount of wealth and run. Instead I narrowed my eyes at her and demanded, "What's that for?"

"Your two oxen. It's a fair price and I'm paying for 'em."

Cat ran off with my tongue then. Ran clean off and away. I stood there staring at those gold coins, chewing on the inside of my lip, not knowing what to say. After a spell all I could muster was, "Why?"

Tender, like she was my own ma, she opened my clenched fist, put the coins in it, and closed the fingers over. "I didn't know they were butchering *your* oxen," she said, and by the way she spoke, I believed her.

"It's been so long since we tasted something other than beans that nobody was asking any questions."

A look came over her face like she'd just been poked by something sharp. "Oh, no," she cried, covering her mouth with both hands. "You must think I was playing a cruel trick on you, serving up your own oxen to you on a plate. Honestly, I had no idea until this very morning that that supper came at the expense of your team. I'm truly sorry."

I looked down at my fist. The coins were cool and heavy inside my fingers. Like a poultice on a wound. But they wouldn't pull a wagon.

"You and yours gonna be okay?" she asked.

I guess maybe I nodded. That's what you had to do out here. Keep nodding and keep moving. Never admit that you'd been beaten—by anything or anyone.

"How many oxen do you have left—two?"

"Yes, ma'am."

She looked toward the mountains. "Long way to go still with just two oxen. But you empty out that wagon of yours. Tell your ma I said so. Unload all the heavy things, the bed and the bureau and the trunks and the tools, and just leave 'em behind. Leave 'em sitting right here in the middle of the desert. Then you and your sisters walk, mind you, and stick together. That way, I expect, you'll make it."

She took her fingers and pulled my face round 'cause I was staring off at the mountains too, starting to believe they were just another mirage, something you could reach for your whole life and never ever actually touch. "I know your family name," she said, "but what's your given name?"

"Colton, ma'am."

"Colton Wescott." She spoke with the authority of a preacher and repeated it loudly. "Colton Wescott. I expect I'll hear about you someday when you're all grown up. And I'll be able to tell people that I traveled west with you." She looked puffed up and confident, like the future was all settled just because she'd said so. "Well, the sun's going to work. Guess we should too. Best of luck to you, now. Get that wagon unloaded." She hurried back inside the circle that was now buzzing with activity.

The dirty white dog had lain while we talked, chewing on the bone. When I walked off, he rose up like a good fellow and followed me. He left the bone behind.

The other wagons didn't wait for us to get unloaded, of course. The rifle was fired and the circle started unwinding, the train heading west, always heading west. It'd be another long day of playing catch-up.

Althea was watching for me outside the wagon. She was wringing her hands 'cause she knew something was wrong. "What is it, Colton? What's happened?"

I explained it best I could. Told her matter-of-fact that two of our oxen were killed and we had to get along without 'em. I told her we had to empty the wagon. Something kept me from showing her the money, though, and I don't know why that was. The coins were certainly a piece of good luck, more than we'd had in weeks. Maybe I just wanted to feel their weight in my pocket awhile, feel like there were four good-size pieces of hope waiting there. Things couldn't get *too* bad then.

Althea took the news in stride. Her face got stiff, but she didn't cry. She just started pulling blankets and buckets and things outta the wagon and throwing 'em on the ground.

I grabbed her wrist. "Not here," I said. "Let's get a little closer to that stone building."

Still not speaking, she gathered up the litter and tossed it back into the wagon. Then she coaxed Jewel out into the morning and had her make a game of helping get the last two oxen yoked and hitched. I think my sister was tougher than I was at times.

That pair of oxen acted real surprised when I shouted "Get up!" to 'em. They swung their heads round, searching for their teammates. Their eyes got kinda big when they didn't find 'em. Unless that was my imagination. I had to take the goad to 'em and shout again, but then they did try, bless 'em. They leaned into their yoke by their lonesome, dug their split hooves into the sand, and pulled. The pair of 'em could barely budge the big wagon, loaded as it was, but inch by inch they got it moved closer to where I wanted it. The rising sun was just painting the desert a cold yellow.

Mustering my courage, I went to the back of the wagon to tell Ma she had to start parting with her treasures. That everything we'd paid so dearly for back in St. Joseph, and packed so carefully for California, was now going to be left to rot in the desert.

Althea stopped me. "She doesn't know," she murmured. "She's fogged up—been talking nonsense all morning. Better to just leave the things and get her to a doctor, if we can find one."

It was a guilty relief at best. At least I didn't have to *tell* her we were robbing her while she slept. Quiet as we could, and working round her, we lifted out the chairs and the headboard, emptied the trunks of books and linens and candles, before straining to lift the trunks themselves. I set the pails of leafless rose cuttings next to the chairs, but Althea lifted 'em right back into the wagon.

"Not these, Colton," she said firmly. "She's got to have something."

I was too beat down to argue.

Carrying out Pa's carpetbag and setting it in the sand gave me a real shiver. Made it seem all the more like he was dead, 'cause he'd surely never be using these clothes again. Over and over I wiped my hands on my pants, but they still felt sticky with shame and fear and worry. "Keep unloading," I told Althea. "I'll be right back."

She nodded and kept climbing quietly in and outta the wagon, stacking all that we owned in the open wasteland.

The dog was still glued to my side as I walked up to the stone house and then, hearing the sound of splashing water, past it. Out by the corral I found a man emptying a bucket into the horse trough.

"Pardon me, sir."

"Thought you folks was all gone," he said without looking up. "Whaddya need?"

Huh. What did I need? How long was that list? Well, a doctor was surely at the top of it. "Would you know where the nearest doctor could be found?"

"Somebody get hurt?"

"My ma's been sick for a while. Her baby died yesterday."

That made him set down the bucket and turn around. "I'm sorry to hear that, son, but the only doctor we got is a woman over in Chinatown, 'bout thirty miles from here. They say she's pretty good. Pretty to look at, anyway." He grinned and winked, picked up his bucket, and returned to his work.

Another thought struck me. "Could I borrow one of your horses? Ride to fetch the doctor?"

His laughter was so scornful it made me grit my teeth.

"Borrow one of *these* horses? Hah! Son, these horses are owned by the Central Overland California and Pikes Peak Express Company, under government contract to deliver the United States mail."

He must've seen the words fly right past my ears, 'cause he bent down to speak to me like I was some kinda invalid. "The Pony Express, son. You never heard of the Pony Express?"

"I heard of it," I answered, all abristle. "Riders carry the U.S. mail, going at a gallop, from St. Joseph to California."

"And back again. One went through here yesterday. You didn't see him?"

Now I remembered the hoofbeats. I'd been so relieved we

weren't being attacked—and so awed by the hawk on my shoulder—that I'd forgotten the people shouting 'bout the Pony mail. I nodded.

He grunted and walked back for more water. The three horses had come to the trough as the water was being dumped in, but they weren't drinking it. Having tried it myself, I didn't blame 'em. It smelled like rotten eggs and tasted worse.

They certainly were fine animals to look at. Lot of meat on their bones, sharp look to their eyes. The roan was the biggest. He had a short back and big, powerful hindquarters. I'd bet one of the gold pieces in my pocket that he could outrun 'most any horse he met. I'd *give* one of the gold pieces, maybe, just for the chance to sit on a horse nice as him. Lordy, wouldn't that be something. The two bays were equally as fit. The one had a white star and strip going down his face and a couple of white socks, and the other, so dark as to 'most be black, shone with health even in this dusty corral.

"This here's a relay station," the man explained as he returned with another bucket of water. "Got a couple hundred of 'em across the territory. Rider gets a fresh horse at each one."

"Who brings the horse back?" I asked.

Like I was thickheaded, he answered roughly, "The rider goin' the *opposite* direction, course. Mail's movin' all the time, east and west. That is, 'cept when the Paiutes get stirred up." He nodded toward the stone house. "Tried to burn us outta here last week. Shot my wrangler, so I sent him on to Chinatown with your wagon train this morning. I'm havin' to do all the work till the company replaces him."

Althea sidled up behind me, trying to hide herself from the man I was talking to. "We got most of the things out now," she whispered. "Can't see the other wagons anymore." That meant we better hurry up. I nodded and she skittered away.

The man raised his eyebrows. "That your own slave? You're kinda young, ain't ya?"

You could've hit me over the head with a shovel and I wouldn't have been more taken aback. Slave? "She's my sister," I corrected him.

He looked me over closer, up and down, then pulled back like he'd seen something awful. "Why, I'll be! You got colored blood, don't ya? I knew it," he said, shaking his head. "I knew it right away. Say, you better not be tryin' to pass yourself off as a white boy, or you're gonna find yourself strung up one of these days. Not everyone's as tolerable as I am. Where are your folks?"

Something inside of me warned not to tell him everything. "Pa had to ride on ahead," I sorta lied. "And my ma's sick in the wagon." I motioned for him to follow me round the house, and he did.

The dirty-colored dog rose up at just the wrong moment and got himself tangled under the man's boots. To my surprise, the growl came outta the man. He kicked the dog sideways, catching him in the ribs and lifting him clean off the ground. Swallowing a yelp as he hit the sand, the dog ran off a ways. If I'd had any qualms 'bout taking to the trail again, they were gone now.

Just as she'd said, Althea had most of our belongings piled neatly beside the wagon. There was the headboard to Ma's bed, the bureau, the one broken chair and the two good ones, a pair of empty trunks with their lids open and their fragile contents stacked alongside, one partially used fifty-pound bag of flour, a sack of nails, the tent, some coils of rope,

Pa's carpetbag, and the pretty white washbasin with the flowers painted on the sides.

Self-conscious, I deepened my voice. "How much will you give me for all this?"

"Ain't got no money to give."

That flattened me. I was hoping to get something, at least *something*, for all our worldly goods. No man would walk away with *nothing* to show. "Then, what will you trade me?" I countered.

"Got nothin' to trade."

He was fighting a smile now. He knew he had me, knew he had me certain as if I was hanging upside down from a tree with my pockets turned inside out. We both knew I couldn't load up and take everything with me.

He waved me away, like he was chasing off a fly, and turned to leave. Not watching where he was going, he came near to stumbling over that little dog again. The creature bolted, just in time, and I, without thinking, reached down and scooped him up.

"I'll trade you for *him*," I called in the direction of the man's back. The dog was trembling in my arms like he was having a seizure or something. The man never turned around. He just swatted his arm at me a final time. So I let myself be chased away.

Waving the goad at the oxen, I set them to huffing and struggling and bellowing. After I'd set the dog down, I didn't have to so much as whistle for him. He chose for his work protecting Jewel and Althea and padded along between the two of 'em. With the sun at our backs, we aimed our sights west once again.

CHAPTER EIGHT

If that little hawk was flying round up there somewhere, he must've thought we were a sight. Two skinny oxen creeping cross the desert, slow as molasses. A lonesome boy and two girls holding hands and a scabby, dirty white dog traipsing beside. He might've flown off to tell the buzzards to get their forks ready, but he would've been wrong. We were still moving. And that meant we hadn't given up.

I'd be lying, though, if I said I wasn't thinking 'bout it some. 'Bout giving up. Seemed that ever since I got in the way of Pa's bullet, everything I laid my hand to went south. First the wagon, then the oxen, then 'most all our supplies and furniture. Not to mention Willie dying and Ma heading the same direction. I had myself in a pretty good sulk by the time the full sun was painting the mountains orange.

With the chill melting from the air, wrens came hopping outta their pebbly nests to bob their heads and chase after black beetles. Long-tailed lizards hugged the rocks, waiting for a bigger helping of the warmth that was on the way. Spotting a particularly pretty red-and-white-striped stone, I bent to pick it up. Its smooth shape felt good in my hand, and taking a big drink of the sweet desert air, I started to soften some.

There was a whole community of squirrels round us, well matched in their black collars. They whistled and scurried through the brush, touching noses in greeting before diving back into their tunnels. Two of the younger ones stayed out playing a wild game of tag, jumping clean into the air and doing somersaults and such, until their mother shrilled a warning and they had to go scampering underground with her. It was entertainment enough to raise my spirits.

Noticing that the dog seemed to have adopted Jewel especially as kin—he was padding along tight on her heels—I asked her, "What'll we call him? Jocko? Or Tex? Or Ugly Joe?"

"His name's Lucky," she said, just as matter-of-fact as anything.

That made me laugh out loud, causing a jackrabbit to stamp his foot in alarm and go hightailing. "It is? How do you know that?"

"He told me."

Not a smile or nothing. Just as serious as Sunday, she was. I laughed again and, as long as there was no one but Althea to see, took hold of her free hand. For being only four years old, Jewel had a lot of spit in her. And heck, who was to say the dog *hadn't* told her his name?

As the sun pulled itself higher, our two pitiful oxen fell to pulling slower. We were hardly making any progress at all by then, and those mountains began to shimmer in the heat like a taunting dream. The squirrels disappeared, and the birds sat silent and still on their nests.

"Hold on there," I called out finally, and everyone, human and animal alike, was only too happy to stop. The oxen's ribs looked like bellows squeezing air in and out. The creatures themselves were too tired to complain. I passed round some of the smelly water from the relay station—suitable, at least, for splashing on faces—and wet the mouths and noses of the oxen.

Althea and Jewel took the opportunity to collapse in the hot shade under the wagon. As for me, I had to shove aside my worst fears, soak a clean handkerchief, and climb up and into the back of the wagon. The musty, sickly smell that clouded its insides near choked me. Ma was curled motionless on her mattress, one hand touching her cheek. There was no sign of her breathing. In a dizzying rush my world narrowed to jumbled images of waxy fingers, a sun-striped quilt, a near-empty bag of cornmeal, and an irksome cluster of tin pails sprouting leafless, thorny stalks.

She was gone. We were alone.

Slumping onto the floor in defeat, I yanked my hat off and wiped the sticky sweat from my forehead. I dragged a sleeve across my eyes. They stung like needles were poking 'em. For the longest time there was no sound anywhere at all, and it seemed like the whole world had stopped breathing.

When I'd settled myself enough to open my eyes again, I found that Ma was staring at me. I couldn't hardly believe it. In a whisper I ventured, "Ma?"

She blinked.

"You got to hang on, Ma," I said, scrambling on my knees to get the wet handkerchief to her cracked lips. "We're 'most there. You got to hang on." Her skin felt hot as sand under my fingers.

She nodded, the tiniest bit, and even tried to smile, I think. But it was too much. She closed her eyes and went still again.

I was more scared than ever. I had to get her to a doctor.

Climbing outta the wagon in a hurry, I announced, "We're gonna make some changes." I handed Jewel the braided leather goad. "You think you can keep these two fellas moving?"

She nodded once and grabbed the handle with a fiery enthusiasm. "Get on up there!" she hollered loud as any field hand, and jabbed the near ox in the flanks. The dog, Lucky, rose to life at that. He snapped at the surprised animal's ankles and barked and growled and just worried him in general. Poor creature didn't know what was happening to him, but he sure leaned into his yoke and started putting some effort into his work.

"And we're gonna have to help push," I told Althea. "At least through the heat of the day."

She nodded too, and we took up shoulder-by-shoulder positions at the back of the wagon. Spreading our four palms on the splintery wood panel, we leaned into our own invisible yokes. My heart was pounding and my leg was burning fiercer than ever, but step by step we started pushing more of the desert behind us.

Most of that day I kept my head down, watching the shadowy ruts trickle past my feet like a torturous, never-ending stream. I tried not to let it get to me how slow we were moving, but it was hard. Specially when one of Ma's confused cries jerked me outta my trance. At least she was still alive, but her pain tore through me afresh every time, and I cursed that devil's trail and our achingly slow progress.

The wagon was still too heavy for only a couple of oxen and three kids, and I wanted to empty it of everything that was left but Ma. "Why can't we heave the roses?" I grumbled to Althea. "They're dead anyway. Nothing left of 'em but dirt and thorns, and there's enough of that round us already." I was looking for a fight, I suppose, but she wasn't taking the bait.

"They're *not* dead," she whispered back, smooth as a summer breeze, which riled me all the more. "They just look that way. Besides, like I said, Ma needs to keep *something*."

"Doesn't need to be roses."

"We're keeping the roses, Colton."

Mule! I thought.

We put our heads down and kept plodding, but I wasn't through feeling ornery. You see, every time I looked up at our hands—Althea's and mine—pressed against the wagon, a new worry gnawed at me. I'd never taken much notice of it before, that my sister's color was darker than mine, but the man at the relay station certainly had. When I'd first gone up to him, he'd thought I was white. And he'd been angry when he learned otherwise. "You better not be tryin' to pass yourself off as a white boy," he'd warned. There was solid threat in those words, and my throat got tight at the memory. I knew what he meant 'cause back in Missouri I'd seen a hanging once. I didn't ever want to be caught on the end of that rope.

Step after crunching step the accusing words rolled round in my head like marbles, making it ache, making me feel guilty for something I hadn't even done. A choice I hadn't even made. Pricking me too was the fact that those words built on a troublesome afternoon back in St. Joe, before we'd got ourselves mixed up with this trip west.

On the same day that Pa had announced we were paid up for California and had hurried off for more supplies, Ma had shooed my sisters outta the room. She wanted the two of us to "have a talk."

Ma wanting to talk meant I must've done something wrong, so I was running through my mind all the things I'd figured she couldn't possibly know about. To bring the sweat out on me more, she left me standing in the middle of the room while she stayed kneeling on the floor. She was taking her time with packing and repacking her trunk, making hard decisions about a lot of woman stuff. A cream pitcher would go in and a clothes iron would come out, and she'd give a little high-pitched sigh and switch the two. But her lips kept pinching up tight, so I knew she was angry 'bout something, and I came real close to admitting that *I* was the one who'd broke the handle off one of her teacups. (I'd been reaching for a sack of peppermints that was hidden behind 'em.)

"Colton," she said in a preacher's graveside voice, "in the top drawer of the bureau there's a hand mirror. Will you bring it to me, please?"

I'd never been privy to Ma's things before, and it made my face hot to even pull the drawer open. To my relief, I found the looking glass right away, lying on a stack of folded handkerchiefs, and I handed it to her.

She handed it right back. "You see yourself?"

I glanced at the reflection and nodded. Course I saw myself. When was the punishment coming?

"Tell me what you see."

"Ma!"

"All right, then, I'll tell you." Leaving me to stare into the oval, she closed her eyes and rocked back and forth. Speaking real solemn, she said, "I see a twelve-year-old boy with a good head on his shoulders. He's an old soul. Been here before, I expect. He's got green eyes like his pa and black hair like his ma, but he's got something else that only God could give him. Something special. The creatures know it, 'cause they come swarming to him like bees to a blossom and aren't afraid.

"The boy's not big; he's small and wiry like his pa. Small enough to be a jockey if we could only afford the racehorse." She allowed herself a chuckle. "And I reckon he's the kind that'll get where he's going, 'cause he's got a whole lot of determination."

She opened her eyes. "There's something else you'll see in that mirror, Colton Wescott. You're 'most as white as your pa."

That made me squirm. I hated any talk of how one of my folks was white and one was mixed blood, like they were some kinda dogs, purebred and mongrel. They were just folks, is all. "Why are you talking like that?" I began, but she shushed me up.

"Because it needs talking 'bout. And the sooner you realize it, the sooner you'll understand 'bout your opportunities." She flashed her black eyes at me, and I thought right then she was one of the prettiest women I'd ever seen anywhere, angry or not. "What it means," she went on saying, "is that people are gonna look at you and they're gonna look at your sisters and they're gonna treat you different from one another. Different from me, too. Not all of 'em, but some of 'em. Maybe even most of 'em. They're gonna look at your light skin, Colton, and welcome you into their houses, and they're gonna look at your sisters and their dark faces and tell 'em to wait outside."

"But that's not fair," I said, and right away heard how childish I sounded. Here she was trying to tell me something she thought was important, trying to pull me onto the grown-up side of the river, and I was whining 'bout it. There was no wading back cross now. I could tell that. So I shut myself up.

"Guess I've lived long enough to know what's fair and what isn't," she grumbled. "But there's no fixing that. The world is what it is." She rested a pair of small leather-bound books in her lap and looked up at me. "What I'm trying to tell you, plain and simple, is that when we move to California, you're gonna have some opportunities . . . and some choices to make. And I'm telling you now, Colton, it's all right with me, whichever you choose. Even if it's your pa's world. You hear me? It's all right. 'Cause the world is what it is, and no one can change that."

CHAPTER NINE

The day that we pushed on with just the two oxen ended up being the hottest we'd had, I'd swear to it. The sun was pouring fire down our backs and heads and hands; the sand was burning up through our shoes; and there wasn't a breath of wind. Not a breath. Sweat rolled off us like syrup.

If someone had offered it to me, I would've happily exchanged one of the gold coins in my pocket for only a piece of cool shade. Maybe two of 'em. But peering round the wagon and up the trail showed there was no shade to be had, not by a long shot. And there was no one to offer any either. So we kept our heads down and kept walking and pushing.

Must've been a couple of hours after we'd set out that a pair of claws hit my shoulder and I jumped and Althea screamed. The little hawk was back! Holding still as I could ('cause I was trembling), I shushed Althea hard. The wagon stopped moving 'cause Jewel left the oxen to come running. Soon as she saw the hawk, she stopped in her tracks with a face full of wonder and a lopsided smile. "Your birdie's back," is all she said.

I didn't move. I was so happy he'd shown up again, even if it didn't make a bit of sense, that I only watched him outta the corner of my eye. His beak was gaping open, showing his little leather tongue, like he'd been flying somewhere fast and furious. Now that he'd stopped, he seemed anxious. The way he was squeezing his claws into me, first one set and then the other, sent a pleasant chill skipping down my spine.

That's when I did something kinda crazy. With my heart pumping faster, I slid away from the wagon. I spread my arms out like wings and started slowly twirling round, grinning from ear to ear. Althea was covering her mouth with both hands, plain horrified, but Jewel was laughing.

The bird seemed to enjoy it too. He crouched and stuck to me, adjusting his balance as we went. Till, all of a sudden, he tipped his head away from me. Listening, I guess. I stopped spinning. I knew he was getting ready to go, and I got all filled up inside, wanting him to stay.

No, that wasn't it. I wanted to go *with* him. I wanted to taste the wind in my face and see the ground blurred beneath my feet. I wanted to forget all my troubles and escape this earthbound prison I was caught up in.

Sure enough, with a flapping of wings he lifted off, light as smoke. Spiraled up and up into the hot blue sky. His *klee-klee-klee* was like a call to me to follow, and it pained me something awful that I couldn't.

None of us moved for a spell. We stood there, the three of us, shading our eyes and watching him go. Till we heard the hoofbeats. Like I'd been splashed with cold water, I came to. What fools we were to not keep a lookout! What easy prey we were out here in the open! From the time we'd set out on the trail, we'd all heard whispered tales of children carried off by Indians and made to work as slaves—or worse, scalped alive and left to bleed to death in the sand. Was the hawk trying to warn us 'bout that? My heart was pumping with a whole different sort of excitement now.

Althea, Jewel, and I dived under the wagon, and Lucky joined us, wagging his tail and barking like it was all a game. I pinned him tight under my arm and held his mouth closed. Why had I let Mr. Haphorn take Pa's gun? How were we gonna defend ourselves and Ma now? Peering through the wheels and spokes and ox legs, we tried to get a glimpse of our fate.

After what seemed like an endless wait, down the trail from the west came a lone rider on a horse, galloping full out like the devil was on his tail. I let out my breath. It wasn't Indians after all. In fact, I was pretty sure it was another Pony Express rider. No one to cheer him on this time 'cept us.

In a low voice I asked my sisters, "You know what that is coming toward us?" Their fearful expressions said they'd rather not hear the details.

"A Pony Express rider. You've heard of the Pony Express, haven't you?"

They both turned to me and nodded, and maybe Althea was being truthful, but I know for certain that Jewel had no idea what I was talking 'bout. The rider was coming closer, and they were twisting their pigtails, eyes wide, ready to bust outta there and run.

"You see, there's no way to get letters and telegrams and such cross the territory. Unless you count wagon train—and I reckon people could die before they got their mail *that* way." I added a chuckle there, but considering our situation, it wasn't all that funny. "So the Pony riders carry it horseback, galloping all the way from St. Joseph, Missouri, to Sacramento, California."

"Oh, Colton, you're fibbing," Althea said. "No one can gallop all the way from Missouri to California."

"Not *one* person," I shot back, "but a whole passel of horses and riders. They trade off horses and riders for fresh at relay stations, like the one we left this morning."

She still looked doubtful.

"I remember," Jewel said. "I saw the horse with the white face there that was galloping yesterday."

"You're right," I said, surprised at the things she noticed. The world wasn't gonna be able to pull one over on her.

The Pony rider sped by, giving us only a curious glance. I was shocked to see he was just a kid, not much older'n me, though he looked tougher. He was dressed head to toe in buckskin, with his trousers tucked smartly into his boots. His shallow-brimmed hat was pulled down past his ears, and the saddle—what I could see of it—was little more'n a scrap of leather and a pair of stirrups. He was traveling light, as they say.

Just as we were crawling out to take our places again, I heard the fading hoofbeats break their rhythm. I looked over my shoulder, and here comes the rider, galloping back toward us.

Stinging us with a spray of sand, he reined his horse in tight and frowned. "You in some sorta trouble?"

Lucky barked, and I glared at him for a traitor. "We're making our way to Chinatown," I said. "Can you tell us how much farther it is?"

His horse was dancing and shaking his head, like he knew they'd turned the wrong way and needed to make up lost time. The boy sat him slick as a whistle. "You mean Dayton? Left there a couple of hours ago," he said. "It's due west. But you won't make it before nightfall." His horse pawed the ground with growing fury. "You sure you're okay? You want me to send someone for you?"

"We're fine, thank you."

He touched the brim of his hat, saluting Althea and Jewel and making 'em blush. Nodded to me and loosed the reins. The horse spun on his haunches and, just like that, bolted into a dead run. In a matter of minutes they'd disappeared.

With the hawk come and gone, and the Pony rider come and gone, the hot, empty trail seemed all the quieter and lonelier. I looked in on Ma, but she was asleep, her skin still hot, her breath still perilously faint. My sisters and I took up our positions without words. Jewel weakly swung the goad, and Althea and I slumped against the wagon, and with a shudder and a creaking it slowly got to moving.

Our shadows stretched longer and longer with the waning day. There was still no Chinatown or Dayton on the horizon. I was beginning to wonder if we'd had another trick played on us and was growing fretful 'cause I didn't relish the thought of spending a whole night alone in the open desert. As the air cooled, we stopped a spell to rest our feet and to eat the leftover steak. It didn't taste near as good knowing the price we'd paid for it. With the sweat dried on our bodies and our bellies leaden with food, we returned to our plodding.

Everyone was plumb tuckered out. The oxen took up some halfhearted bawling, and Jewel fell dead asleep at the walk. I halted the wagon long enough to lift her in. Don't think she even opened an eyeball. Lucky was quick to give me a pitiful look and hold up one paw—the rapscallion—so I lifted him into the wagon too, and didn't he look like royalty then! Althea picked up the goad and took Jewel's place beside the team.

The moon rose, sickle shaped and silver white. All the desert's coyotes greeted it with an earsplitting chorus of hallelujahs. Guess they woke up Ma, 'cause when I peeked over the back of the wagon, I noticed her lying with her eyes open, just staring into the moonlight.

Quiet, 'cause I wasn't sure if her mind was awake, I asked, "You thirsty, Ma?"

Her head lolled to one side and she looked at me like I was a stranger. Blinked and kept looking.

"Are you hungry? We saved some steak for you."

Althea heard me talking and came back, allowing the oxen to come to a stop for another breather. She climbed into the wagon and sure-handedly tended to Ma, lifting her head up so she could drink some, then wiping the dribbles off her cheek. She took a piece of dried apple and soaked it in water and, real gentle, put it inside Ma's cheek so she could take a little nourishment. At the ripe old age of ten, Althea was all growed up.

When Ma had closed her eyes again, Althea crawled over Jewel and Lucky and outta the wagon. She looked dead on her feet. "You think we're almost there?" she asked, and I didn't have the heart to stomp on the flickering hope in her eyes.

I looked up the dark trail, the twin ruts like giant snakes sleeping side by side. "Dayton's probably over that next rise," I answered, wanting to believe it myself. "We better keep moving if we're gonna get there before they close up the town for the night."

She nodded. Funny thing was, before she could get to 'em, the oxen started moving. Almost seemed eager. I'd heard of teams knowing where water was or where their kin were waiting, even without being able to see 'em, so I crossed my fingers and hoped our two oxen were that sensible.

The coyotes carried their howling closer. First one would send out a call, yip-yappy and delirious, on one side of us, and then another would answer from the other side. Then they'd all join in. Then it would start over, call and answer, each time the chorus sounding nearer, each time more voices joining in. It almost seemed like they were planning something. I was getting that rabbity, run-away feeling again.

I decided to match their singing with my own, hoping that might persuade 'em to move on. "As the blackbird in the spring," I began, and Althea joined in, "beneath the willow tree." Together we warbled, "Sat and piped, I heard him sing, singing Aura Lee."

Slowly, agonizingly slowly, the wagon began rumbling up the rise. And the coyotes began letting themselves be seen. First they were just shadowy forms with yellow eyes glinting outta the darkness, but then their silvery backs and their dripping tongues began showing in the moonlight. Althea and I sang louder and they fell silent, but I felt 'em drawing their noose tighter. Lucky crept to the back of the wagon to watch, but there was no barking this time.

Still singing, "Aura Lee, Aura Lee," Althea sidled back toward me.

"Don't act scared," I warned. "We got to keep the wagon moving. They won't attack as long as we keep moving." She nodded but nudged me aside to help push, rather than return to the oxen.

So we sang and pushed, the words coming from memory 'cause my mind was spinning in fear and doubt. The coyotes kept gathering and we kept climbing. I wanted that town to be on the other side of that rise so bad that if it wasn't, I was afraid I was gonna cry. And I knew I couldn't do that. I had sisters.

One of the coyotes broke from the brush to trot directly behind me. I swear I could feel his breath on my leg. A couple of the others picked a fight among themselves and set to growling and snarling and tearing each other to bits. Althea and I threw all our strength into pushing toward the top, finally heaving the wagon and ourselves over. I was scared to look, scared I'd only see more desert. *Please, God,* I prayed, *no more desert.*

Taking a deep breath, I peered round the wagon. And it was there. Right there by the mountains. Not more'n half a mile below us, sitting beside a silvery river in a wide valley, was the finest-looking town—by any name—that I'd ever seen.

CHAPTER TEN

O nly a few horses and mules penned on the town's edge saw us coming. They stood silhouetted in the faint moonlight, ears pointed, watching. Our oxen dragged the wagon up beside 'em and stopped, and the near one swung his head round and let out a long groan that faded away to nothingness. *We can't take another step,* he was telling me. *Not a single nother step.* I shared his sentiment exactly.

Giving 'em each a grateful slap, I whispered, "It's enough for now. Have a rest." My hand met only bone and hide; all the meat, it seemed, had been worked off 'em. At least they had no fears of being served up on someone's dinner plate. But until they fattened up, or we found fresh oxen, our wagon wasn't rolling another inch. We were pretty much stuck.

Althea sagged against one of the wheels, her dark eyes showing big and glassy. She was done in too. All round me, it seemed, everything was crumbling. "Wait here," I said, pumping cheer into my voice. "I'll go raise the doctor and hurry right back." She nodded wearily and crawled up onto the wagon seat, hugging herself against the desert cold. Squaring my shoulders, I set off.

It was all playacting. After what the man at the relay

station had said, I was none too confident about the reception I would get. Here I was, a stranger—and not a full white one at that—walking into a sleeping town in the dead of night. I didn't know where the doctor lived, didn't even know if she'd agree to help us. Maybe she'd take one look at me and wave me away. Maybe she'd wave me away with her gun.

Thinking 'bout that made me hitch my shoulders up some more and draw out my stride. She could shoot if she wanted, but she best have good aim, 'cause Ma needed her help and I wasn't gonna be run off easily.

In hurrying past a smallish stone building, something like a cellar built into the side of a hill, I realized not all the town was asleep. There were voices inside. That brought me to a standstill with a fresh thought: Maybe someone in there would prove friendly enough to point me in the direction of the doctor. While I was trying to muster enough courage to knock, I came to realize that the snips and scraps of conversation I was hearing were part of some strange language. And the gibberish was being spat so fiercely that it sounded like a roomful of cats fighting. Just what and who was I 'bout to interrupt? Spying a knothole halfway down the door, I stooped to peer through it.

At that instant the room went silent as a graveyard, and I jumped away, thinking I'd been discovered. My heart kicked up and raced so fast that I probably could've pulled the wagon a few more miles down the trail all by myself. But when no one rushed the door—and I'd calmed down some—I let curiosity press me to that knothole again.

Never had I seen such a sight. Hunched over a makeshift table were twelve or fifteen of the oddest-looking little men, each with a single braid of black hair trailing down his back.

In the glow of the room's many candles I could see that a pattern had been drawn on the table and that the men were now wordlessly arranging coins on it. Somebody mumbled something and the men stood back. From the center of the table an upside-down pail was ceremoniously lifted, revealing a pile of reddish stones. A solemn man with a white cloth draped over his shoulders began dividing the stones to points on the pattern. No one made a sound.

Until I did. Guess I forgot how tired I was, 'cause my shaky legs unexpectedly gave way and I thudded against the door. A cry of alarm snuffed out the candles. The men skittered like rabbits into the room's corners.

For several heart-thumping minutes we waited, each of us, I suppose, wondering and worrying 'bout what lay on the other side of the door. The silence was so complete that in the distance I heard coyotes fall upon their prey. Unearthly squeals pierced the night.

The territory, I'd learned, was full of all sorts of dangers, not the least of which was the people in it. You just didn't go banging on doors in the middle of the night. And you certainly didn't open 'em. The men inside didn't trust my intentions, and I'd be a fool to trust theirs. Best to walk away. So, dusting off my knees, I climbed to my feet. But one glance at the darkened windows and closed doors of the sleeping town showed that my prospects there weren't any better. At least these men were already awake. I wouldn't face a pistol by startling 'em.

Gathering up what was left of my courage, I knocked. Course there was no answer. I laid my hand on the iron handle, its cold metal almost pleasurable in my sweaty grip, and slowly pulled on the door. I stuck my chin through the narrow opening and, polite as could be, asked, "Can you tell me where the doctor lives?"

I couldn't see the men in the darkness. I could tell, though, that fear had a choke hold on 'em all. "Please, I just need to find the doctor." Nothing but silence.

Maybe they couldn't understand me. Or maybe they didn't want to understand me. Either way I'd wasted precious time. Feeling foolish, I let the door swing shut and started a hobbling jog toward town.

Wasn't more'n twenty steps on my way when the door opened. "You need doctor?"

I spun. There was one of the little men, half hidden by the doorframe, eyeing me as cautiously as a child does a vicious dog. *Me*. Now, that was an odd feeling. "Yes," I answered fast, before he could pull back. "My ma's real sick. She's in that wagon over there." I pointed.

The man seemed afraid to leave the doorway. He turned and spoke to someone inside, then hesitantly stepped into the night. Eyeing me again, he hurried toward our wagon in a peculiar, choppy gait. I followed at a reassuring distance. With only a quick glance inside, he scuttled away.

Althea frowned. "Was that the doctor?"

"I don't know," I answered, honest enough. "I told him we needed one."

An anxious, breathy whistling, like the sound a dove makes, came from the wagon. Ma! Althea plunged inside and I hurried to the back, expecting the worst.

You could hardly see her. It was like the darkness was swallowing her up, and she was gasping, trying to hold off the drowning. Althea crouched over her and murmured. I found myself stiffening and fighting for air myself. Here I'd done everything I could and still it wasn't gonna be enough. *Where* was the doctor?

With each of Ma's breaths cutting through me like a newly sharpened knife, I faced the town. I clenched my fists and willed for the doctor to come. Although Jewel went on sleeping, Lucky rose up to rest his chin on my shoulder and stare toward town as well. It was all the comfort he could give.

The stars showed brittle and icy bright overhead. The cold, cold air quietly worked its way under my skin, chilling my very bones, preparing to take me, too. My leg, which had fallen numb with all the walking, throbbed dully. And still the town slept. As each empty minute passed, I began to believe that we'd crawled this far only to fail.

A ways down the street a bobbing light poked a hole in the darkness. It was a lantern, and as it came closer and the flame grew larger I saw that it was accompanied by two figures: the little man with the braid and a woman wrapped in a shawl. To my surprise, she looked just as tired and worried as I felt. Her long, papery cornhusk of a face, in fact, seemed to be permanently creased with worry.

"What's happened?" she demanded.

"My ma's sick. Her baby died—yesterday, I think it was." Is that how recent it'd been? I wasn't sure.

She searched the darkness behind me. "Where's your pa?"

Oh, no. She wasn't gonna waste her time on a bunch of kids. "He's . . . he's seeing to another matter," I stammered, hoping that wasn't a lie. "He left me in charge. Told me get help for Ma."

She wasn't buying my story; I could read that much on her face. But she climbed into our wagon anyway. I waited for her to climb right back out and say she couldn't help us. I waited for her to say she only treated white folks. But that didn't happen. "Fong," she called from inside the wagon, a welcome urgency to her voice, "bring some more help. And hurry."

The rest of that night was like a waking dream. People I'd never seen before surrounded us; hands lifted Ma and Jewel outta the wagon. The oxen were led away in one direction, and Althea and I in another. Lamps were lit and food heated and plates set under our chins. The napkins smelled clean and soapy. No dust at all.

"A bit of good luck, that," someone said. "Doctor just returning from Carson City and all." And in the stupor of so much food and so many faces and too many voices, I did feel lucky. We'd made it to civilization. We'd gotten Ma to a doctor and done ourselves proud. Hadn't been killed in the process, or eaten or starved or heated to death. Yes, we'd done good. *I'd* done good. And lifting off the yoke I'd been carrying since Pa galloped away, I laid my head down on my arms and slept.

CHAPTER ELEVEN

Next thing I remember noticing was how scratchy the wool blanket was that was bunched under my face. And how the room I was in, a strange room, was as sunlit and hot as high noon. Where was I?

Blinking my eyes open, which was like clawing sand through 'em, I saw Althea and Jewel sprawled, arms and legs akimbo, in a mess of blankets beside me. They were still sleeping. I blinked again—dang, that hurt!—and looked around, trying to make sense of all the wooden legs I was seeing. They weren't ox legs or wheel spokes. They belonged to a desk and some chairs and a table and a bed. We were sleeping on a solid wood floor. Indoors! In a real house! How many months had passed since we'd slept with a real roof over our heads and a real floor under our feet? Wouldn't Ma be happy?

Where was Ma?

That sat me up straight, and my stirring made Althea moan. Pushing Jewel's leg off her, she sat up too, sleepy eyed as a cat.

We were both taking stock of things when the strange little man from last night came into the room. Carrying a tray with a yellow cloth draped over it, he shuffled like his feet hurt, or like he was crossing ice and afraid of falling. In the light of day I saw that there was something odd about his face, too. I didn't want to stare, but . . . well, it was flat. He had dark, narrow eyes that were set on kinda crooked. And while he wore pants like most men, he was also wearing a blue silk cap pulled down tight on his head. Coming out the back was that braided pigtail. Althea and I looked at each other in bewilderment.

Nodding and smiling, and making little bows from his waist as he crossed the room, the man set the tray down on the desk. He removed the cloth and a cloud of fragrant steam escaped. Colorful bowls and dishes heaped with food filled the tray. In a hushed voice the pigtailed man said, "Good morning!" The words sounded funny. "Happy to see you awake. Here is rice with syrup, and fried ham and cinnamon buns and nice milk. You eat."

Not a dried apple in sight, thank the Lord.

Without taking her eyes off him, Althea nudged Jewel awake. They each accepted a bowl of rice, a fine silver spoon stuck in its middle, and I took one too. The thin china was hot to the touch, so we balanced the bowls between our upraised knees and burning fingertips. Althea began spooning small bites into her mouth, and Jewel and I followed suit. Seeing that we were enjoying it—I nodded our thanks—the little man walked to the bed. He leaned over its pillow, cocking his head and listening.

That's when I noticed it was Ma lying there, so thin and so still that the sheets hardly rose to pass over her. I set my bowl down and started to get up, but the man immediately flapped his arms like an angry bird, motioning me to stay seated. Tiptoeing cross the room, he whispered, "Your mother sleeping again. She eat some already this morning.

Now you eat. But"—he held his finger to his lips—"you, shh."

I did as I was told. We all did. The little man stood over us the whole time, hands clasped behind him, humming. He smiled confidently, unlike when we'd first met, and something told me that in this house he was as accustomed to giving orders as he was to having them followed.

I must've fallen back to sleep after that, 'cause the next thing I remember, the sun was slanting in the opposite window and the room wasn't near as hot. Althea and Jewel were already awake, tearing the meat off a roasted chicken that was sitting between 'em on a fancy white and blue platter. Another tray was waiting on the desk, this one loaded with powdery biscuits and churned butter and some kinda cooked greens and more rice. My mouth started watering. I could get used to this royal treatment. Seeing me awake, Jewel offered an oily, skin-crackly drumstick. "It's *good*," she mumbled with her mouth full. One bite into the juicy meat told me she was right.

When the three of us had been nourished enough to try out our feet again, and the little man wasn't there to stop us, Althea and Jewel crawled up onto Ma's bed. She blinked awake and managed a mother's ready smile, but she was too weak to talk. Sweat beaded her forehead, and the way she clutched a wad of blanket in one hand told me she was hurting. A lot. No one mentioned Willie or Pa—I'd warned my sisters against it—but you could see the unasked questions stinging Ma's eyes. Next to her on the nightstand stood a big blue bottle of medicine, a bowl, and a rag, which provoked some questions of my own. So leaving the three of 'em to sit together, I carried those questions and a tray of licked-clean dishes down a set of narrow stairs in search of the doctor.

It was the doctor's own house we were staying in, and her office below was bustling that afternoon with activity. I'd been wondering why she'd taken no notice of our color, but one peek into the waiting room gave the answer: Folks in this town seemed to come packaged in all sorts of colors.

Seated on one of the two long benches was a flat-faced man with a pigtail and a hacking cough who could've been the twin of the man bringing us food. Next to him was a grimy soul—only half human, I'd swear—that looked to've climbed outta the ground. He had watery eyes staring from a leathery face and a bedraggled beard that fell past his belly. His mud-covered pants were worn through at the knees. A snowy-haired lady who'd taken a bath in her perfume sat on the opposite bench. She looked like a queen from a foreign land, and her silk skirts rustled as she fanned herself. In the corner, kinda bobbing up and down, was a thin, brown-skinned girl wrapped in an Indian's shawl. She held a baby who was wailing at the top of his lungs. That gave me a stab of pain 'cause it made me wonder if this doctor could've saved Willie.

I was desperate to ask 'bout Ma and did some pacing of my own. I wanted to find out what was wrong with her and if she was gonna get better and how much that fancy blue bottle of medicine was costing us and if we could afford it. But throughout the day ailing folks streamed through the waiting room, and all I could do was watch.

I saw that the man who'd brought us the trays of food worked as the doctor's assistant, too. He quickly followed whatever orders she spoke to him, then stood against the wall, hands clasped, when she didn't need his help. I noticed, too, that it seemed to reassure some of the men patients that there was another man in the room, even if he was no taller'n a woman and braided his long hair like one.

Twice I thought I'd be able to speak with the doctor, but first came a person with a rheumy eye and I had to step aside, and then came one with a mangled hand. Round about the time a clock chimed half past four, a boy some years older than me drove his clattering wagon right up to the door. He rushed in and grabbed the doctor's arm and simply wouldn't let go, jabbering on about his ma having a baby and his pa saying they needed to hurry. Dragging the boy with her, the doctor calmly packed some things into a satchel. The pair of 'em clumsily climbed into his wagon, where she finally shook him off and took hold of the reins herself, and they rumbled off at a gallop. My questions had to wait.

The sun was going down, and since the rooms were emptied, the little man busied himself sweeping them. I joined in. He gathered up the doctor's tools, wiped them with a cloth, and put them back in their hinged boxes. Then he showed me how to wash the windows till you couldn't even tell there was glass there, and how to fill the small medicine bottles from larger ones kept in a storeroom. It was when I followed him out to the storeroom that I discovered where Lucky'd spent the night. I figured he wasn't allowed inside the house, which was okay. I wasn't gonna push the doctor's hospitality. After we'd finished, though, I showed Jewel where he was, and those two knotted themselves into a tongue-licking, arm-hugging, laughing, barking mess. Acted like they'd been parted for a year. I left 'em there to slobber on each other while I hurried out to see to our oxen and our wagon before dark.

Didn't have to look far; the two animals were penned with

the same horses and mules we'd seen on the edge of town last night. They were lying in the corner, back to back, as if joined by an invisible yoke. After a whole day's rest they still looked mighty spent. If they noticed me coming, they took pains not to show it. Couldn't blame 'em. Just inside the barn was a man scooping feed into buckets, and I went over to settle things with him.

"Those are our oxen you have out there," I said, which wasn't a very good way to start. Pa did a sight better'n me talking with people.

The man pushed his hat back on his head and smiled anyway. "Are they, now? Then how come they're in *my* corral?"

That got me. Felt like my mouth was full of pebbles as I stammered an answer. "I mean . . . thank you . . . for looking after 'em. They *are* ours. I've . . . I've come to see to the bill."

"Did I give you a bill?"

Why was he funning me? 'cause I was young? Or was he gonna try and claim our oxen as his? "I need to pay you for their feed," I insisted. And to impress him, I pulled one of the gold coins from my pocket. Even in the barn's slanted light it gleamed.

That gleam jumped straight up into his eyes and he whistled. "That'll pay for a whole lot of feed. How long you plan on keeping 'em here?"

"Until my ma gets better and we can move on to Sacramento."

He threw back his head and laughed, and my face flushed hot. "Hope you're hiding more oxen in your pocket along with that money."

"Huh?"

"Those two skinny fellas you drug in couldn't make it over the Sierra Nevada on a good day. Why, even if they was pulling behind three yoke of good oxen, they couldn't do it. You ain't going nowheres."

What a ninny I was. Of course we were gonna need more oxen. "Can I buy a couple of pairs of oxen from you? I have more money." Soon as I said that, I knew it was a mistake.

"Hmm." He dug a finger into his ear, sizing me up at the same time. "You must've found yourself a gold mine. Where's your ..." I didn't know whether he was gonna ask 'bout my supposed mine or my pa, but either way he suddenly seemed to think better of it and the finger came outta his ear. "Let's never mind 'bout that. Now then, I could probably find you some more oxen in a day or three, some real good ones too, but that's not your only problem. See, I was looking over your wagon, and you're gonna need a new wheel for it. Lucky for you, I can fix that myself." He paused, trying, I think, to dim the gleam in his eye, but it was no use. Opportunity had walked right into his barn and spilled its pockets. "So, everything together," he said real smoothly, "along with the feed for these two oxen and at least four new ones, would come to ... oh, say, one hundred ninety-five dollars." He reached for the coin.

I shoved it in my pocket fast and took a step backward just in case he was gonna hit me. "I . . . I don't have that much money," I stammered.

"Well," he growled, "you got to pay something for me feeding your animals if you're gonna keep 'em here." He returned to scooping feed, leaving me cooling my heels and wondering how I was ever gonna pile up enough money to pay for Ma's medicine and the oxen's keep and the wagon repair, and then still manage to buy more oxen to get us outta this town and on our way. "Or you can sell 'em to me." He kept scooping, not even turning around. "You know, cut your losses and just settle in here. What's so almighty important 'bout Sacramento, anyways? It's too crowded. Why, I heard you can't hardly cross a street in Sacramento without fear of getting run over." He stood up now and turned to give me a look as hard as iron. "You want to get run over?"

The whole way back to the doctor's house my face burned like someone was holding a torch to it. I'd done what the man had coaxed me to do; I'd sold him our oxen. Just didn't know if that was right or not. "Cut your losses," he'd kept saying over and over. And it seemed to make sense. The animals weren't strong enough to get over the mountains, and I'd need to buy more oxen anyway, so there was no use in feeding these two while I figured out a way to get more. So I was walking away with another twenty dollars in my pocket, a fourth of what we'd been paid for our butchered oxen, which added some heat to my face. I felt like I'd failed.

Well, just what was I supposed to do? I argued with myself. Keep feeding two scrawny oxen that were no help to us? With Ma needing so much care? At least we had a solid hundred dollars now. That was good seed money.

I tried to take pleasure in the heavy feel of my pocket. As I stepped onto the dusky boardwalk, brushing shoulders with others, I tried to walk tall, a man of wealth. But instead of buoying me up, the weight seemed to drag me down. With each echoing footfall it seemed that I was sinking into the trap of this little town that was so far from where we'd started and so far from where we needed to be.

CHAPTER TWELVE

Early next morning the doctor still hadn't returned, and after seeing that Ma was as comfortable as could be expected, I slipped out to do some exploring. Dayton, or Chinatown—I realized now it was Chinese men I was seeing everywhere—was only middling size, but it was abristle with hardworking people scratching out a living. That's what I had to do. At least for now. It's what Pa would've done.

I'd been thinking 'bout him a lot while walking in his shoes, growing angry and teary and then just thoughtful in turns. Since yesterday I'd been thinking back on a time when all of us were living on a small farm in Missouri. We'd had an agreement with the lady that owned the farm that any eggs laid inside the chicken pen belonged to her, while any eggs found outside the pen could belong to us. Course, not many eggs were laid outside the pen. There was this one day when Pa and I were hunting through the bushes. I was bellyaching that it wasn't fair that we should have to work so hard for a few measly eggs when that lady could just walk out and pick eggs off a nest any old time she wanted. Pa went on searching through the bushes, real slow and steady, like he hadn't even heard me. Till he said, "Complainin' don't fill a man's stomach, Colton, and it just tires the tongue. You gotta gather the eggs given you." And that's what I set out to do in Chinatown: gather eggs. Somehow, some way, I was gonna earn my family's keep.

Now that I got a good look at it in daylight, I thought the town itself was kinda ramshackle, like it'd been nailed together in a hurry. The setting was pretty enough, though. It'd been built hard on the banks of a shallow river, and the golden trees lining it glinted in the morning sun. But the buildings themselves were crammed together like books on a shelf. Some were tall, like Mrs. Minsky's Boardinghouse and the Union Hotel. Squeezed in between were some smaller ones, like Zang's Saloon and Victor Wisehart Saddlery and the tiny building with just the word BARBER in the window. I supposed mining offered opportunity, 'cause there were several stores selling supplies. And I guessed that was dirty work, too, 'cause there were twice as many signs offering to wash laundry. Wondering if the livery would have work for me, I headed toward it. But as I walked past Hallsworth's Emporium— WE HAVE WHAT YOU WANT—I caught the word *roses* in the window display and stopped to examine a pamphlet on the subject. And that got me thinking in a different direction.

Hurrying back to the doctor's house, I motioned for Althea to leave Ma's bed and follow me down the stairs and out the back door. That's where Jewel was. In the short time since she and Lucky'd been reunited, she'd assembled her own little lean-to and makeshift fence with scrap lumber. The two of 'em were setting up house, it seemed. Lucky was hang-tongued happy, even though he was wearing an apron round his middle, which no self-respecting dog should've done. I don't think he cared how Jewel humiliated him, long as he kept getting her table scraps.

I told Althea and Jewel to sit down. Acting like part of the family, Lucky sat too.

"How's Ma doing?" I asked Althea.

She made a face that read neither good nor bad. Hopeful maybe. "She's wore out still," she answered thoughtfully. "I think she knows that Willie's dead. She sure does sleep a lot, though."

I watched her run her finger round the toe of her shoe while she was talking. It was split clean open, just like the other one. All that walking did it. Leather shoes just couldn't hold up to the desert. Guess that's why they nailed iron shoes onto horses.

"And how's Lucky doing?" I asked Jewel.

"Good," she answered, beaming just as happily as he was. "He's the mama and I'm the papa and this is our house."

"Looks like your house could use a little outfitting."

All three of 'em looked at me funny. See, while I was walking the town, I was thinking 'bout Pa and feeling the weight of the gold coins in a different way. Some of the money had to go to the doctor, I knew—probably most of it. And some of it had to be saved up for more oxen and a new wheel. But before it was all gone, I wanted to do something nice for Ma and my sisters. Pa would've.

"They got an emporium here."

"So?" Althea responded testily.

"Well," I said, "winter's not far off, and by the way she's been eating of late, Jewel's probably growed outta last year's coat. And . . . snowflakes'll be setting up house between *your* toes if you're not careful."

"That's not funny, Colton." She pulled her skirt down tight over her knees and past her shoes to hide 'em. "Don't tease us when we got nothing to pay for new things."

It was the moment I'd been waiting for. Reaching into my pocket, my deep one that I checked every day to make sure it hadn't developed any holes, I pulled out the four gold coins, along with the paper money I'd got for selling our last two oxen. The coins looked even bigger and shinier and richer than before.

Althea gasped. "*Where* did you get those?" She leaned close, afraid to touch 'em, then pulled away. "Did you steal 'em? Oh no, Colton!" All in one breath.

I laughed. "No, I'll explain it. Come on," I said. "Let's go see what this town has for sale."

It was still only September, so I guess you could say that Christmas came early to the Wescott family. As we walked up and down past the stores, pointing and giggling, it was like I could hear Pa laughing too. He'd always said, "There are necessaries and there are frivolaries, and in this life a person needs some of both."

Before noon we were walking back down the shaded boardwalk feeling like royalty. Althea had on a pair of brand-spanking-new shoes with grown-up heels and made a show of lifting her skirt a little higher than usual to negotiate steps. She had a new wool coat, too, just like Jewel did. Jewel insisted on wearing hers, even though it was hotter'n blazes. I found a packaged set of six miniature plates and teacups and presented it to her and Lucky for their "new house." That made her laugh, and the laugh alone was worth the price. For Ma we picked out a pretty blue shawl—

that was her necessary—and the pamphlet on *How to Grow Splendid Roses in the West*. That was her frivolary. And there was peppermint candy for each of us.

Me? I was having a hard time spending anything on myself. More'n anything I wanted my own horse. There was a gaping hole inside me that only the feel and smell and breath of a horse could fill up. But that would've set me back some fifty dollars, not including a saddle and bridle. Too much of a frivolary. Just knowing I had enough money in my pocket, though, was making it torturous not to look. So I left my sisters staring at the blacksmith's orange sparks to saunter over to the town's main livery yard.

It didn't have much to offer. There were more mules, in fact, than horses, maybe 'cause of all the miners in the area. A bunch of the horses were dozing in a corral, swishing their tails at flies, while others waited, saddled and tied to a rail, swishing their tails too. I began working my way through the prospects in the corral, when one of the saddled horses lifted his head and pulled against the tied reins to watch me. My throat caught. The horse was a chestnut, on the smallish side, with a white blaze on his face and little pricked ears. He looked exactly like Ned. That would mean Pa was still alive. Pa was right here in Chinatown!

I yipped with joy, which sent the horses scattering in all directions, then banging together in a confused frenzy. Pushing through the herd, I tried not to lose sight of the chestnut. If I could just get to him, just check the scar behind his ears, I'd know for certain. He kept watching me come, and the closer I got, the more certain I was. And just when I was ready to reach for his bridle, a stranger walked up, climbed into the saddle, and rode the gelding away.

The jolt of pain near knocked me flat. It was like losing Pa all over again, which didn't make any sense. He was dead. I knew that. But still I felt cheated. Kicking a pebble outta the way and hearing it thunk against the barn didn't help. I just grew angrier. All over again I was angry at him for leaving us. Angry and hurt that he'd leave me. When my eyes started burning hot and wet, I turned my anger on myself. *Stop being a Nellie boy,* I scolded.

Smoking with fury, I stalked into town again. This time my heels on the boardwalk sounded hollow. The coins in my pocket didn't feel near as weighty or special. I didn't know where I was going, just felt like I wanted to run.

That's when I saw it. In the telegraph office. A large poster with a horse and rider galloping furiously across the top of it. The words were set in bold type: WANTED. YOUNG, SKINNY, WIRY FELLOWS NOT OVER EIGHTEEN. MUST BE EXPERT RIDERS. WILLING TO RISK DEATH DAILY. ORPHANS PREFERRED.

My heart pumped double fast 'cause the words were speaking straight to me. They were speaking to me strong as if they'd reached out and grabbed me by the collar. With my palms growing sweaty, I read 'em over once more before going on to the small print. Sure enough, it was an invitation to ride for the Pony Express—for the princely sum of one hundred dollars a month *and* room and board! "Apply to the Pony Express office in Carson City," it said, "on Tuesday or Friday before 3:30 P.M."

A sudden memory of the little hawk filled my mind. I could almost feel his claws digging into my skin, hear his shrill cry that urged me to follow. Tomorrow was Friday, and that got me all stirred up.

I read over the poster again. "Orphans preferred," it said,

and I guess I qualified in principle. I'd always been told I was skinny, and I wasn't over eighteen. "Expert rider." I'd manage. All of a sudden, and more than anything, I wanted to sit on the back of a galloping horse and watch the ground fly past my feet. To run and run and run. "Willing to risk death daily." Huh! When *hadn't* I been doing that?

With my heart pounding so loud in my ears that it drowned out the sounds of the street, I made my way back toward my sisters. They were safe now, I told myself. Ma was safe. And it looked like she might be staying with the doctor a long time. So I needed to earn money for my family. Shoving away the guilt, I knew it was mostly that I wanted to gallop. Just for a while I wanted to gallop away from all my troubles. And I knew, somehow, I was going to.

CHAPTER THIRTEEN

D on't be thinking 'bout leaving us, Colton. You're all we got—much as it pains me to say that."

"Oh, come on. You still got Ma here, and heck, you're almost a ma. You nag like one."

Althea rolled her eyes and blew air through her nose.

"See what I mean?"

Dusk was surrounding the town as we talked, setting a quiet space between the bustling day and the boisterous night. Behind the mountains a last spattering of fiery orange clouds was being snuffed out by a purply sky. Although we were on the stoop behind the doctor's house, I knew that Chinatown's dusty street out front was clearing. Wagons had stopped their rattling, horses had stopped their trotting, people had stopped their clomping up and down the boardwalk. The stores were closed and the business folks had gone home for the day. Soon the saloons would be stirring to life. Come the first glittery stars, piano music and laughter would dance through the air.

Usually I relished this time. It was relaxing. But tonight I was so itchy a person would've sworn I had ants in my pants. It didn't help that the conversation was hitting some snags. I stood up to shake out my legs.

Althea was just staring at her lap, wearing a look of pure anger. Since Jewel was playing house nearby, we had to keep our voices low. There was a lot of silence between times. Lucky grabbed a moment of freedom to pad over and flop at our feet. Stretching and yawning, he rolled onto his back and lay there looking like a fool, grinning just as wide as one. That dog had the foulest-smelling breath I'd ever known on any animal or person.

"And you got Lucky here," I said. "He'll look after you, if his breath don't kill you first."

Althea's stabbing glare told me she didn't share the humor.

"Listen," I said, talking serious, trying to convince her as well as me that my going was right, "I gotta earn us some money. I talked to the doctor this afternoon, and she said Ma had the childbed fever and it could take her a month or more to get better."

It was true. I'd met the doctor coming back from the birthing that'd hauled her off and that had lasted a whole day and night. She looked limp as a wrung-out cloth. Spoke to me nice enough, though. Steadying herself against a bookcase, she'd told me that medicine and time and God's will would heal Ma, but there'd be no traveling over the mountains for another month or two, and by then it would be winter, so we'd all be staying on until spring. She had the room, she assured me, and promised to work out a fair price for the board and care. And then, before she could get some rest herself, somebody else was pulling at her sleeve and needing her help.

"We can't all of us just sit around eating her food and sleeping in her house without working for it," I said.

"What about all that money you're carrying?"

"It won't last forever. And what're we gonna do when it's gone?"

She made a face that would've looked proper on a mule, and her bubbling anger percolated all the way down to her foot, which started tapping hard and fast. Pretending to study her new shoes, she asked, "How're you gonna get to Carson City? Do you even know where it is?"

"Not exactly," I began, and she looked up right away, thinking she had me. "But I was told it's south and west of here, 'bout twelve miles on. I can just follow the wagon tracks. They seem to lead to all the towns worth passing through."

"So, *how're* you gonna get there—walk?"

I felt for the coins in my pocket, rubbing them through my fingers. Even with our little spending spree I still had better'n eighty-five dollars. I could manage to buy a horse and saddle and ride to Carson City, but I'd already decided not to. Better keep the money for emergencies. "Yeah, I'm gonna walk."

"Ha!" Althea looked relieved. "Now I *know* you're funning us, 'cause you can't just up and walk all the way to Carson City by your lonesome."

I smiled. As the last light faded from the sky, shrouding me apart with my thoughts, I told myself to let her think that. *Let her think I'm just funning.*

Later, when the lamps were turned low and the upstairs floor of the doctor's house was quiet, I sat with Ma awhile. For the first time in a long time she looked something like her old self. She was even raised up a little bit on a mess of pillows, though she couldn't lift her head off 'em.

I was sitting in a chair pulled up close to the bed, leaning over to her, and she was resting her hand on mine. Kinda scared me how light and bony it felt. No heavier than a bird's wing. I'd always thought of her as being the strong one.

"Colton." She murmured my name and smiled. "Guess you're the man now."

She didn't even mention Pa. Naming me as his replacement only added to my itchiness. And to my nagging guilt. Was my leaving to find work the same as his running off? Would I be deserting my family too?

No, I told myself straight out. This was different. I was doing this for my family. Still, I squirmed and tried to pull my hand free.

She closed her fingers round mine. "Seems it's dangerous times we're living in."

"Whaddya mean?"

"Dr. Bekins was reading to me from a newspaper 'bout the coming election for president. She's a nice lady. Smart. There's a Mr. Lincoln, it seems, who's stood up and said he's against having slaves, and a Mr. Douglas, who's all for it. And the whole state of South Carolina says it'll pull outta the Union if it so happens that Mr. Lincoln wins. They're talking of war." Her chest was going up and down with the effort of breathing.

"Guess that won't trouble us," I said, giving her a reassuring smile. "We're a long way from South Carolina."

She looked stone-cold serious. Sick as she was, there was something that had her back up. "I don't expect Mr. Lincoln'll win the election. Seems as if there's always been slaves. Far back as the Bible there's been slaves." She was rubbing my hand with her thumb while she was talking, rubbing her own worries into me. "World is what it is and you can't change that." Her words stayed soft enough, but when she looked up,

I saw a storm brewing in her eyes. In the lamplight they burned black as two bits of coal. "Colton," she said all of a sudden and urgent, "I want that you do something for me."

"Sure, Ma." I tried to laugh a little, like if I did, she'd stop being so serious, stop scaring the pants off me. But her look stopped me flat. Lifting one hand, she fumbled with the buttons on her dress.

"Turn your head," she scolded.

Course I did, and when she spoke my name again, I saw that she was holding a small, yellowish envelope, stained with sweat and worn at the corners. Nothing 'bout its appearance said so, but I knew right away it held something important.

"Colton Wescott," she said, and her using my entire name made the fact doubly clear, "I don't know what's going to happen to me—shush now! I need you to listen—but I can't let this letter stay hid any longer. I'm putting it in your care. If, for some reason, we all don't make it to Sacramento, I want you to promise to deliver this envelope into the hands of my sister there."

I didn't take the envelope at first. I was still trying to keep things light. "But nothing's gonna happen to you now, Ma. The doctor's looking after you. You're getting better."

Like I hadn't spoken at all, she pushed the envelope toward me. A new worry chased the storm outta her eyes, and for a moment she looked longingly at it, like a child who's been made to give up a prize. Producing a pin, she motioned for me to put the envelope inside my shirt.

"I don't see why you think—"

"None of us knows our time, Colton," she interrupted. "So you listen close. Inside that envelope are some papers setting my sister, Luzenia, free from her master. She's been paid for in full, and she's free to live life as she sees fit now. She doesn't have to run anymore. Only, she doesn't know that."

"You never told us you had a sister who was a slave."

"She *isn't* a slave!" Beads of sweat popped out on her brow. "And I didn't tell you 'bout her 'cause I hardly know anything 'bout her myself. She's my half sister, and I only saw her twice, when I was near your age. Our ma had already died by then. But I swore when I saw that strangled look in her eyes that I'd find a way to buy her freedom. Only, she ran away before I could do it."

"Then, why does she need this paper?"

"Because the way the world is, any white man can walk up to you at any place and at any time and accuse you of being his runaway slave. Me, you, your sisters, anybody. Next morning you find yourself working under the whip. That's not gonna change. But that paper you're carrying, which the Reverend and Mrs. Winstrom helped me get with their own money, can protect her some. I'd have gotten it to her sooner, but I didn't know where she was living till she sent word to me last spring." She let out a breath and blinked, looking weak again but determined. "No one in my family is gonna be a slave," she said firmly. "So if I can't make it to Sacramento, I want you to find a way to get there and get that paper to my sister. But you have to hand it to her directly. Can you promise me that?"

"I promise, Ma."

"Good." Immediately she closed her eyes, as if our talk was all that'd been keeping her awake. Her grip on my hand eased and her breathing came regular.

Studying her wearied face, I wondered if I should tell her 'bout my plan to ride for the Pony Express. In a way it was carrying out her wishes, 'cause I'd be headed toward

Sacramento. But I knew she'd worry about the danger. The poster'd said, "Willing to risk death daily." To tell truth, that was worrying me some too. What if I never made it to Sacramento? What if I was killed before I could hand the letter over? What if this was the very last night I ever looked upon my ma or my sisters? I was getting myself pretty worked up and teary when she opened her eyes. Gave me a chill 'cause it was like she knew my thoughts.

"You're the man now, Colton," she said solemnly and with confidence. "You do whatever it takes."

And then she was asleep for certain, 'cause a few minutes later there was a soft and regular rattling to her breathing. I tried laying myself down on the floor beside Althea and Jewel, but that itchy feeling had me jumping. What's more, Ma's envelope was pressing its need into my skin too.

For what seemed like an hour but was probably no more'n a few minutes, I tossed and turned. My blanket twisted into a knot. Heaving a sigh, I gave up on sleep and lay staring at the shadows on the ceiling. Out on the street a man's loud laugh burst into the night. There was some talk between others, words I couldn't make out, then another laugh. They got on their horses and rode off, the quickening sound of hoofbeats making my heart gallop. In the silence that followed I realized Althea was awake. Good Lord, didn't she *ever* sleep?

"Don't you be thinking of running off," she warned in a whisper. Rising up on one elbow, she gave me her best hard look. Even though it was dark, I could feel it try to bring me to rights. "You hear me, Colton?"

I did, but I didn't say so. I just kept staring at the ceiling. The inside of me was already outside with those hoofbeats, running fast through the night. She knew it, I suppose, 'cause she suddenly flopped onto her side, purposely turning her back to me. There was a distance growing between us. I'd been feeling it all day. The pulling apart was hard on both of us.

It took a long time until her breathing grew regular, but when it did, I rose up real quiet. I'd already wrapped three gold coins, along with some bills, inside a handkerchief, and I laid the small bundle beside her pillow. The remaining gold coin was riding inside my left boot. It gave me a measure of security as I pulled it on.

I'd spent part of the day testing out the squeaks in the upstairs hall and found there were too many of 'em to pass unnoticed. So I'd left a window open earlier in the evening, one of a pair that looked out onto a narrow balcony. Grabbing my coat, which'd also been outfitted earlier in the day with a fair helping of food, I climbed through the window. My heart was hammering so loud in my ears I couldn't hear if I was making any noise. Testing the railing, I threw my leg over and shinnied down the post, landing hard in the dirt street. A couple of saddle horses pricked their ears, but when I looked round, I didn't see any human eyes watching.

There, I'd done it. I was free. Out at the end of the dark street, where the town emptied into the desert, I heard a coyote yip and another one answer. That prickled my skin, made me look back up at the balcony. A pillow and a blanket were waiting for me there. And safety. Who knew what was waiting for me in the night?

Taking a deep drink of the chilled air, I turned away, started putting one foot ahead of the other. "You do whatever it takes," Ma had said. For that I needed to keep heading west.

CHAPTER FOURTEEN

The sky was mostly clear, just a few straggly clouds glowing silver against the black. A fat slice of moon sat low on the horizon. It lit up the sand enough to cast the twin wagon ruts in shadow, making 'em easy to follow. Seemed like they were angling southerly now, still pulled toward the mountains in a sorta homeward migration. The air was awful cold and, once I left town, awful silent. The *cr-runch, cr-runch* of my boots sounded alarmingly loud in the darkness.

Didn't take long for the coyotes to find me. I'd tried tiptoeing, but one by one they came congregating outta the night. First there were three, then five, then a whole pack. I wondered if it was the same ones that'd followed us into town. These yellow-eyed fellas were hanging off a ways, following in a sorta half circle. Just knowing they wanted me to run made my heart skitter like a rabbit's.

But I wasn't planning on running, and I ordered my jittery nerves to settle. "When the sun comes up," I said real loud to my four-footed audience—and while I didn't turn round, I imagine it put 'em back a step or two—"it's gonna be Friday. And on Friday applications are accepted till 3:30 P.M. in the Pony Express office in Carson City,

Utah Territory. And I, Colton Wescott—you'll do yourselves well to remember that name—plan to be waiting first in line when the sun comes up in Carson City."

Course, I was more scared than I sounded. But something had gotten into me—it was like I had ice in my veins—and I was filled with such determination that no coyote, not even a whole pack of 'em, was gonna stop me from trying out for the Pony mail.

Remembering the little hawk and how it felt to have him digging his excitement into my shoulder, I spread my arms. I imagined myself flying. Slowly I began twirling round, hoping I looked to've taken leave of my senses—at least to a coyote's way of thinking. With the bunch of 'em standing glassy eyed and curious, I suddenly lifted my arms over my head. "Git! Git! Git!" I shouted at the top of my lungs, and those prowlers tucked tail and scattered in all directions, the way fish do when you drop a stone in the pond.

They joined back together soon enough, though. Guess they were determined too.

When I saw they were gonna keep following me, I took a different approach. I turned my back to 'em. Acted like they didn't concern me at all, and just kept walking. I sang some too, all the songs I could bring to mind. You could say I was showing more sand than sense, but I fully intended on getting to Carson City in one piece. And I made a vow this'd be the last walking I'd do. Tomorrow I was gonna throw my leg over the back of a Pony Express horse, and from then on I'd just be a blur in the yellow eyes of these slobbering beasts.

We must've traveled more'n a mile that way, me walking and talking and singing. All the time they came padding closer and closer. One of 'em was chattering his teeth off and on, like he was already tasting me, and that *did* prickle the hairs on my neck. Another one started growling and making little stabbing lunges in the direction of my ankles, trying to hurry his supper.

Again and again I swung round and threw my arms up in the air. "Git!" I shouted, and stomped my foot. "Git!" Each time they scattered, though each time it wasn't near as far. They were swarming together now and coming right up close. Their glowing eyes seemed soulless, nightmarish in the moonlight. Saliva glistened and dripped from their black lips. One lifted his pointy snout into the air and sniffed.

That's when I smelled it too: the mouth-tickling aroma of the meats and breads I had hid inside my coat. How daft could I be?

With their noses near to touching my boots, I took out a packet of steak slices. The rustling of the paper made dozens of ears rise up. I carefully peeled off one slice, waved it in the air, then heaved it into the night far as I could. Most of the pack chased after it. I pulled off another slice and heaved it in the opposite direction. The others followed. Little by little I tore the steak into pieces and hurled it all over the place. I ripped the bread into chunks and sent it flying too. In seconds you would've thought there was a coyote convention taking place, 'cause there was yipping and growling and snarling to beat the devil. I didn't wait round for thanks. Tossing the juice-stained paper into the brush as dessert, I turned and took off at a dogtrot. I needed to put some distance between them and me, and now was the time.

I surprised myself with how fast I could run, and how far.

Lucky for me the ground was fairly even, just little rolling hills that made it feel like I was getting a lot of land put behind me. When I fell to a walk, wheezing like a leaky bellows, I spooked a jackrabbit and he took up running where I'd laid off.

If I had to guess, I'd say it took me somewhere over three hours to find my way to the outskirts of Carson City. The framework of civilization began appearing in scraps—a lone ranch house here, a barn there, and a few scattered outbuildings—before I reached the town proper. And it *was* a proper town I found as I entered the main street, with a formal plaza and white picket fences and brand-spanking-new buildings going up right and left. Even in the middle of the night I could smell the sawdust—a good, clean smell that meant people were happy. They were building their dreams, settling in and making homes for themselves. I hoped Ma and the rest of us would be doing that someday.

Figuring I'd find the Pony Express office somewhere along here, I headed farther into town. It made me a little nervous being out and 'bout at this hour—whatever this hour was—'cause it seemed like if someone were to see you, they'd say you were up to no good. Who else was out this time of night 'cept rustlers and robbers and coyotes? So I kept to the dirt street and stayed clear of the rattly boardwalk, praying I'd make less noise that way.

Saloons seemed to be mighty popular in Carson City. They were lined up on both sides of the street and mostly painted white. At this hour of the night, or morning perhaps, they were finally empty, though through an open door to one of 'em I saw a stove still glowing orange and the silhouette of a man curled up asleep on the bar.

The other popular establishments in the city seemed to be assay offices. Gold fever must've struck hard in these parts, 'cause there sure were a lot of 'em. Many of the offices had signs in their windows bragging that *they'd* been the ones to weigh out so-and-so's two-pound or three-pound gold nugget. For a moment I was tempted to swap dreams and try my hand at mining, but then I stumbled upon the Pony Express office.

It was 'bout halfway through town, near Fourth Street, tucked between a good-size hotel and another assay office. Painted letters on the door's window read PONY EXPRESS OFFICE on top, and below that, MR. BOLIVAR ROBERTS, SUPERINTENDENT. Posted inside the window was a list of names of people having mail waiting for 'em. And there was the same poster, too, that I'd seen in Chinatown. The galloping horse and rider sent the same finger of excitement running along my spine as they'd done before. I was ready to sign up. *Now.* Where was this Mr. Roberts?

Glancing at the eastern horizon, I found no sign of the sun rising any time soon, so there was no telling when Mr. Roberts might show up. I plopped down on the bench outside his office. The night air was still and cold. Somewhere in the darkness a horse squealed and several others whinnied in response. My heart bucked.

Time would go by faster if I slept, so I tried curling up on the bench. It was like my eyes were propped open with toothpicks, though. Tired as I was, I just couldn't settle my bones. Sleep stood off a ways, just watching me. I shivered. Wrapping my arms round myself, I wished I had a blanket or a quilt or even Lucky, foul breath and all.

Outside of town a lone coyote yipped, a call to the world that he was waiting. I listened, waiting with him. He yipped again, but still there was no answer. Of a sudden the night seemed extra heavy with lonesomeness. I shivered again and forced my eyes shut, tried to stop listening. Sometime before that coyote found his friends, I managed to find sleep.

CHAPTER FIFTEEN

It was the sound of boots scraping wood that jolted me awake. Or at least jolted me upright. Before I'd fully come to, I was trying to rub the fog outta my eyes and at the same time trying to unkink my bones, which felt like a horny pile of hog's knuckles. I blinked into the sunlight, which produced a swirling mess of hot colors, then shaded my eyes and blinked again. A man wearing a black coat and necktie was standing over me. Since he was silhouetted against the morning glare, though, I couldn't make out his face.

"You get throwed outta your bed?" he asked, and at least by his neighborly tone I guessed I wasn't in any immediate danger.

"No, sir," I answered. "I'm waiting on the Pony Express man."

"The rider or the desk jockey?"

"Huh?"

"What do you want?"

I climbed to my feet and stood where I could look into the man's face directly. And that's just how I'd have to describe it: direct. 'Cause everything 'bout its formation seemed honed to a purpose. The cheekbones, set high and flat, smooth as copper. The sand-colored hair flowing away in waves, like he was accustomed to riding head-on into the wind. A perfectly straight nose that split shadowy crevices harboring a pair of steely blue eyes. It was a face that had been carved from determined living. I knew without being told that even though he was smiling at me now, this man wasn't the sort you wanted to cross.

Rattling the doorknob to draw attention to his question, and to the fact that I was keeping him waiting, he raised an eyebrow. I glanced at the lettering to make sure, then asked, "Are *you* Mr. Bolivar Roberts?"

"Guilty," he replied. And right away, in a conspiratorial whisper, "What'd I do?"

"I'm here to ride for your Pony Express."

He let out a good laugh, which was not quite the reaction I was expecting. "You are, are you? Well, just how old might you be, son?"

"Twelve," I shot back, "near thirteen."

He laughed louder. Opening the door—indicating the conversation was nearly done—he said, "You want to think that one over again? You more favor ten, maybe eleven."

My face got blistering hot. "I'm . . . I'm twelve," I stammered like a royal fool. "Really."

He chuckled, though not in a mean way. "I'm sorry, son," he said. "Riding for the Pony Express is man's work. Tell your pa to send you back when you've growed up some." With that he walked into the office and closed the door.

And there I stood on the wrong side of it, dismissed. After I'd gone through all the heartache of leaving Ma and Althea and Jewel. After I'd walked the whole night and fought off a pack of hungry coyotes. Given the boot.

Feeling stunned—like I'd been slapped hard—I plopped

down on the same bench I'd been sleeping on. And I sat there. Just sat there, staring cross the street but not seeing a thing. It wasn't supposed to happen this way. What was I gonna do now? Seemed like my mind was mired in mud, 'cause I couldn't grab on to whatever it was I should do next.

Voicing its own opinion on what I should do next was my stomach. It began gurgling and growling, reminding me how long it'd been since I'd tossed *it* some food. I was feeling so sorry for myself that I dug down in my boot for the gold coin. Then I searched out a place serving breakfast, which happened to be the hotel next door, and splurged on a frivolary: a fried steak followed by a plateful of corn dodgers dripping in honey. These were served up with a steaming cup of coffee—extra cream and sugar, thank you.

Well, there's nothing like a cup of hot coffee to warm your spirits on a dismal day—not that the weather itself was dismal. In fact, as I strolled along the boardwalk afterward, feeling pleasantly full and jingly, dodging elbows and stepping clear of skirts, I noticed that the morning sky was painted an especially pretty color of blue. Troop after troop of fluffy white clouds marched cross it in fine order. Somehow that made me feel positive, like things were progressing as they should and I needed to be progressing with 'em. So I made my way back to the bench outside the Pony Express office. It sorta felt like "my" bench now, and I sorta felt like I could protect "my" job by sitting on it. Besides, if no one else showed up to apply, Mr. Roberts'd *have* to let me ride, wouldn't he?

But of course someone else showed up. In fact, over the next few hours several someones showed up.

The first was a rough-looking man with leathery skin

and legs so bowed he must've spent his whole life on a horse. At the sight of him my heart wallowed down round my knees. Soon as he stamped into the office, leaving the door wide open, I scootched across the bench to listen.

Mr. Roberts was polite through and through. He asked the man a few questions 'bout his abilities, listened to him brag 'bout a couple of incidents. Nudging the conversation in a different direction, he reviewed the advertisement. "Not over eighteen," I heard him muse slowly and by way of introduction, like maybe the man wasn't aware of that requirement. The bowlegged man laughed uncomfortably. "You know," Mr. Roberts went on, "you get to be a certain age and a person gets too wise for a job like this. Course if I can't fill the saddle with someone young and foolish, I'll look you up." The man chuckled again and came strutting outta the office like he'd been promoted rather than turned down. So the job was still open. My heart lifted up.

Some time later two brothers—at least I think they were brothers by the way they were talking and joshing with each other—came stumbling down the street toward the office, each with an arm flung cross the other's shoulders. And they were big shoulders. The two of 'em walking side by side looked like a yoke of oxen. Although it was morning, I expected they'd been drinking some. The way they were laughing and weaving was turning heads. Anyway, they managed to squeeze into the office, still yoked, and announce together that they were here to apply, together, for the Pony Express rider position. Together.

Mr. Roberts wasn't as polite this time. He asked 'em 'bout their knowledge of horses and of the surrounding land but interrupted their rambling answers by saying, "You gentlemen may not be acquainted with the oath required of all our employees. Let me familiarize you with it." Behind me I heard a rustling of papers, and then in a more severe voice he recited: "'I do hereby swear, before the Great and Living God, that during my engagement I will under no circumstances use profane language; I will drink no intoxicating liquors'"—Mr. Roberts paused here purposefully, and though I couldn't see him, I could imagine his point-blank stare— "'I will not quarrel or fight with any employee of the firm; and in every respect I will conduct myself honestly, be faithful to my duties, and so direct all my acts to win the confidence of my employer. So help me God.'"

There was another pause. One of the brothers let out a raw oath, along with a belch, making the other bust out laughing, and then they came bumping through the doorway again and went stumbling down the middle of the street, not caring about horses or wagons or anything, and just laughing and laughing.

I decided to give it another try. Gathering up my gumption, I straightened my shirt, smoothed my hair, and stepped quietly inside the Pony Express office. The room was small, made all the more so by the huge desk sitting in its middle. Papers were strewn all cross its surface, and Mr. Roberts was bent over 'em, studying 'em before penning figures into a ledger. He hadn't heard me come in, so I cleared my throat, real polite like. "Yes?" he said, looking up. "Oh, it's you. What is it now?"

"I'm sorry 'bout before," I began. "I'm really fifteen, sir. It's just that I look young. But . . ."

His frown stopped me cold. His eyes narrowed, and I could've sworn they flashed hot blue sparks. Dismissing me with a wave of his hand, he grumbled, "I've no time for your tall tales. Why don't you run along back to your ma's apron strings?" He bent over his figures, leaving me shame-faced and with nothing to do but shuffle toward the door with my tail between my legs.

This time when I took to sitting on my bench, I thought Carson City looked a whole lot less happy and friendly. It didn't help that I was squirming with guilt. I'd just lied, something I prided myself on not doing. Lied straight out. And I was feeling more and more like I'd run off, just like Pa. Now I'd failed at getting a job. What was I gonna do? Where was I gonna go?

Feeling 'bout as worthless as a flea on a dog's backside, I sat on that bench for hours, my mind mired in pity. I watched homesteaders ride into town in their wagons, then out again. I watched the stagecoach pull up at the hotel. The driver's assistant hopped down to load two trunks and to hand in a lady, followed by a gentleman. Climbing to the high seat, he snugged his hat on his head and nodded, and the horses were hollered into a gallop. A cloud of dust boiled up behind 'em, leaving a haze that hung over the street for a long time after they'd headed west. I watched a bay horse get loose from his tie and go ambling off by himself. As the heat of the day picked up, the town slowed. I think I dozed some.

Later in the afternoon, when a fitful wind was spinning little dust devils along the street, someone else came clomping down the boardwalk. He was older'n me, probably round sixteen or seventeen. Built lean. He walked like he knew where he was going, and he must've, 'cause he walked straight into the Pony Express office without even reading the sign on the door. I sat up straight and cocked an ear.

"I'm here for the job," I heard him announce.

Mr. Roberts's chair creaked, so I pictured him leaning back in it. "Can you handle a horse?" I was anxious to hear the answer myself.

"Yes, sir. Been breaking stock for Mr. Chappie Barnes for over a year now."

"You quit or get fired?"

"Haven't quit yet and I don't aim to get fired. Chappie knows I'm here."

"Hmm." Mr. Roberts's chair thudded onto all four legs, and I heard him shuffle through some more papers. "Well, you look fit enough," he said. "And you don't smell like you've been bedding the bottle." His chair creaked again. "Let me tell you what I'm looking for. The route I need filled is 'bout the toughest in my division—it's up and over the Sierra— at heights topping seven thousand feet—to the next home station, Sportsman's Hall, on the other side. Trail's not half bad in the summer, but it's cold as hell in the winter, and the mail keeps moving whether it's blowing snow or not."

"I don't mind a little snow."

"I'm not talking 'bout a little snow." The chair started creaking with agitated rhythm. "I'm talking 'bout snow so deep you can't even see your horse's ears. I'm talking 'bout blizzards so powerful your whole world turns upside down and white. I'm talking 'bout winds so loud you can't hear your own self scream—and I've *known* men to scream. That's the kind of snow I'm talking 'bout."

The chair stopped creaking and the boy stopped talking. He was thinking, I suppose, thinking 'bout that snow, just like I was. Only, I was thinking how I wanted to try it. I wanted to see the top of that mountain. I wanted to push through that snow and bring the mail to the other side. *Me*. On the back of that horse.

"Yes, sir," he said finally. "I understand 'bout the snow." The hitch in his voice, just a shadow of doubt, spoke otherwise. "That the only route you got open?"

"Yes, it is."

There was another pause, and if I'd been a horse, I'd have been getting ready to dump this rider, 'cause his hand on the reins was starting to tremble. "I had a friend," he said, "who signed up to ride a few months back—Billy Lawton. He quit?"

"Disappeared," Mr. Roberts answered abruptly. "Horse galloped into here the other day without him, and there's been no sign of Billy since. Luckily the mail wasn't lost. That's why we attach it to the horse—horse gets through, rider not always."

"You think he was killed?"

"I'll put it this way: Last Friday was payday and he didn't collect. Still got the money right here." A desk drawer was opened and closed. "If he's got family to claim it, I'll send it on. You got family?"

In the silence that followed I pictured him nodding.

"That's why we prefer orphans, son. Says so right in our advertisement." The chair creaked again, but this time there was a finality to it. Sounded like a door being gently closed. "Listen," Mr. Roberts was saying, "I'm not trying to talk you outta the job, I just want you to know it's a tough one.

And it doesn't shame your manhood none if you don't take it. Folks with families have got other considerations, is all." Another silence. "You still want to apply?"

"Yeah, I think so."

"Then, bring your horse round here in, say, another thirty minutes. We'll put you through your paces and see how well you stick a saddle."

So that was it—you had to prove you could ride. I jumped to my feet, bumping into the older boy as he was coming outta the office. He shoved past me—hardly even noticing, though I expect he would soon enough—and strode off down the street. With the blood rushing through my veins, I glanced at the Pony Express poster one more time and headed off in the other direction.

I needed to find a horse. I didn't have enough money on me to buy one, so I was hoping the livery would let me borrow one—just long enough to prove I could ride. My palms got a little sweaty at that. I'd been able to ride Ned as well as Pa had—maybe better—but that was Ned. He was mostly a nice horse. Sure, he had his prankish moments—and if you didn't keep your wits 'bout you, he'd leave you sitting on air—but probably anybody could ride him. The question was, could I ride a strange horse at what I figured to be a dead gallop? Or a strange horse at a dead gallop down the middle of Carson City? Now, that remained to be seen.

CHAPTER SIXTEEN

Drinking whiskey and counting gold must've been the prime pastimes for the people of Carson City, 'cause I sure had a hard time finding a livery. I had to trot the whole length of town, in fact, before I found a low-slung barn painted with the words

Frank Bucher
Livery, Feed, and Stable
Horses Bought and Sold

There was only one horse out front, but I judged him right off as being good enough to gallop. And bending over his upturned hoof was a man, probably Mr. Bucher himself. I hurried cross the yard.

"Pardon me, sir," I began, and the man glanced past his shoulder. "Can you lend me a horse? Please? I don't need him for very long."

"Not in the business of lending horses," he grumbled, and returned to his work.

Jingling the change from the gold coin for proof, I replied, "I have money."

That got his interest. He let the hoof drop and he straightened, grabbing at his back for coming up too fast. His round melon of a head sported bulgy brown eyes that began hungrily measuring me up and down for the exact amount of money I might be carrying. This was getting familiar. "You got money," he said, "you can *buy* yourself a horse." And, just in time, he remembered to smile.

My heart did skip over a beat. Dangling those words in front of me was an awful kinda temptation. But even though the coins grew damp inside my clenched hand, I knew I didn't have enough money. Unless . . .

No, I told myself. And to him, firm as I could, "I can't *buy* a horse right now—"

"Then, whaddya botherin' me for?" he cried. Shaking his head in exasperation, he stomped off.

Those coins were like to burning a hole through my hand. And if I got the job, there'd be more. "Wait!" I called, and his boot practically hovered in midair. "I . . . I guess I could look at what you got."

This time he was all teeth—smiling big—even before he turned around.

I learned soon enough that my first sight of the place pretty much told the tale: There wasn't a lot to choose from at Mr. Bucher's Livery, Feed, and Stable. Only 'bout fifteen or eighteen head of horses stood slack hipped and sleepy eyed in the corral out back. As he walked in among 'em, swinging his rope, I tried to look 'em over quick as I could so I'd make a good choice. It wasn't easy 'cause these horses were one mangy, bony, hammerheaded group.

The lasso started whirling with more purpose. I took a

deep breath and, kinda casual and confident, like I'd done this a time or two, said, "Think I'll give that bay horse in the corner a try, the one with the three white socks."

Mr. Bucher grunted. "Naw," he said as his lasso landed. "You can have this black one."

This black one? My eyes raced over the herd. I hadn't noticed a black horse. But as the rope came taut and the other animals scattered, I saw that there was indeed a small black horse there. An ornery one! Soon as the rope settled round his neck he swung his haunches toward Mr. Bucher and clamped his tail tight, getting ready to kick out. "Here, now!" the man hollered. He scooped up a pebble and threw it at the horse, stinging him good. The animal jumped sideways. He had his ears pinned, and he snaked out his head and shook his teeth at the man. My jaw went slack, and I think if I hadn't been near thirteen, I might've cried. With this black horse my hopes of winning a job with the Pony Express were pretty much shot through.

Mr. Bucher, looking smug as a cat, came leading the mean horse outta the corral.

"I still think I'd rather try the bay," I ventured, but he shoved my druthers aside and asked, "Where's yer saddle?"

"I don't have one." That played right into his hand, of course, and I could 'most feel the lasso tightening round my own neck.

"I can sell you one of those, too," he said with a smile. He added a wink. "And I'll throw in the bridle for nothing." Handing me the end of the rope, he disappeared inside the barn.

The black horse focused his smoldering fury on me.

I'd have to say he wore the most sullen expression I'd ever seen on an animal. His heavy-lashed eye was small—you could rightly call him pig eyed—and he held it half closed, like he was trying to ignore the world round him. Already prepared to fight the bit, he had his mouth clenched and his lips wrinkled up tight. He wasn't truly black, 'cause the sun had long ago faded his coat to a dried-up brown. The bristly tips of his mane and tail had burned to a dull orange.

But—and with me there was always a *but* when it came to horses—outside his scrawny build he wasn't put together half bad. His right front leg turned out some, and his feet were awful big and pancakey. They could use a good trim and a new set of shoes. But the rest of him, even rib thin, was kinda okay. I wondered what some regular oats and brushing would do for him.

Mr. Bucher returned, lugging a saddle as dried up and forlorn looking as the horse. He had a bridle, too, which he presented to the black's face. All of an instant there was a flash of huge yellow teeth, followed by a holler of rage. A sickening thud as fist sank into flesh, and before I knew it, the bridle was yanked into place and Mr. Bucher was flapping his injured hand in the air. Spitting out curses more colorful than I'd had the privilege to hear, the man flung the saddle cross the horse's back, kneed him hard in the ribs, and yanked the cinch tight.

"There you are," he said, boldly turning his back on the stunned horse and holding out his hand. "That'll be forty-five dollars, and I'm selling him to you cheap."

I half expected a punch in the face too for what I was 'bout to tell him. Although the coins in my pocket had been heavy enough when I was looking to borrow a horse, they didn't add up to buying a horse, even this pitiful excuse for one. Pulling out all the money I had, I showed it to him. "I've got something less than twenty dollars here," I said. And right away, before he could hit me, "But I'm gonna be riding for the Pony Express, and that's good money, so I'll give you the rest soon as I get paid." I took a step backward, just in case.

To my surprise he didn't shout. He got a funny look on his face, and I couldn't tell if he was more curious or amused. "Mr. Roberts hired *you* to ride for him?"

"Well, not yet." I was doing the measuring now, trying to figure out how long his arm was and just how much farther away I should be backing. "I'm trying out for the position. That's why I needed to borrow a horse."

He frowned as he looked down at me, then cross to the black. "And you're gonna ride *this* horse to prove your skills?"

Something 'bout the way his face was twitching gave me a sense that he knew what I didn't, and it wasn't good. I stood straighter. "Yes, sir," I answered him. "I can put this money down on him now. But if you want to buy him back when I'm done, that'd sit all right with me."

"Uh-huh." The man ran his tongue over his teeth, sucked on his lips, and spread 'em in a secretive sorta smile. Jerking his head toward the main street, he asked, "You gonna ride right now?"

I nodded, my heart starting to jump round a little.

"Well, this I gotta see." Grabbing my money fast and stuffing it in his own pocket, he said, "Let's go." His sudden high spirits scared me more than I cared to admit.

News of the riding exhibition seemed to've made its way through town, 'cause people were spilling out doors and crowding the boardwalk, watching and waiting. Mr. Bucher darted into a saloon, where a loud laugh seemed to come at my expense. My hands started sweating. I knew it had to do with this horse I was leading. Just how bad was he?

In front of the Pony Express office the other rider was already sitting atop his horse, a handsome grullo, and talking to Mr. Roberts. I noticed he had his pants tucked inside his boots like a real race rider. Quickly I stuffed mine inside my boots, though not to the same effect. I sized up the animal he was on as being not *that* much bigger than my black horse, though he was obviously better fed. Better muscled, too. He looked through the bridle with an air of easy confidence, not pinning his ears like mine was.

"Okay, Mr. Stockley, let's have you—"

I led my horse up, interrupting Mr. Roberts, and they both looked over in surprise. "Pardon me," I said. "I'd like to try out for the position too."

I'm sure I saw a twinkle in Mr. Roberts's eye, but he kept his face serious. Glancing over at my horse, he said simply, "Okay, mount up."

That's when I realized the stirrups were set too long for my legs. With the whole populace of Carson City looking on, and my face burning, I fumbled with the saddle. I adjusted the leathers short as I could and, even though it wasn't enough, climbed up. Soon as I lowered myself into the seat I knew for sure that I'd been had.

Arching his back real stiff, so I was like to sitting on a hill, the horse took a couple of fast, skittery steps sideways. His head dropped outta sight. I knew enough to yank the reins up—hard—before he started bucking, but that didn't stop him from shaking his head and picking up speed. Not being able to reach the stirrups, I clamped my heels into his sides. Lordy, did that make him mad! He bunched up again, buried his head between his knees, and started bucking to kingdom come. Like a far-off noise, I heard people whooping and hollering.

Funny how when you're in a situation happening too fast and dangerous, you see everything real slow and clear. Even though the saddle was bouncing beneath me and there was a whole lot of daylight there, I knew I was staying on. I thought back to the time when Ned had got his tail tangled up in a stickery bush and started bucking like crazy, and I'd pulled his head one way and the other before kicking him into a gallop to get us outta the mess. And while I was remembering that, I was yanking on the black's head and thumping my heels into his sides just as hard as I could without falling off. Pretty soon—or maybe it happened right away, I'm not sure— he gave up bucking and we went galloping down the middle of the street, faster'n a bullet. I grabbed hold of the reins *and* his mane, dodged a wagon coming our way, leaped over a dog that'd strayed from the crowd, and we raced outta town.

I thought we might gallop for a long time. Heck, I thought we might gallop all the way back to Chinatown, but I found the scrawny little horse had more sauce than substance. He just wasn't fit. When he started chugging like a locomotive, gasping for air, I spun him round and kicked him back toward town.

Guess the folks there had forgotten 'bout us, 'cause they were all watching the other fella make short runs up and down the street. I saw that the grullo was behaving himself perfectly, stopping and starting without any kinda fuss, while his rider leaped outta the saddle and then back into it.

We kept galloping toward the pair, slower and more rambly now, while I worked my mind fast. We had to do something. A couple of faces in the crowd turned to watch us come, and we thundered into town on those big pancake feet and caught the other pair just as they'd finished sliding to a stop and were turning away. I nudged the black shoulder-to-shoulder with the grullo, and when that horse sped up, the black found the grit to stay with him. I hadn't really formed a plan, so when I reached up and knocked the hat off the other guy, toppling it from his head and just snatching its brim with my fingers, it probably surprised me as much as him.

I reined the black to a stop as laughter boomed from both sides of the street. "The Pony Express doesn't deliver hats," Mr. Roberts shouted, though he was laughing too. As I expected, the other rider came rushing up, madder'n a bull that's had his tail twisted, and grabbed his hat outta my hands. He spun his horse in a fancy circle and trotted over to Mr. Roberts.

I guessed I was licked. Feeling shamefaced, I climbed off my horse and led him back to the livery. Dirty brown foam lathered his chest and flanks, which were sucking in and out like a bellows. Soon as I got there, I loosened the cinch and let him take a drink at the trough. That's when Mr. Bucher came walking up. He was laughing hard and slapping his leg over and over. My anger started bubbling 'cause I figured he was laughing at me.

"Now, that *was* a show, I tell you. Lifted the hat right off of that uppity Johnnie Stockley! Whew!"

More'n anything, I wanted to just climb back into the saddle and ride outta town. Now that I had a horse, even one as sorry as the black, I didn't want to give him up. But I had no prospects for more money, so I couldn't finish paying for him.

"You want to buy this horse back?" is all I said.

He swung his head from side to side, and I think there were actual tears coming from his eyes. "No, sirree," he said. "He's all yours and paid in full. Saddle, too, though I'll punch a couple more holes in the stirrups so they'll fit you better."

For a second I wondered if there was another trick in all this, but the way I figured it, at least I was getting a horse. "Thank you," I said. "I'll . . ." I'll what? What was I gonna do now? Where was I gonna go? "I'll be back for him in a bit," I finished, and walked away from the livery, not having any more sense of my future than a blind bat in the night.

The whole day seemed to've been one disappointment and embarrassment after another, and I was feeling pretty low. After tromping along the boardwalk awhile and getting my share of slaps on the back, I found myself back at "my" bench in front of the Pony Express office. I plopped down on it, crossed my arms, and waited. For what, I don't know. But it's where I wanted to be, and at the end of the day I was still waiting.

Mr. Roberts knew I was there 'cause he could see me through the window. He let me sit. Not until the sun started sinking did he push back his chair and get up to pull the curtain and close the office door. I kept staring straight cross the street, mad at the world, I guess. It surprised me when he took a seat on the bench too. He was wearing a look of satisfaction, and I supposed that was because he'd found himself a rider, a good one, to fill his empty Pony Express saddle.

"You got nothing else to do but polish my bench?" he asked after a bit.

I shook my head. "No, sir."

"That was quite a show you put on for us this afternoon."

I was in no mood for funning.

"Where you from, son?" he asked kindly.

"I walked over from Chinatown last night, but I was born in Lancaster, Missouri."

"Lancaster? You don't say! Why, I spent some time there myself when I was a young'un. How did you get all the way out here?"

The humiliation I'd been through on the wagon train warned me not to tell him 'bout what drove my ma and pa to look for a more peaceable life. Besides, since he didn't know anything 'bout my family, he probably didn't see me as colored. "Got relatives in Sacramento," is all I said by way of an answer. "That's where we're headed."

"If you're heading for California, why are you putting in for a job here?"

"'Cause my ma's sick. Her baby died, and I need to earn money for the doctor's bills. I got two sisters to look after too."

"What's your pa doing? You have a pa, don't you?"

I thought about that question for a second. My heart squeezed a bit as I answered, "He's dead." There, it was getting easier to say.

"I'm sorry to hear that." Mr. Roberts crossed and uncrossed his legs, scratched behind his ear, and breathed a sigh. The silence that had taken up sitting between us was getting awkward when he said, "You *really* fifteen?"

The way he said it made it seem like there was a chance at something if I said yes. And I *did* want that chance, but lying just didn't sit with me, never had. "No, sir," I answered, and I was surprised when he didn't just stand up and go. "Only twelve."

There was more silence, and he, at least, seemed comfortable with it. "What did you think of that other rider?"

Now, having seen the truth, and knowing it, didn't make it any easier to admit. "He sits a horse real good," I said. My hands were clenching and unclenching, I wanted his job so bad. Mr. Roberts didn't appear to notice. He acted calm as the coming night.

"I think so too," is what he said. Heaving another happy-tired sigh, he leaned back against the bench, palms flat on his trousers, and stared out at the pink and orange sky. "Isn't that pretty?" he asked. The shrill howl of a coyote split the twilight. It was answered by another. "You say you walked here last night from Chinatown?"

"Yes, sir."

"There's been a mighty bold pack of coyotes roaming that stretch of late. Not natural. You run into 'em?"

I had to laugh. "Yes, sir," I answered again. "Treated 'em to dinner, in fact."

He pushed his hat off his forehead and studied me with those sparking blue eyes. "You know," he said, "you remind me of *me* at your age. I took my share of foolish risks a time or three, especially when I'd set my mind to something. But hang it all, I wish you were more than twelve. At least fourteen."

He shook his head and went back to staring at the sky's shifting colors. I didn't know whether to get up and leave or not. The fact was, I was starting to get sleepy, and another night on this bench was seeming better than riding back to Chinatown in the dark.

"Looks like the mountains will be getting some weather,"

Mr. Roberts said. "See those clouds stacking up? That means a storm's coming. And that means delays in the mail. Folks in California will be squawking 'bout not getting their newspapers from back east in a timely manner."

Why, I wondered, was he telling me this?

"Well," he said, "seeing as how you've filed for squatter's rights on my bench, I guess I'm going to have to put you to work for me. But what I want to ask you is, *why* are you so set on riding for the Pony Express? It's dangerous work. I've scared off bigger ones than you today."

My heart started bucking wild as that black horse. Was I hired? Trying to stay calm, trying to act more than twelve, I answered confidently, "These are dangerous times." Those were Ma's words, but I guess they worked. Then I shrugged. "I reckon I can outgallop most of 'em."

Mr. Roberts grinned and shoved his hand out. "Then, I guess you can gallop for the Pony Express." Just as I reached for his hand, though, he pulled it away. "Wait a minute! What's your name?"

"Colton Wescott, sir."

"Colton Wescott," he repeated. "And *how* old are you again?" I saw that his blue eyes were twinkling.

Maybe lying was worth this job. "Would fourteen do?" I answered.

"Fourteen it is! Welcome aboard."

CHAPTER SEVENTEEN

Till my head was sinking into it, I never really thought 'bout how welcome a pillow could feel. But when you added a real mattress underneath, one with more spring than straw alone can provide, and a bulging full belly, well, it becomes a feeling that's just this side of heaven.

And that's the feeling I was having as I lay on my back that night, staring up at the ceiling of my very own hotel room. My very own! Bought and paid for by Mr. Bolivar Roberts, district superintendent for the Pony Express. And just down the street was my very own horse. Boarded on credit with Mr. Bucher till I collected my first pay.

The lamp on my bedside table was still lit, and a moth, jumpy and wide awake as me, was dancing round its glass chimney. His gyrations were casting moving shadows on the walls and ceiling. Locking my arms behind my head, I sighed like a dog that's finally got its rabbit, and ran over the events of the day one more time.

Course I was thrilled to be hired on as a Pony rider. But even after we'd shaken hands on it, I wasn't too sure *why* I'd been chosen. I'd had to ask Mr. Roberts.

"Well," he'd answered, "it's a couple of things, though

I'm not going to fill your head with all of 'em. Let's just leave it at the fact that I know you can sit a horse."

"But so can the other rider—Mr. Stockley," I said, instantly regretting my words, 'cause they surely weren't in my favor.

"Oh, I hired him, too," the man said, "as a backup. But he'll be riding in the other direction. I've got a temporary spot on the Fort Churchill to Carson run. I think he's just too spooked about his friend gone missing to send him up through the mountains." He must've seen a fearful look on my face, 'cause right away he added, "Now, don't you go listening to any talk of mountain fairies or one-eyed ogres that'll boil your bones for dinner. That's all a bunch of hogwash."

I nodded, but for a while there, when he went on talking, I wasn't listening. I was wondering how you outgalloped a one-eyed ogre through the mountains. Specially if you were riding in the pitch black of night.

"Well, then," Mr. Roberts had said, slapping his trousers again and standing up, "let's get you sworn in and settled in so you can get some sleep. Looks like your eyelids are gathering sand."

Reaching cross the wool blanket covering my hotel bed, I felt for and found the little calfskin Bible that Mr. Roberts had given me, compliments of the Central Overland California and Pikes Peak Express Company, operators of the Pony Express. In his office he'd had me lay my hand on it and swear to be a good and honest employee, and I'd done so. I had to set an example, he told me, and I nodded again. I wasn't to drink intoxicating liquors—which was an easy enough promise, since I never had—and I couldn't use profane language, which prompted another ready nod 'cause I didn't know enough colorful words. I had to promise to treat all the horses well, and you wouldn't have needed to hold my hand to a Bible for that one. Mr. Roberts explained they'd been carefully chosen from all across the territory, and top dollar paid for 'em—as much as two hundred dollars each. That must've been why the horses at the burnt-out relay station, where we'd buried little Willie, had looked so fine. I nodded enthusiastically along with that final promise.

Flipping through the Bible's onionskin pages, I sniffed at the fresh ink. Ma sure would be happy if she knew I was carrying it. Thinking of her gave me a lonesome feeling. I was suddenly sad 'bout being so far from her and Althea and Jewel. Sad 'bout not having Pa round to be proud of me. I rested the Bible on my chest and closed my hands over it. I had to find a way to let 'em know I was okay. Riding my new black horse over to Chinatown would be easy enough—well, it'd be *close* enough, but with that ornery piece of horseflesh, who knew if it'd be easy. 'Cept that Mr. Roberts had informed me that I had to stay within a couple hundred yards of the Pony Express office at all times, just in case I was needed.

I wouldn't mind staying a couple hundred nights in this bed, I thought as I rolled onto my stomach. The tan envelope I was carrying for Ma crackled 'gainst my skin, and that got me stirred up again. I was finally headed toward Sacramento. I could deliver freedom to Ma's sister and get paid to boot. Things were definitely looking up.

As I was rolling onto my side, my knee bumped the other gear I'd been given, compliments of the Pony Express. Ma definitely *wouldn't* be happy 'bout this one: It was a pistol. A Navy Colt, Mr. Roberts'd told me, and it was big and black and mean looking. I lifted it off the blanket. Feeling its deadly weight in my hand gave me a case of the allovers. But at the same time it gave me a powerful feeling. I sat up, wrapped my fingers round the handle, and pointed it at the mirror hanging over the washbasin. In the darkness of the room the dim reflection could be anybody. It could be me, or it could be someone I didn't even know, a stranger pointing a gun straight at my heart. All that had to happen to snuff the life outta one of us was to squeeze the little half-moon trigger.

That took me back to the morning when I'd been shot. All over again I felt the iron ball tearing the skin off my leg and heard the hoofbeats carrying Pa away. The fun went outta the pistol, and I laid it carefully on the table beside the bed. But no matter which way I turned it, it always seemed to be pointing at me somehow, and so I rose up and carried it over to the small dresser to hide it in one of the drawers.

That's when I found out who'd slept in this room last: the Pony Express rider who'd gone missing. 'Cause right below my eyes, all ajumble in the top drawer, were his things. Instantly it was like there was someone dead in the room, and I was breathing fast and wondering what I'd got myself into. With shaky fingers I looked through the pile. There were two wool shirts, one tea colored and one gray, both small enough to fit me. There was a set of broken suspenders and a beat-up copy of a book called *Robinson Crusoe*. Digging round, I uncovered one silver spur, minus its mate, as well as a hinged case hiding a faded image of a worried-looking ma. At least, I figured it was his ma. The gruesome fates that were crashing through my mind looked to be going through hers, too. I folded the case shut and laid her to rest on one of her son's shirts. I laid the gun beside it. Then I pushed the drawer closed and tried to push all those blood-filled, broken-boned, head-bashed-in images outta my mind. I went back to my bed.

For the hour the hotel was still pretty noisy. Time and again people tromped down the hallway past my closed door, talking and laughing loud. There was some singing below. In the room next to me someone was sawing logs for the coming winter. Guess the noise didn't bother him at all.

The fullness of my belly and the plumpness of my pillow finally began to beat out my jitters, and the moth's banging against the glass chimney finally sounded soothing. My eyelids started to droop. I must've dozed off soon after, 'cause next thing I knew, the room was coming light and I hadn't even crawled under the covers! I'd been dead to the world, as Ma would say, though it gave me a shiver to think that.

First thing I did after washing my face and smoothing my hair was head down the stairs to the hotel's dining hall. One of the benefits that came with riding for the Pony Express, I'd learned, was that I could eat all I wanted and the hotel would just bill it to the COC & PP. I hoped I didn't put 'em into debt!

The hall that Saturday morning was bustling with chatty people, clanking dishes, and steaming food. I was served right away, like royalty, and was working on my second plate of potatoes and sausages when Mr. Roberts walked in and sat down.

"You sleep well?" he asked.

"Yes, sir. Best sleep I've had since leaving Missouri."

Glancing at my plate, already licked clean, he grinned with mischief. "You do recall the poster in my office, don't you? *Skinny, wiry* fellows wanted? The way you're eating, I'm afraid you're going to be soring my horses' backs."

Course he was funning, but I set my fork down right away, awful red faced, and said I was finished.

He stood up. "Good. Because the mail will be here soon."

"Mail?" I echoed, jumping to my feet.

"Yes, the mail. The Pony mail. What we're paying you to deliver. The westbound rider should be arriving"—he took out his pocket watch—"in about fifteen minutes." Snapping it shut, he returned it to his pocket. His cold blue eyes shot through me, and suddenly all the food I'd swallowed was clawing its way back up my throat. I was gonna gallop off this very morning?

"The speed and dependability of the Pony Express has never been more vital," he said, low and urgent. "Newspapers from back in the States are saying that a war may break out, a war within our very own country, in an effort to divide it in two. Everyone wants to know which side California will take. It's our job, and yours, to deliver these important communications." He paused, scanning my attire. "Where's your gun?"

Hang it all! It was still in the drawer in my room.

"I took a great risk in hiring you, Mr. Wescott. I hope I wasn't in error."

I shook my head, my stomach heaving. "Just give me a minute, sir." And I went racing up the stairs, all the way praying to God to please—*please*—don't let me get sick this very first morning. In two fumbling tries I had the Colt weighing heavily on my hip, and, still feeling greenish, I managed to dash down the stairs in time to catch up with Mr. Roberts as he strode outta the dining hall.

Right next door, in front of the Pony Express office, was a saddled horse, and was he ever a sight! A man was gripping

133

the reins, but the horse was prancing and fretting and spinning on the end of 'em like a wind-tossed kite. He was a bright bay with shiny black stockings and a thick, glossy mane and tail. His neck, which he kept twisting round, looking for something, was already dark with sweat. His nostrils were blooming wide, and when the early-morning sun shone through the tender skin there, they glowed red as fire.

Mr. Roberts ducked inside his office and came out carrying some clothing. "Here," he said, handing me what turned out to be a fine buckskin coat. "It's a whole lot colder in the mountains."

I pulled it on, though I didn't need it. I was plenty warm with excitement and nerves. Mr. Roberts was watching me with narrowed eyes, real critical. At first I thought it was 'cause the coat was too big—the sleeves did hang past my wrists—but then I realized he was studying me for grit. He wanted to see if I had the brass to climb aboard this piece of desert wind. *This* was why riding the black horse had inspired him to hire me.

"Where's the mail I'm supposed to carry?"

"It's coming," he said, pulling out his watch and checking the time again. "Henry there has the rest of it." He nodded toward the man jerking uselessly on the reins.

It was the horse who heard 'em first, 'cause just at that moment he stopped his spinning and stood still as stone. His little ears pointed toward the edge of town. We heard 'em next: hoofbeats, coming hard and fast.

All of an instant, with the fury of a storm, a lathered horse blew into town. He rushed past other horses and riders and wagons and people and slid to a stop beside the bay, breathing hard. The rider, looking kinda wild eyed and weary, jumped off and lifted a leather contraption off his saddle. He handed it to Henry, then took the reins to both horses. Quick as lightning, Henry opened one of the four bulging pouches sewn onto the piece of leather and scanned the letters inside. He stuffed a few under his arm, pulled some more from his pocket, and returned the lot to the pouch. I think he locked it with a small key. Rising up, he slapped the whole contraption over the bay's saddle, making sure it fit tight over the horn at the front and the cantle at the back. Three heads turned toward me then, four if you count the restive horse.

My heart was banging out bullets. I suddenly couldn't get enough air. "How do I know which way to go?" I asked in choking fear.

"You don't have to," Mr. Roberts said. "The horse knows."

And in the blink of an eye I was hoisted into the saddle, handed the reins, and sent galloping toward the mountains.

CHAPTER EIGHTEEN

A prayer of thanks was swept from my lips as we galloped, gratitude to an unknown someone who'd done me the kindness of tying my stirrups up shorter, giving me a fighting chance to stay on this runaway locomotive. Even so, I found myself having to grab hold of the bay's reins *and* his black mane. I could feel the heat of his body burning right through the skimpy saddle to my legs. It was like he was stoked with real fire. I hoped Mr. Roberts was right, that the horse *did* know where he was going, 'cause the measly pieces of leather wrapped round my fingers would be useless to stop him.

The helplessness of my situation was made doubly clear to me as we galloped through the middle of Carson. The bay didn't even blink as other horses leaped and spun outta our way. A stiff-kneed donkey wasn't as quick, and we shaved a few hairs off him as we sprinted by, the man leading him shaking his fist and shouting. A long wagon loaded with timber pulled into our path and I hunched for the killing crash, but the driver saw us and yanked hard on his reins, and his horses lifted and twisted their heads such that we sped just under their whiskers. In a few heart-stopping seconds we were clear of town, blazing along the dirt road that skirted the wide valley.

When I found myself still in the saddle, still in one piece, I took a deep breath—my first, really, since I'd climbed aboard—and dared to lift my eyes. Rising up ahead of us, like a sky-high wall, were those sharp-peaked mountains that'd been taunting me for weeks. Some were already capped with snow. A shiver ran along my spine like ice had been dumped down my shirt. How in the name of God were we supposed to climb over 'em? There wasn't any path that I could see. There wasn't so much as a ledge for carving out a path on those sheer walls.

We kept galloping, though, and as we did I began to feel the ground swelling beneath us, slowly rising. As we got closer and closer to the stony wall, me worrying that we were gonna charge headlong at it, the road swerved to the left and contented itself with running alongside the mountains for a piece. It seemed to be taking measure of 'em, biding its time, as it were, by skimming over hills and dipping through hollows. That was fine with me.

We must've covered several miles by then, and the bay horse wasn't even breathing hard. After his first burst of speed he'd settled into a steady gallop, and he acted like he could do it forever. He was a real veteran, I could tell. And with the big stride he had, the two of us were eating up the ground like a prairie fire.

I'd settled too, finally finding my balance in the saddle, soaking up the bounding rhythm in the small of my back. What had started out as sweaty-handed fear turned into awe and then joy. Pure, skin-tingling, heart-hollering joy. *I could do this all day*, I thought as we galloped. *All day and every day*. Me and this horse—we were one helluva pair—and I think even

Ma wouldn't mind the swearing if she could see the world go rushing past like a river, all in a colorful blur, like I was.

As we were coming over the next rise, me drinking in the great expanse of valley that stretched ahead of us, I spotted something small and dark pinned against the cloudy sky. Off to the side, only lower, was another something. It was an odd sight, and I couldn't wrap my mind round it at first. I kept watching and we kept galloping, dropping into a shallow basin now and again and losing sight of the twin silhouettes, then riding up and out and finding 'em closer, still hovering. When we got near enough that I could make out fluttering wings, I realized with a squeeze of joy that it was a pair of those little smoke-colored hawks, the same kind I'd seen back on the trail. A good omen.

Our thundering approach, though, caused the birds to lift higher, part company, and swoop clean outta sight, which left the huge sky empty and me kinda sad. But the very next thing, one of the birds dropped outta nowhere to fly shoulder-to-shoulder with me. Right off I knew he was racing us. *Klee-klee-klee!* he shrilled. Like a bullet fired from a twin pistol, the other bird appeared at my opposite shoulder. The challenge was echoed: *Klee-klee-klee!* An explosion of joy busted through every inch of my skin. Laughing with the two of 'em, I doubled over the bay's neck. "Hee-ya!" I screamed, and that horse dug down and found even more speed, and we lifted up and became the wind.

For miles we flew like that, two of us in the air, two of us on the ground. Only when the next town was coming into sight did the hawks spin away, whistling a good-bye. Gave me a rush of warmth right through to my belly. It was a special moment, something that I could pack away and carry with me the rest of my life.

I don't know whether it was the brisk weather or the thrill of my first Pony Express ride, but the town—whatever its name was—made just the prettiest picture that morning. It was nestled against the base of the mountains, protected on the windward side by a grove of black-trunked trees. In the morning light the leaves fluttered and twinkled, glinting like dangling jewels in brilliant greens and yellows and oranges and reds. As we came pounding right into the heart of town—me admiring the twin rows of fine buildings, some brick, some wood, all with welcoming porches and balconies painted fresh and shiny—I found myself thinking that I could settle down and live in a place such as this.

Wasn't hard to spot the Pony Express station 'cause there was a bearded man holding the reins to a restive, saddled horse and watching me come. Outta the corner of my eye I noticed some children waving and saw a blacksmith pause his hammering and look up. I wished I could've put on a better show, but the bay galloped up to the station so fast and stopped so sudden that I was thrown up onto his neck, my chin buried right behind his ears. Red faced, I jumped down from the saddle—and near fell to the ground, my legs shaky as jelly! I had to grab hold of the stirrup to steady myself.

"Get the mochila," the man barked.

"What?"

"The mochila!" He waggled a finger toward my saddle. "What yer carryin' the mail in."

"Oh." I turned and tugged at the specially made saddle cover with its four pouches, heaving it off and delivering it to the impatient man. He handed me the reins to the fresh horse, knelt down on the spot, and opened a pouch different from the one that'd been opened in Carson City. He didn't need a key for it. He quickly searched through the letters once, then once again, before returning the entire stack to the pouch. His shoulders sagged in disappointment.

"You a new hire?" he asked as he rose to his feet.

"Yes, sir."

He grunted. "Roberts so desperate he's hirin' brats to ride for him, huh?"

I knew enough to keep my mouth shut.

Another, younger man hurried up to take the reins of the tired bay. Leading the horse away, he petted his neck and murmured pleasantries, things like, "There now, what a good fella," and, "Got a big bucket of oats waiting for you," and, "You'll sure sleep good tonight."

The horse I was left holding, a creamy yellow gelding with a slightly paler mane and tail, stopped his dancing to whinny after the departing bay. There was a mulish quality to his expression, and sure enough, when his call was ignored, he squealed and sat back on the reins.

"Cut that out!" the man cried. Reaching past me, he gave the reins a hard yank, and the gelding's mouth gaped in pain. He followed that with a boot to the animal's stomach. The yellow horse quit his bellowing, all right, and he paid attention, but Lordy, did he look mad!

In short order the mochila was fitted onto the saddle and I was boosted on top of it. To tell truth, I was more'n a little tired myself and wished I could've sat awhile and caught my breath. But that wasn't offered. A fist-size packet was.

"Some jerky for ya," the man said. "Long climb to Friday's." Looking up at a cloud-pocked sky, he said, "Probably rain before you get there, so watch the rocky patches. It gets slippery fast." He shoved the reins into my hands and slapped the horse on the haunches, and just like that we were hurtling away like we'd been shot outta a hot cannon. "And stay off his back!" were the closest words I got to a happy send-off.

I gripped the saddle and readied myself for another hour's gallop. This horse was just as fast and powerful as the first one, and the ride should've been much the same, but it wasn't. That was 'cause these stirrups hadn't been shortened to fit my legs. If I pointed my feet down, I could kinda touch the hard leather footholds, but that did 'bout as much good as trying to walk tippy-toe cross a rope bridge that was bouncing in the wind. Only pride kept me from grabbing the saddle horn with both hands. That and the fact that I didn't want anyone telling Mr. Roberts I couldn't stick a horse. So I gritted my teeth, looked through the furry yellow ears, and focused on a point far down the road. If I was fated to fall off, I was at least gonna make sure it happened outta sight.

"You keep it together!" someone close by shouted, and that startled me such that I nearly *did* tumble outta the saddle on the spot. Looking down, I caught a glimpse of a stoutish woman in a white-collared black dress. What surprised me even more was that she had a face the color of my ma's, only darker. "You keep it together!" the woman said again, and she was looking straight into my eyes, like she was giving an order. Both her hands waved in the air as I galloped by.

Those words stuck to me like cockleburs, and maybe they helped me stick to the saddle, too, 'cause I was still on board well outside of town. My knees were being rubbed raw from gripping so hard, but I was staying in the saddle. Over and over I kept hearing the woman's words as we galloped: *Keep it together, keep it together.* The horse's hooves pounded out the words. *Keep it together, you keep it together.*

But what did they mean? That I should keep myself together with this horse? That would make sense 'cause it *was* a slippery pairing. Setting pride aside, I grabbed hold of the saddle horn and gave my knees a break. Who knew how much longer I'd be able to hang on? Or maybe it was that I should keep myself together with my family, that I should go back to Chinatown. That's what the woman on the wagon train had said, more or less. "Stick together," she'd said, "and you'll make it." Or maybe it was something else, something completely different. Maybe the woman, whoever she was, had something to do with the Pony Express. Maybe she just wanted to make sure I'd keep together with the important mail I was carrying. That was probably it.

I kept galloping alongside the mountains, in and outta shadows, and the words kept up their pricking. Somehow I couldn't shake the feeling that they meant something more, something pertaining only to me, Colton Wescott. That they were telling me 'bout something I still had to do.

CHAPTER NINETEEN

Closer and ever closer to the mountains we galloped, until the jagged peaks loomed directly over our heads, iron gray and sharp as knives. The sick feeling in my stomach burrowed deeper. Against a darkening sky only one of the peaks was sunlit. It stood out like a beacon 'cause it was scarred by a huge, horseshoe-shaped hollow lined with snow. It looked like a giant sky horse had stomped on the mountaintop in making his leap over.

That's 'bout what it would take, I was thinking, when the yellow horse cut his speed of a sudden. He veered sharp to the right, almost unseating me, and I had to grab for mane. And there it was: a trail—if you could call it that—scratched upward at an angle cross the mountain's face.

The galloping ended right quick then. Coiling himself up tight as a ball, the horse hurled us at the grade. I knew enough to lean over his shoulders to ease the weight on his back. I held my breath, too, as if having my lungs full of air would help lighten the load.

Lordy, it was a climb! As I focused on balancing myself, his iron-rimmed hooves scraped and slid on the rocky soil. With the wind whistling past my ears, I felt his sides heaving and his haunches bunching. The power was such that it was like sitting on a war cannon as it fired and recoiled, attacking the mountain over and over.

Until the cannon emptied. Gradually the lunges ate up less ground. The horse's breathing came in loud, ragged gusts that challenged the rising wind. He reluctantly slowed to a grunting trot and then a purposeful, head-bobbing walk. He was still trying to hurry, mindful of his work, bless him, but it was a murderous hard task. That devil of a trail liked to rise straight up and up and up and outta sight. I'd swear it disappeared into thin air.

Course, it didn't. What it did do, I found, was zigzag up the mountainside in a sorta stairway of treacherous, tight switchbacks. You just couldn't see the turn till you were one step shy of toppling into the hereafter.

Which we almost did. Arriving at the first switchback, and knowing full well that I shouldn't, I looked down— down at the flat, hazy valley that already seemed a whole nother world away. We were so high! The dizzying height immediately grabbed me by the collar and coaxed me close to the edge. Caught in its spell, I pictured myself falling, could see my fingers splayed against clouds as I went tumbling headlong through the air. I couldn't breathe.

Just in time I came to my senses. I hauled those reins up tight and kicked the horse away from the drop-off. He shook his head. Grabbing the bit firm in his teeth, he yanked the reins loose and returned to picking his own way, which was much too close to the edge for my comfort. I held my breath and let him go.

What else could I do? I was at the horse's mercy. I had to

risk death by trusting him, 'cause I'd sure enough be dead without him. I shook with the thought of what'd become of me if we got separated. I didn't know my way through the mountains. Heck, if I fell, I didn't even know this horse's name to try calling him back. So each time a pebble was knocked loose and went pinging down the slope, my stomach knotted itself one loop tighter. I grabbed on to the saddle horn and prayed silently to the horse: *Please stay on the trail, please stay on the trail. Don't fall and leave me; just—please—stay on the trail.*

Slowly we climbed outta the desert world and into the steep, windy one of the mountains. The yellow pincushion bushes that had dotted the lower slopes by the thousands were replaced by leafier plants with hot orange and red spikes. Scrawny pine trees began sprouting up. The higher we got, the taller the pines got, and at one point I was surprised to see telegraph wires stretched between their tops like some sorta ambitious spiderweb. They were the first wires I'd seen since leaving St. Joseph. I didn't dare let my gaze follow up or down to see where they went. We just kept climbing.

It seemed that the yellow horse and I had this hairpin trail to our lonesome, until we were squeezing round a real narrow switchback. That's when we found ourselves horse face–to–mule face with a pack train headed toward the valley. The man on the lead mule hollered, "Whoa," and tried to organize his animals over to the side to give us room to pass. But the yellow horse had no patience for that. Without missing a beat, he shoved his chest into that string of mules. Trouble was, he challenged 'em on the outer side of the trail, so that for several agonizing, dizzying, suffocating minutes we were back tippy-toeing only inches from the edge. I clung to the saddle horn with both hands then—you couldn't have pried 'em loose—and leaned all my weight toward the mountain, hoping that one mule or another wouldn't be having a temperamental sorta day and suddenly decide to shoulder us over those last few inches . . . those few inches between us and death.

Took me a while to recover from that one. I was hoping we were near the top, 'cause my legs were getting kinda shaky from clinging to the saddle. But I could almost hear the mountain's rumbly laugh as it chose to give me a cruel glimpse of what lay ahead. Coming round the next switchback, I got to look plumb into the heart of the Sierra Nevada. My jaw dropped to my belt buckle. Stretching away before us was a deep, rocky meadow, blanketed with bushes so thick you couldn't possibly have walked through 'em. And rising beyond the meadow were layers upon layers of more mountains, the closer ones green and blue, the farther ones hazy purple fading to gray. Their caps were frosted with blazing white snow.

Huh. We hadn't even begun to get through the mountains.

Only thing that kept my spirits from drying up and blowing away then was the cool air. It was so moist I drank it in like water. It had a tangy flavor, too, like horse liniment. Sure opened up your breathing passages. After endless weeks choking on the dust and heat of the desert, breathing this air was like plunging into a clear lake and feeling the dirt and sweat just wash away.

And then we were up. The path leveled off and I sat back in the saddle and it was like we were moving on clouds. The yellow horse gasped for air. He was reeking of sour sweat, so I let him rest. I didn't know if that was allowed, but he'd sure enough put his back into his work and deserved it.

Immediately he dropped his head to nibble along the sides of the trail. There wasn't much nourishment there—only a few yellow green seedlings managed to poke through the heavy carpet of pine needles. I tore some of the jerky from its wrapper and stuffed it inside my cheek, letting it soak and soften there, enjoying the salty flavor. Sitting on top of that mountain, breathing in the crisp air, listening to the bit jangling and the grass being ripped, I felt good. We'd made it. Life was good.

Guess the mountain needed to set me down a peg or two again, 'cause while I was resting there, a long, warning rumble sounded overhead. A glance up through the treetops showed heavy clouds rushing in and closing out the sky. They looked like boiling steam, they were coming so fast. The man in the town below had predicted it right: It was gonna rain. I gathered the reins, but the yellow horse needed no encouragement. In one leap he was back at a ground-covering gallop.

A stormy gloom clamped down over the mountaintop, so sudden it was like someone had snuffed out the sun. In one heartbeat lightning bathed it in white, blinding us, then vanished, leaving us groping in the dark. Thunder rumbled and banged so close over my head my teeth rattled. It banged again and again, and we were galloping so hard I didn't know which was hooves and which was storm. Then the rain began. Maybe it was 'cause we were closer to the clouds, but those first drops came down hard and heavy as bullets. I snugged my hat on my head and turned up my collar, but the drops stung my thighs and the backs of my hands. Must've stung the horse, too, 'cause he pinned his ears and flattened out like a hot-blooded racehorse nosing the finish line.

When we were little, Ma used to tell us bedtime stories

'bout children who got lost in forests, 'bout the strange things that could happen to 'em there in the dark. Specially when they happened upon enchanted cottages. But when a cabin and shed appeared outta the downpour, I was so wet and miserable I didn't care a whit if they were enchanted. I wanted outta that storm. My legs were rubbed raw, my back ached, my fingers and face and feet were numb from the cold. *Do what you will*, I thought, *put a spell on me, but let me inside.*

The yellow horse splashed to a stop and whinnied, like he'd done this a time or two. Right off, a man came hurrying out into the weather. I disconnected myself from the saddle, remembering to grab the mochila this time, and handed the reins over. As the horse was being led away, the front door of the cabin was swung open and I was beckoned inside. Believe you me, I didn't have to be asked twice.

The two people waiting there were friendly. They set a chair by the fire for me and thrust a steaming bowl of beans into my reddened hands. They clapped me on the back for making it through the weather, which made my chest swell some. Then they left me for the mochila.

I didn't care. The fire-warmed room was melting away the cold, and the food—next I was handed a wedge of corn bread and a stinging-hot cup of coffee—tasted so good as I don't think I've ever had. I gulped it down fast. Just as fast, sleep started working through me, relaxing me all over. I stretched my legs closer to the fire, ready for a good rest.

Somebody shook my shoulder. Hands tugged at me, dragging me outta the chair, and I started to believe I *was* in some sorta wicked, enchanted cottage. Too drowsy to struggle, I let 'em pull me toward the door and shove me out in the rain. It was still coming down fast, like someone wouldn't let go of the pump handle. I couldn't see the trail at all. Another saddled horse was coming from the shed, a brown one, unless it was just the mud that was already splashed on him. The mochila was fitted into place. A look at me and the stirrups were quickly shortened. A couple of pairs of arms hoisted me up and there was hollering and then we were galloping again. After the warmth of the cabin, the rain felt extra cold and punishing.

If I thought the climb up had been treacherous, I now had a chance to reconsider. 'Cause the path going down this first mountain was steep and slick as a log flume. The brown horse didn't so much gallop as scramble, hunching his back to keep us upright while we slipped and slid down the muddy trail. I couldn't make out anything round us. It was all a water-stained blur of brown and black and green. Seemed like we were tumbling through some kinda nightmare, the kind where you're falling and flailing and running and not really getting anywhere. This horse seemed to feel that way too. He held to his job steadily but joylessly.

Over the course of the afternoon the rain stopped and started several times. More Pony Express stations appeared in the wilderness, providing more fresh horses. No fresh riders. I didn't know the names of either of 'em—the horses or the stations—but I didn't have to. All I had to do was sit on the back of one and let him carry me toward the other. Without the sun I'd lost track of time, but it seemed that 'bout every hour or so the horse I was riding slowed and there would be a little cabin or inn or a small settlement even. And there would be another horse saddled and waiting. More food would be shoved at me and the pouch searched again.

Sometimes letters were added, sometimes letters were taken out. That's what made the people smile. Not my coming, but what I was carrying. Newspapers, especially, made eyes brighten, made faces soften with the prospect, I suppose, of entertaining evenings ahead. This even though I'd heard back in Carson City that the newspapers were weeks old and hard to read, being printed on paper fine as onionskin so as not to weigh down the mail. But thinking 'bout the smiles made the endless galloping a little easier to bear.

As night fell, we were still hurtling up and down, up and down, through the mountains. I wondered thickly when it was going to end—*if* it was going to end. My mind was numb with cold. I'd lost all sense of where I was or even how many horses I'd been on. What was this, the sixth or the seventh? He was shorter than the others, that much I knew, 'cause when we splashed cross a river, my boots took a good dunking—not that I wasn't already soaked through to my toes from the rain. Scrambling up and over the bank, we turned to gallop alongside the river. We were at the bottom of a deep gorge, galloping through the underbelly of the mountains, it seemed, and it was a world that was black and cold and awful lonely.

Sometime that night the horse slowed again, and yes, we were at another station, a huge inn fronted by a large work yard. Knowing the routine well, I dropped outta the saddle, numb to the pain of my feet hitting the ground. I tugged the mochila off and waited for another horse to be led out. This time when the mochila was set cross the saddle, however, another rider climbed aboard and galloped off. In my stupor I raised my hand to try and stop him.

"You'll be wantin' a place by the fire, then, won't ya?"

a friendly voice said. The words were accompanied by a slap on the back, one that nearly knocked me over. I was led, stumbling in my soggy boots, into a large room, wrapped in a buffalo robe, and set by the fire with a bowl of venison stew. I was too done in to eat.

The room was crowded. And hot. There was a buzzing sound that could've been all the people talking, or it could've been the drumming of hooves in my head. I couldn't tell. Peeking over the edge of the robe, I saw that this Pony Express station was set up inside a bustling mountain inn. Travelers were coming and going and calling out orders and packing and unpacking like it was broad daylight. It made me dizzy to watch 'em. My head wouldn't stop banging, and I couldn't make my throat swallow the stew. Got it in my mind that I had to be on my way, so I threw off the robe and stood up. I wavered like a drunkard and plunked down in the chair again.

"Here, now," a woman's voice soothed in my ear. "I've your room readied." Her hand touched my forehead, and it was so cool and refreshing it was like being on the top of that first mountain again, feeling the crisp air on my skin. "Poor boy," she cooed as she nudged me back to my feet. I followed where she led, weaving in and out and round people who didn't pay us any mind. Climbed a flight of stairs and stumbled down a hall and into a small room dimly lit by a table lamp. There were two beds there, separated by a sheet hung from the ceiling. A dark, lumpy form filled one of the beds. The woman guided me past it and pointed to the empty one. "Here you are, now. Is there anything else you'll be needin'?"

Maybe I shook my head. I don't know for sure. Her words sounded so far off, like someone was speaking through a fog or calling out in a dream. I made as to plop down on the bed but couldn't control my fall and kept toppling over until I sprawled in a heap on the mattress.

"You keep it together now," the voice murmured. "Keep us all together."

Or did it? The words tried to worm their way into my understanding. But I was too worn out to try to figure 'em out. Tomorrow. Tomorrow would come soon enough.

CHAPTER TWENTY

It could've been the needle-sharp kitten claws that jerked me awake first. Or maybe it was the blunt words hissed so close to my ear that I smelled the rotting teeth: "I know your secret, boy. Could tell right off. But folks downstairs don't know 'bout you, do they?"

My heart skidded to a stop. Where was my gun? Tugging at the cocklebur of a kitten on my neck, all the while yelling to myself, *Come to! Come to!* I swung upright. My feet hit the floor with a thud. I rubbed my eyes—Lordy, my arms were sore—and tried to focus on the hazy shape in front of me.

It hardened into the silhouette of a gaunt, leathery old man hunched sideways on the room's other bed. The curtain had been pushed open, and he was watching my every movement like a cat ready to pounce. The hairs on the back of my neck stiffened. Now I remembered: My gun was under my pillow. Outta casual reach. Trying to buy time, I stammered, "I . . . I don't know what you're talking 'bout."

The kitten somersaulted down into my lap, batting at the fringe on my coat. I noticed that he was ginger colored and cute in an ornery way, and cupped my hand cross his back. Quick as lightning, he spun and sank his tiny fangs deep into my palm. That sure enough woke me the rest of the way.

The man flicked his attention to the kitten, kinda protectively, I thought, before turning his stare once again on me. He didn't say anything else—just sat there, one leg crossed over the other, skinny and stoop shouldered, breathing loud. He was giving me a case of the allovers with his pointed accusation and his cocksure eyes. But with my gun outta reach, there was nothing I could do 'cept return his stare. So we sat, two strangers, not moving, just looking into each other's faces like a couple of kids in a blinking contest. Only the kitten jumped round in a beam of sunlight, amusing himself. In the dusty silence I felt my heart banging 'gainst my ribs. I heard myself swallow. I held my stare.

There was an odd, weathered appearance 'bout the man on the other bed. It was the kind you see on stubborn old trees that have stood by themselves year after year, far from the forest and alone against the wind. All the sharp corners had been worn away to a smooth gray shell, and his face was frozen into an expressionless mask. Only his eyes— pale, watery blue, like pieces of colored glass at the bottom of a stream—glimmered with excitement. He'd never win a real blinking contest, I found, 'cause those eyes of his just twitched and winked, almost working independent of each other. They were searching me all over and up and down, storing away information, I thought, like nuts for the winter.

"I know the folks downstairs don't know 'bout you"—his gravelly voice startled me into a blink—"'cause of what took place before you rode in. See, a couple of 'em near came to blows. Over the election." He sat back, smug, like I was supposed to understand what that meant. Not getting a rise outta me, he leaned closer. "Some of 'em stand behind that Lincoln feller and free states and all, but one of 'em"— he paused, sorta snorting and chuckling and wheezing at once—"well, he swore he'd sleep buck naked in the snow before he'd share a roof with a colored person." His voice narrowed to an eager whisper. "How'd you slip by 'em?"

My heart started thumping harder, warning me to run, 'cause I'd been caught—doing what? What exactly had I done? Mr. Roberts hadn't questioned me 'bout my background when he hired me on, nor had anyone at any of the Pony Express stations on the way to this one. The man had to be bluffing. He couldn't prove anything. He was just some crazy old coot outta the woods, bent on scaring me.

While I was putting together my own bluff, I picked up the kitten and cradled him in front of my face. The greenish eyes looked at me with wonderment. The pink mouth started to yawn, but then, to my surprise, the kitten jumped outta my hands like he had springs and went tumbling head over tail through the air.

"Hey!" the man said, coming to life and lunging for the creature.

I reached out and snatched the kitten up before he hit the floor. In a fury he righted himself, growling and scratching and spitting, and I happily passed the little hellion over to the man's outstretched hand. Immediately the animal balled himself up and looked content. Rubbing my stinging palms on my pants, I presented my bluff. Coolly I asked, "Who says I'm not white?"

The man cradled his kitten close to his belly. He leaned over him, 'most wriggling with anticipation. The gray hair that circled his head like a halo and stretched past his belly in an untamed beard seemed to quiver as well. "I do," he said, and his eyes widened for the effect.

The certainty in his voice knocked a few cards outta my fingers. I was sure the sudden panic swirling all through my insides was showing on my face. Something bad was going to happen. I just knew it. Right there in that room I could suddenly taste the water on our wagon that had mysteriously gone salty, smell the dark stench of the desert station where Ma and the rest of us had been left behind, hear the wagon boss sneer, "Damn mongrels." I was found out. Trapped.

And then, clear as day, I heard Ma's words to me: "You're 'most as white as your pa," she'd said. "It's all right." I could choose his world.

And Lordy, did I. I was so nervous sitting in that room with that strange man making accusations that all of a sudden I couldn't think straight. It was like I saw an open window and just jumped through it. Made my choice. Boldly I thrust out my hand. "I still don't know what you're talking 'bout, mister, but I'm Colton Wescott. I ride for the Pony Express."

He studied my hand, like he was a tracking dog searching for clues, but didn't take it. His eyes worked me up and down. "Nobody can keep a secret from me," is all he said.

A knock sounded at the door, and as far as I was concerned, it couldn't have come at a better time. "We're runnin' outta breakfast fixin's," a woman said. "You boys want some, you better hurry along." It sounded like she started to leave, but before I could stand up, she was back. "And if that cat of yours is in there, Jeremiah McGahee, I want it put out. *Now.*" I didn't wait for a second invitation. Hastily fishing my gun out from under the pillow, I headed for the door.

The weight of the pistol lent me enough confidence that I could mosey past those watchful, glassy eyes.

The hall outside my room was long, with at least ten other doors and what looked like more round the corner. Clomping down the stairs into the mostly empty main room, I realized this station was even bigger than I'd remembered from last night. Long timbers, splotched like a leopard and glowing a pinkish yellow, formed a high, angled roof overhead and a wide, polished floor below. Heavy, hand-hewn furniture was scattered round, most of it circled near the giant stone fireplace. The hearth itself was so big you could've roasted two pigs in it side by side. There was a crackling blaze going in it now, even with the station's double doors thrown wide, welcoming the crisp, piney air.

The morning was blindingly bright, like the sun was having to make up for sleeping through yesterday. Most of the activity was outside, with people and animals and wagons coming and going at a steady clip despite the mud. Everything smelled wet and clean, though there was a strong odor of lye boiling somewhere out back. I guess having a lot of soap was a high priority here.

Competing with the outdoor smells were the indoor ones of frying meat and sizzling onions and boiled coffee. They lassoed my stomach like it was a long-lost calf, and I followed right along, past the front desk and a rack of damp coats and underneath an entirely unnecessary sign that pointed the way to the dining hall.

The main room was empty, I found, because everyone that wasn't working outside was sitting round tables in this room. People seemed to be taking their time this morning, smoking pipes and talking, poring over maps or reading newspapers.

"You can sit right here," a girl called to me, and I walked cross the room and took the offered chair by a window. She was back in a minute with a pot of coffee and a china cup and saucer. If she saw anything other than a white boy in my chair, she didn't show it. "Menu's over there," she said, pointing to a wooden board with a hand-lettered list of food items, "but we're outta the cinnamon rolls. Gotta get up with the miners to get those. Say"—she looked me over with some distaste, and I froze—"you want those clothes of yours washed, we can do it for you."

For the first time that morning I realized what a sorry mess I was. Dried mud splattered my pants to the knees, completely caking the bottoms. The crackling creases had left a splintered trail all the way into the dining hall. The buckskin coat, which I'd slept in, was stiff from the rain and damp at the seams. Althea and Jewel both would've accused me of being neighborly with a skunk, though the only thing I could smell was onions. All I knew was I was warm and dry for the first time in a long time, and I didn't feel like shedding any clothes.

"Thanks anyway," I said. Clearing my throat, I asked politely, "Where am I?"

She threw back her head and laughed. "Just how much did you drink last night?"

I shook my head. "No, I wasn't drinking." But she was pretty, which made me add, "At least last night." I grinned in what I thought was a sly, grown-up manner. "I rode the Pony mail in. Left Carson City yesterday."

"Oh, I see." She looked suitably impressed, and I flexed my shoulders some, feeling proud. "Well, you must be new, so

I'll tell you. You're in California. You made it cross the Sierra Nevada to here, which is called Sportsman's Hall." She looked round. "It's an inn and a trading post and a Pony Express station and, well, 'bout anything else you want. I guess you covered something better'n seventy-five miles. Snowshoe says it's 'bout that far to Genoa, and I think Carson's farther on. It's a good ways no matter how you cut it. Hungry?"

I nodded.

She touched my shoulder and winked. "I'll rustle you up something."

The coffee tasted good. It was thick and syrupy and, with a good helping of sugar from the painted china bowl on the table, a real mouth pleaser. Only drawback was that I heard the black liquid plunk into the emptiness of my stomach like drops of water in a well. That reminded me that I hadn't eaten any of the stew last night, and I got a wave of hunger pains. With all the wonderful smells filling up the room, my poor stomach was fairly writhing in complaint. I kept pouring coffee into it, though, and before I'd finished a second cup, a platter of flapjacks was set in front of me.

"Got some steak and eggs, and some hash, on the way for you," the girl said, filling my cup a third time. "Don't you worry none 'bout going hungry here. The two Mr. Blairs— Mr. John and Mr. Jim, that's them over there—say to always treat the Pony riders good, and I do!" She winked again.

Looking over at the two men and then scanning the rest of the tables, I wondered if old Mr. McGahee's rabble-rousers were somewhere nearby. It made me a little nervous, but I was a lot more hungry. I tucked into my flapjacks with fork in one hand and knife in the other. While I chewed,

I sneaked glances round the room, all the time making sure that no one had any reason to look in my direction.

The place was constructed all of pine, and no expense had been spared on the details. Someone with a love of carving, and a talent for it, had cut designs into every third beam. Even some of the support timbers were girded with cleverly carved animal faces. On two sides of the room broad windows let the sun stream in. The one next to my right shoulder looked out onto an ocean of forest that lapped right up to the glass panes. Ahead of me the other window offered a view of the front of the station and the road. That's where the activity was. Wagons of all sorts, with teams of horses or oxen or mules, jammed the yard, waiting to be loaded or unloaded. Horses whinnied in recognition. Men called out their own hellos. There seemed to be a fair number of miners round too. At least they looked like the miners I'd seen back in Chinatown. They'd come riding up one at a time—they always seemed to travel by their lonesome—sometimes leading a pack mule behind 'em. I noticed that they didn't holler at each other. Like wild animals drawn to the flames of a campfire, they looked interested by the spectacle, excited even, but in the end they were none too comfortable with crowds.

Another platter was set before me, this one heaped with sizzling steak and onions and potatoes and fried eggs and biscuits. I tore into it with no thought to manners, and the smiling girl teased, "Whoa, there, little man. No one's gonna take it away from you." That made me go red, but it didn't stop me from shoveling in the food.

I ate and ate, till I thought I would bust, and then I ate some more. The girl kept bringing coffee and I kept drinking it, smiling and chewing and nodding each time. This day was starting right fine, I thought, even allowing for mysterious Mr. McGahee.

As if the mere thought of him could conjure up his appearance, he walked into the dining hall. Scanning heads—for me, apparently—he slunk straight over to the table nearest mine and sat down. I wondered if that wild kitten of his was stuffed inside one of his pockets. I knew he was staring at me, but I kept looking out the window, fiddling with the spoon in my coffee, trying to ignore him. That turned out to be not so hard because the two Mr. Blairs, joined by another man, seemed to have picked up the heated argument from last night.

"I know there's plenty of runaway slaves in Sacramento," the newcomer was growling. "Plenty. So if I don't find mine, I'll certainly find others to replace 'em."

One of the Mr. Blairs threw down his fork, which clanged sharply against his plate, bringing other conversations in the room to a halt. "You can't just ride into town and haul off anyone you please," he warned. "The U.S. government will have something to say about that."

"Like I told you last night," the man countered, "the U.S. government can keep its nose outta *my* business with *my* slaves. I bought and paid for 'em, damn it, and I'm owed two slaves." He pounded a fist on the table.

I didn't want to look. I kept scolding myself not to all the while my head was turning. And then I nearly couldn't stop looking. That was 'cause the man chasing after his runaway slaves was sporting the biggest set of ears you ever saw. They were sticking straight outta the sides of his head like they'd been nailed on as an afterthought. People all through the room were glancing over, looking away, then glancing over again. No one could help it. The rest of him was fairly ordinary. Not too tall, thick chested. Limp brown hair that stuck to his sweaty forehead. But those ears.

"If my horse jumped his fence," he went on arguing, "and ran away, wouldn't you allow me the right to chase after him and get him back? Even if he ran into your state? I've paid for him; he's mine. So what's the difference if one of my slaves gets the itch to run off? Shouldn't I be able to chase after him or her—or both, as in this case? Even if they've run cross some invisible border and into a so-called free state?"

The room was so still it could've been empty. Everyone was listening.

"No," replied the quieter of the Blairs—either John or Jim, I didn't know which—"you shouldn't. Because there's an error in your reasoning. You're trying to equate the colored man with a mere animal that—"

Again a fist slammed the tabletop. "He has the faculties of an animal! He's not human, like you or me."

"Now really, I don't think you mean to say that—"

"Tell me," interrupted the slave chaser, "just tell me if you've ever met one of these black devils that you'd sit down to a meal with. One that you'd welcome right into this room. Tell me, have you?" He sat back in his chair and glared his challenge to everyone in the room. Heads quickly studied their plates.

In the tense silence I couldn't help looking up at my roommate. His face was holding to its mask, but his eyes were laughing.

That trapped feeling, the feeling of being a cornered

animal, was pushing the breath outta me. If the folks in this room knew 'bout my family, they wouldn't allow me to sit here. Heck, if they knew the truth, they might drag me outside by way of a lynching rope. Wasn't that what the man at the desert relay station had warned? "You better not be tryin' to pass yourself off as a white boy," he'd said, "or you're gonna find yourself strung up one of these days."

I tried to level a stare at Mr. McGahee, but my bluff had fallen apart and he knew it. Shoving away from the table, I stood so suddenly that the chair tipped over with a noisy clatter. Every head turned toward me, and my face burned. Scrambling to set the chair back in place, I nodded a thank-you in the direction of the surprised girl, turned, and bolted outta the dining hall.

CHAPTER TWENTY-ONE

Tired as I was, and sore as I was, I clomped outta Sportsman's Hall ready to ride on to Sacramento. Suddenly I didn't want to spend any more time here than necessary. I hurried through the crowded yard, weaving my way round and past and between the horses and oxen and wagons. On a normal day the sweet-hot smells of sweaty coats and the comforting sounds of nickers and stamping hooves would've settled me. But on this day I felt chased. I headed to the stables.

They were set at the bottom of a slope behind the main building—a whole city of barns and sheds and corrals. Hundreds of horses, parceled out among the pens, stood ankle-deep in the mud. Most of 'em were dozing, their heads drooping and their eyes blinking open and closed. The sun's heat had to be a pleasure after a night of freezing rain. Slipping and sliding past 'em down the churned-up path, I made my way into the largest barn.

It was still ice cold inside, even more so than outside, where the sun had begun to chase the mountain chill from the air. But it was dry, and the horses and mules lucky enough to be bedded down in these stalls looked well rested. I figured the Pony Express horses were in here somewhere, 'cause I knew they always got the best of care. Starting up the aisle, I casually tried to find the horse I'd ridden in on last night.

A tall, lanky boy, some few years older'n me and colored, came carrying a rake. "You needin' a horse?" he asked.

"No, not really." I wasn't sure whether I needed to shield my face from him. Suddenly I didn't know what the world saw when it looked at me. Mumbling, "I'm the Pony Express rider from Carson City," I half turned my back to him. "Came in last night. I just wanted to look over the horses, see which one I'd be riding next."

He had an easy way 'bout him and propped his hands on the rake, ready to talk. "You that anxious for another swim in the mud?"

His sly humor made me relax a little. "Well, no," I answered. I was warming to the idea of talking to someone closer to my own age, closer—in light of things—to my own kind. "The place here is real nice. And to tell truth, I'm still pretty stiff from the ride."

He nodded knowingly. "I hear it's a butt buster. One fella described it as skatin' cross spilled marbles with your tail on fire and your face in a blizzard."

I busted out laughing. "That *is* 'bout what it felt like."

"Don't worry," he said. "You won't have to ride it too many times, 'cause you won't last. No one ever does."

"Won't last . . . how?"

"You'll quit."

He said it like it was obvious, just part of the job, something that happened every day; but the words struck me hard. Quit? That had never occurred to me, even during the worst of the ride.

"Name's Newt," he said. "Newt Perkins." He offered his hand.

I shook it. "Colton Wescott."

"Sure do wish I could trade places with you, though. Just once." There was a wistfulness in his voice.

"Carrying the Pony mail, you mean?"

"Uh-huh. But when I applied, they told me they only used white riders. Sent me down here to the barn."

For a fleeting moment I wanted to tell him my secret; I wanted to tell him it was possible. But seeing as how that wouldn't do either of us any good, I kept my mouth shut. Newt took my silence as agreement with the white-riders-only policy, and his friendliness cooled. Taking a step back and surveying the horses, he walked over to a squatty bay one. "I 'spect you'll take this one," he said, purposely not looking at me. "He's had a rest, and he's a good, solid horse." He slapped the broad rump. "Gets a little stove up in his hocks now and then, so I try to spell him between rides."

"When will the next ride be?"

"Depends on the weather, but the eastbound rider usually comes through here on Tuesday afternoon. That gives you time to rest up. Eat up too, if you're smart. The hall has the best kitchen from here to Sacramento."

I patted my bulging belly. "Yeah, I've already learned that. Or maybe I should say, learned too late?"

"You get one of them cinnamon rolls?" Newt ran his tongue over his lips, then smacked 'em together. Already he was forgiving me the seeming inequalities in our lives.

"No. Guess I slept in some this morning." Ducking in beside the bay, I began scratching his withers. That made him cock his head and wriggle his lips in a shameless display of pleasure. "By the way, how far is it to Sacramento?"

Newt looked at me with a blank stare. "Why you askin'?"

"'Cause that's where I'm headed."

"You are? Well, just when do you plan on goin'?"

"On Tuesday, I suppose," I answered with a shrug. "Isn't that when the mail comes through again?"

He was shaking his head like I was truly some sorry kinda fool. "You got it all wrong. That's when the mail comes through headin' east. And that's when you'll carry it to Carson. See, all *you* do is ride back and forth between here and Carson City, back and forth over the Sierra Nevada. You don't ride any farther west."

It was like a door slammed in my face. Here I was, closer'n I'd ever been to Sacramento, thinking I'd soon be delivering Ma's freedom papers to her sister, and now I was being spun round and shoved back over the mountains. My mind went empty; the food in my stomach soured. I had to be dumb as a fence post. It simply had never occurred to me that I couldn't keep riding the Pony Express route to Sacramento, changing horses along the way, delivering both the mail and Ma's important papers. I knew someone had taken the mochila from me last night and galloped on with it, but somehow I thought *I* could be the one to gallop on west when the next rider rode in. "But I gotta get there."

"Well, like I said, you can always quit. You wouldn't be the first."

That wasn't gonna happen. "How far did you say it was to Sacramento?"

"I didn't say." Suspicion flickered in his eyes. "But I will tell you: It's fifty-six miles. Now let me do the askin'. Why do you need to get to Sacramento so bad?"

"I need to deliver something to my ma's sister."

"Somethin' big? Somethin' small?"

"Some papers." I could feel the envelope warm against my skin as I was talking 'bout it.

"Pay the money and put 'em in the mochila," he said simply. "They'll get there."

I shook my head. "They're pretty important. I think I should deliver 'em myself."

"Listen," he said, leaning past his rake and enjoying knowing more'n me, "there's all kinds of important mail goin' back and forth cross the nation all the time. Nother couple of months and the Pony'll be carryin' news of the presidential election. Good news, I'll betcha. You don't get much more important than that."

I nodded and came outta the stall, letting him think I agreed with him. But I hadn't changed my mind. Ma had said to deliver the papers into her sister's hand, and that was what I was gonna do. I'd gathered that the two men running for president had been doing a lot of talking 'bout kinds of freedoms—states' freedoms and the freedom of slaves— but I couldn't wait for 'em to decide all that. I had the responsibility of delivering real freedom to a real person.

Shifting the subject to something less troublesome, I said, "Seems strange to think I'm in a whole nother state since yesterday."

"Yeah, you woke up in Utah Territory and laid your head down in the state of California. Come Tuesday it's the other way round. Where're you from?"

"Started in Missouri."

"Your family there?"

I shook my head. "No, they're in Chinatown."

"Oh, yeah," he said, "other side of Carson. Never got out that far myself. You know, there's a rumor goin' round they had another big gold strike near there. You hear anything 'bout it?"

I shook my head again.

"Well, I don't lay much store by it anyway." He took on an air that said he'd heard his share of rumors and knew the difference between tall tales and factual ones. "Fella came through here a few days ago showin' off a lump of gold bigger'n your fist. Said he dug it outta Gold Canyon. I don't know, though." He squinted his eyes and looked thoughtful. "Seems to me, if a fella's found a vein that rich, he don't leave it in the first place and he don't go braggin' 'bout it in the second place. Specially when he's not there protectin' his claim."

I didn't know a thing 'bout gold, but I nodded in a way that said, *Yeah, that fella surely had to be lying.* Since Tuesday was still a couple of days off, I glanced round and asked, "So, what is there to do when you're not riding?"

Newt smiled slyly. "They give you the song and dance 'bout not goin' more'n a couple hundred yards from the station at any given time?"

I nodded. And I hadn't forgotten how Mr. Roberts had fired those piercing eyes of his straight at me, so that I'd promised right quick I wouldn't.

"Well, those *are* the rules," he said, "but the two Mr. Blairs don't force 'em here, so you're pretty much on your own." He looked over his shoulder at the other end of the barn, which opened onto the sea of green forest. "There's plenty of good huntin'—lot of deer if you can drop one, otherwise there's always rabbits. Fishin's good too. Or you can pan for gold. So much of it washes down the creeks round here that I figure somewhere out there is an ocean of water lined with pure gold." He grinned at the happy thought. "Oh, and there's a bowlin' alley over in Hangtown. That's what most folks call Placerville. It's another twelve miles down the road. But you gotta watch yourself there. Hangin's a sort of entertainment for those folks, so you don't want to be round when they're bored. Myself, I make sure to ride clear of that place."

Hanging again. I was beginning to feel like I wasn't safe anywhere. Jeremiah McGahee had claimed he knew my secret. Would he go so far as to try and turn me over to the slave chaser? Could he really do that? A shiver raced up my back and down my arms, making 'em twitch. Whether he could or couldn't, I didn't fancy the idea of holing up with him another couple of nights.

"Does everyone sleep up there?" I jerked my head in the direction of Sportsman's Hall.

"Most everyone who's passin' through," he answered. "Those of us who work in the stables, though, we sleep in the bunkhouse. Why?"

Lying sure was a slippery road, but here I was going down it again. "I got a roommate that snores awful loud. Can't get any sleep." I watched Newt's face. He looked skeptical, but I was banking on his kindliness. "Any chance I could sleep down here?"

"It'd be fine with me if we had an extra bunk, but we're full up. Just ask for another room."

"Aw, I don't want to go bothering anybody when I'm so new on the job," I said. "Isn't there anything you can do to help me out?"

Being the good and true person that I guessed him to be, he began looking round the barn. "Well," he replied, "I suppose you could bed down over there. I could spread some straw and blankets in that corner." He nodded toward where some saddles and bridles were hung, then shrugged. "'Bout the best I can offer."

"That'd do fine," I answered. "And I'm obliged to you." Before he could change his mind, I headed for the barn's sunlit back doorway. "Think I'll just go have a look-see at one of those creeks you were talking 'bout. Maybe I'll be rich before nightfall."

CHAPTER TWENTY-TWO

Lolling away a day in the sunshine was just the tonic after yesterday's hard ride in the rain. I found a creek soon enough and sauntered along it, enjoying the burbling water and the tangy air and the brilliant yellows and reds of the season's spindly-stalked flowers. A phoebe, sleek in his black waistcoat, chose to accompany me. He skimmed the waters ahead, picking off bugs, then jumped from bush to bush, flicking his tail and chirping for me to catch up. But I was set on going slow, intently watching for specks of gold in the stream. Who knew if fortune lay within arm's reach? More'n once I bent to poke at a rock, though that whole morning through I didn't come close to finding anything promising.

Round about midday, with the sun baking me to a sweat, I happened upon a sheltered pool, waist-deep and quiet— and it was singing an invitation. A bath and some clean clothes began to seem like a good idea, specially considering the sideways look the girl in the dining hall had given me. Wondering if that phoebe was somewhere nearby, watching with amusement, I yanked off my coat. Ever so carefully I unpinned Ma's letter and stuffed it safely inside the heavy sleeve. Then I stripped down to my skin.

If that phoebe *was* watching, he was laughing, I was sure of it. Probably calling his friends over as well to share in the spectacle. Couldn't blame him. A breeze had painted me all over with pimples, and I was hopping from foot to foot, suddenly chickenhearted. Should I? No, I wasn't all that dirty—well, maybe I was, but still . . . A jay squawked high above me, and from another tree came answering jeers. That was it. Sucking in a deep breath, I plunged—Lordy, Lordy, Lordy, it was cold!—and came scrambling out quick as I went in. My teeth were chattering hard. Sputtering swearwords and gasping for breath and wondering if a person could die from such a shock, I decided I was clean enough and shakily gathered up my clothes.

There was one sunny place on the bank, and I knelt there to vigorously dunk and swish each item in turn. The clear pool turned cloudy from all the mud. Shivering like I had the ague, I wrung out my pants and shirt and socks, and draped 'em over a bush to dry. Then I started jumping round. If those birds were still watching, they were getting a good laugh, 'cause I was slapping my chest and rubbing my arms and dancing like a madman on an anthill. Anything to get warm. Lordy!

After my display there was no sign of the birds, or any other creature, for that matter. Not that I could blame 'em for fleeing deeper into the forest. In the complete silence that followed, though, and while I was pacing back and forth in my nakedness, I got to feeling kinda lonely. The sky yawned endlessly overhead, airy blue and outta reach. Mountainous white clouds lumbered cross it, steadily going 'bout their business. They were followed by even grander plumes. Thousands upon thousands of black green trees towered in every direction.

I felt so small in comparison. So unnecessary, really. No more important than milkweed fluff.

I kept pacing, uneasy, and when the sun had kneaded some heat back into my skin, I found a gravelly spot where I could sit. With my knees hugged to my chest, I rocked back and forth and waited for my clothes to dry. And I let my thoughts wander.

Course they wandered straight to Ma. She didn't even know where I was. Althea would've told her by now what I'd planned on doing, which would set her to worrying, no doubt. "He's too young," she'd complain. "The work's too dangerous." But she'd have to see that I'd gone off only to earn money for our family, wouldn't she?

Or would she see me as just one more person who'd galloped away and left her? One more person who'd failed her. There was the tiniest kernel of truth in that, and my heart squeezed with guilt.

Sinking my chin onto my knees, I thought 'bout Pa. What in God's name had happened to him? My fingers found the scab on my leg and traced its outline. How many days had it been now since the gun went off? 'bout a week, I figured. The wound was healing all right, but the hurt inside of me seemed fresh as ever. Stroking the bumpy crust of skin somehow got me to thinking of Ned. Guess it was 'cause he had a similar scar behind his ears, a remembrance of a time when someone had hurt him. That wound had never healed proper.

I thought back to the day when Pa had come home leading him. He sure was one sorry-looking creature. His tail was thin, his coat was mangy, and his sides were ribby as a fence. Ma rolled her eyes 'cause we certainly didn't need another mouth to feed. Wasn't long, though, before I caught her of an evening rubbing oil into Ned's bald spots and feeding him the burnt ends of her corn bread. She never could turn away from a pitiful face.

The funny thing was, as nice as we treated Ned, he never fully cottoned to us. He was always running off—did it 'bout once a month or so back in the States—like he was expecting something bad to happen to him again. In his eyes, I suppose, all men were just waiting to wrestle him down with a rope. It was hard to fight such feelings.

Miserably wondering what had become of the both of 'em—Pa and Ned—I climbed to my feet and pulled on my slightly damp clothes. The walk back to Sportsman's Hall was a whole lot more solemn.

Bedding down in the barn that night wasn't awful bad, outside of it being awful cold. Newt found me a spare wool blanket, apologizing for it being moth eaten and worn thin.

"Beggars can't be choosers," I answered. That was one of Ma's favorite sayings, and it gave me a jab. I thought 'bout her some more, and 'bout Jewel, and Lucky even, and I spent a lot of time thinking 'bout Althea. I'd sure left her with a lot to shoulder.

Once the horses and mules were seen to, I began carrying armloads of straw into my corner. Then I wrapped the blanket round my shoulders and buried myself deep among the yellow stalks, smelling the sun from last summer and sneezing at the leafy dust and waiting for their warmth. With only my eyes peeking out, watching, ready to run at the first sign of danger, I realized I *was* acting a whole lot like an animal—just like the slave catcher had said—and I squirmed.

After 'bout an hour a thin cloud of warmth built up round me, enough, at least, to sleep. Only, sleep refused to come. In the pitch black of the stable I kept seeing the image of Ma's sister strolling down a boardwalk in Sacramento. Again and again I saw the man with the big ears point a finger at her and holler, "She's mine! She ran away and I'm taking her back." Only, when the sister turned round, it was Ma's face that was stricken with fear, and I was too late to save her.

I tried to chase the images from my mind. They weren't real. And I didn't believe in visions. Ma was way back in Chinatown; and her sister—well, in a town big as Sacramento the slave chaser wouldn't just happen cross her. Besides, in his own words, there were lots of runaway slaves he could claim. It wouldn't be her. It wouldn't.

Trouble was, that big-eared, mean-hearted man was headed toward Sacramento, and I wasn't. I was set to run the other way. That night was a long one, I tell you.

For the next day and a half I kept busy round the stable area. Helping out, I told myself. *Hiding out,* a voice sneered back, *just like an animal.*

I drowned out that needling voice with work. I saddled and unsaddled horses, hitched teams, mucked stalls— whatever needed doing. I took my meals in the kitchen along with the other hands so no one in the dining hall would have excuse to take notice of me. The food looked the same, but my cowardice sure made it taste different.

Come Tuesday morning I let the two Mr. Blairs know, through Newt, that I'd be waiting with the bay horse in the stable, and that as soon as the Pony Express rider rode in from the west, we'd gallop off with the mochila. All that day I perched atop an empty wagon on the sunny side of the barn, waiting and watching. Lordy, was my stomach torn up.

One of the reasons was that even after two days' rest my legs were still purply green all up and down, and sticky with sores. So climbing back into the saddle for another twelve-hour pitch-and-plunge wasn't high on my list.

But the main reason, I knew, was I'd branded myself a failure. Here I was, so close to Sacramento—it was only fifty-six more miles down the road—and I was turning back. I was running. What was I gonna tell Ma? I pictured her lying in her sickbed, breathing on the hope that her sister would soon know freedom. Every time I turned my head away from the west and toward the east, I tell you, her undelivered envelope burned into my skin.

As if that wasn't enough lead in my pockets, by late Tuesday afternoon, I had another thing to worry about: We were running outta daylight. The bay was saddled, I had a couple of slabs of smoked ham and corn bread on me, and I couldn't sit anymore. With the sun sinking through an orange and pink sky, and the air turning blue gray and damp, I left the wagon to look for Newt.

I found him dragging a sack of oats down the aisle, huffing against the weight. Jumping in to help and trying to sound casual, I asked, "Anything I should know 'bout going in the dark?"

He didn't even try funning me. "Naw," he answered, "the horses know the way. All they do is gallop back and forth between the same two stations, so it's easy for 'em. Besides, they see pretty good in the dark, I'm told."

"They see bears pretty good?" I laughed, like I was just kidding.

Newt flopped the bag down and straightened 'cause he knew I wasn't. "Ain't seen a bear round here all year. Mountain lion now and then, but they don't want nothin' to do with you."

I nodded. Yep. Sure. There weren't any wild animals out there that wanted us. Even if there were, my horse would see 'em first, right? So we'd just gallop on by.

While I was talking with Newt, who should come slipping into the barn and surprising us but the slave chaser himself. "I need my saddlebag," he boomed.

My heart skittered like a rabbit's and I near tore off like one, but Newt stood his ground. Looking the man in the eye—and speaking to him like he was just any other man with a horse, instead of one who could own *people*, too—he said, "I'll get it for you." And he turned and walked off, leaving me all alone with the devil in the flesh, sure as if he had a forked tail swishing out from under his long coat.

I pinned my eyes to the ground. Those big ol' ears of his were calling out to me, *Look! Look!* but I refused.

"Don't know what they're thinking," the man said as Newt's footsteps faded, "letting a colored boy run this stable by himself. Bet you a dollar to the penny he's stealing 'em blind."

I felt his gaze fall upon me, seeking agreement. I'd already taken a step back into the shadows, hoping he'd see nothing more in my face than fear.

"What's the matter with *you*, kid? You aren't one of those spineless aa-bo-litionists, are you?" He dragged out the word like he'd tasted something bad. "The sort that thinks slavery's 'oppressive'? That kind of thinking's for the ladies. Remember that."

I think maybe I shook my head, or nodded. I don't know. I was so scared of him I didn't say anything, didn't even speak up to disagree. But that seemed the same as agreeing, so I was hating myself all the more when Newt returned with the saddlebag. He handed it to the man.

"What're you looking at, boy?" the man challenged Newt of a sudden. "You taking a fancy to something of mine?" I knew he was gonna bring up the ears. I just knew it. "Well, let me change your thinking by showing you this."

Like there was a spell cast over 'em, my eyes rose up against my will. Newt and I both stared as the slave chaser slowly pulled a silver watch from his pocket. The gleaming piece had an extra-long chain, and dangling from that chain were twisted ribbons of dark leather.

"They're *ears*," he explained with wicked joy. "Sliced from the likes of you for admiring mine." The devil's eyes turned from Newt to me. "*You* saw him staring, didn't you?"

My head moved up and down. I didn't want it to, I swear, but I was scared. So there I was doing it, betraying Newt and betraying myself. I couldn't look over at him.

The man snorted with satisfaction. "See? And don't forget, boy," he warned Newt, "there's room on this chain for more." He took his saddlebag and left.

After that miserable experience I slunk away from a silent Newt to wait in the stable doorway by myself, soaked in shame. I prayed for the Pony Express rider to appear. I didn't care anymore 'bout bears or the dark of night or sore legs, or even galloping the wrong way, I just wanted outta there. I wanted outta my own skin.

But I was forced to wait. So, twisting and squirming, I waited. Waited as the first stars began speckling the dusky sky. Waited as the black silhouettes of the pine trees soared like church steeples against it. Waited still more as another man came shuffling down the path.

"I want my mule," he whined in a hoarse, whistly sorta voice. A glinty-eyed kitten was crouched on his shoulder, but I didn't need that sight to identify Jeremiah McGahee. Seemed this day couldn't get any worse. When he'd wobbled close enough to recognize me, he exclaimed, "So, this is where you've been hiding yourself!"

Hoofbeats—heaven sent—sounded in the distance.

"I *told* that slave chaser he'd let one slip right . . . past . . . his nose." He skidded his finger along my upper lip, leaving a greasy trail that reeked of fish innards.

"Pony rider's comin'," Newt shouted. He was all business, backing the man's mule outta its stall and trying to get it turned round in a hurry. I ran for the bay, grabbed the reins, and headed outside.

"Did ya have a look at his ears?" Jeremiah called after me. He swallowed a wheezy, coughing laugh. "'Cause he'll be a-wanting yours."

A shiver shook me through and through, and not from the words alone. The night seemed to've turned cold of a sudden and awfully black. I could see my breath, but I couldn't see a moon.

"C'mon," Newt hollered. He slapped the bay's rump, urging us up the slope. The hoofbeats were coming closer.

Just as we got to the front of the station a galloping horse clattered to a stop. Newt grabbed the reins to the steaming animal, and the rider jumped off. The man—he looked past twenty—doubled over, gasping for breath.

Bleary eyed but grinning, he said, "Helluva time getting here. Mail train was late into Folsom, then some idiot went and shot an arrow at me round about Duroc House—just nicked my shoulder, though." He turned, and in the lamplight we saw the torn sleeve, the raw edging darkened by blood. "And if that don't beat all, my horse stumbled crossing the river by the pools and came up with a broken leg. I had to leave him there and walk the rest of the way into Hangtown."

The two Mr. Blairs stepped onto the porch, one clutching a handful of letters, the other a key. I pulled the mochila off the saddle and handed it to them. By the light of their lantern they unlocked one of the secretive pouches, sorted through the envelopes, keeping some and adding theirs, then locked it again. They also checked the one unlocked pouch. The mochila was returned to me, and I sprang toward the bay, throwing the bag over the saddle and making doubly sure it was secure. Wasn't easy 'cause that horse was already dancing round and snorting like he'd been stung. Grabbing hold of some mane along with the reins, I leaped into the saddle.

There wasn't a chance to say good-bye to Newt or to anyone 'cause that horse was done gone. I'd only got my left foot in its stirrup when he took off, so for several rump-thumping strides I clung desperately to the saddle horn while my right foot searched the air. At last its stirrup was found and I could settle in. Sorta. I had to swallow a yelp as the pounding instantly ripped my sored legs raw. The hard leather seat felt foreign too, like I was in some kinda wild rocking chair being dragged through the night sky. Gradually the rhythm came back to me, though, and I settled into the saddle.

Or maybe *settled* wasn't the right word. Galloping headlong into the black canyon of night isn't something that leaves you settled. It leaves you scared. Dang scared and breathless. I grabbed hold of mane with both fists and rode light in the saddle—hunched like a race rider—expecting the horse to stumble on the murky path. If that happened— as it had with the other rider—I wanted to be ready to jump off. I didn't want near a thousand pounds of horseflesh crushing me 'cause my foot was caught up in the stirrup. That thought tore a new hole in my stomach. What if we *did* fall out here, and *I* was the one who broke a leg? Or had my head cracked open? This horse would gallop on to the next station with the mail, that was certain enough, but I'd be left all alone on the mountain in the middle of the night. Who would find me? Or, more likely, *what* would find me?

Just as I was shivering with that dismal thought, something shimmered in the darkness ahead. The bay hesitated, bunched, and leaped forward with a grunt, and we found ourselves splashing cross a river. It was too soon. We weren't supposed to cross the river till a ways farther on, were we? Had we got lost already?

We galloped on blindly, me counting out the minutes in gulping breaths. I'd never felt more helpless. The bay kept going, and lucky for me, he did know the way, 'cause about one hour later he galloped up to a little station sitting right next to the river and stopped. I didn't recognize it from my last ride, but maybe that was 'cause it'd been raining so hard. There was a lantern lit and a horse saddled and waiting. The man said he didn't have any mail, wasn't expecting any. I jumped off the bay and onto the new horse, and in seconds we were galloping again.

The narrow, rolling path was deep inside a chasm now, with black walls rising up to a black sky only lightly sprinkled with stars. Black trees whipped their branches cross my face, tried to pull me from the saddle. Pockets of fog swallowed us whole when the trail dipped, spat us out when the trail rose. My hands and face dripped with cold dew.

As the trail veered and rose steeply, the horse slowed. His breath came in locomotive blasts, and I leaned over his neck to take the weight off his straining back. In the silence of the forest his clattering hooves and roaring breath must've sounded like some ogre from a storybook. With all the noise we were making, you'd think it'd be easy to hear us coming, but no one was waiting when we got to the next station. I think the keeper must've fallen asleep, 'cause he looked addled and more'n a little embarrassed when I banged on the door. I helped him saddle and bridle a fresh horse, and returned to climbing.

It's hard to believe, but after a while I kinda started to take to night riding. I didn't have to think, for one thing. All I had to do was put my faith in my horse, in his sturdy legs and sure hooves and large eyes, and let him carry me, a shadow on his back. It was like we'd melted into one creature, and I moved in the animal's world and not man's.

One by one, hour after hour through the night, we pulled up to the relay stations, both of us panting. The moon rose, three-quarters full, to help light our way. But the air was cold, so cold it almost hurt to breathe. When I went to turn my collar up, my numbed fingers found beads of ice stuck to my hair. Food and a warm fire were offered at 'most every station, but I figured it'd be a lot harder to climb back into the saddle once I'd got off. So I just kept going.

Snow frosted the ground by the time we reached the highest station—Friday's, I think it was called. And an hour after that we were at the small cabin station with the shed. Another change of horses there and we were traveling head-first down the mountain. This was a whole lot scarier than climbing. Galloping uphill felt closer to the ground; you had control 'cause you were pushing against the mountain. But going downhill? It was like the mountain had control of you. It pulled you, harder and faster, and threw slippery pebbles under scrambling hooves and crumbled the very dirt away until you were a hairsbreadth from falling to your death. I had to shove my feet hard against the stirrups and sit way back to keep from plummeting over my horse's head. I couldn't even see his head most of the time, he was so scrunched up, trying to find a safe way down.

Through the darkness we slid and stumbled and made the switchback turns just in time, and my heart never beat so hard in my whole life. The piney smell faded. The dampness evaporated and dry desert air began sucking at my nostrils.

And then, when my bones felt like they'd been rattled and scattered like dice, we were on the flat! The horse made the sharp turn left and we threw ourselves into a final, tired gallop. The sandy desert floor reflected the moonlight well; we could actually see where we were going. It was a straight shot to Carson City, so I'd be there in less than two hours. I had to switch horses one last time, in that little town, the pretty one. And then I'd be galloping along the road to a soft hotel bed and a long sleep.

We pounded our way along the base of the mountains, here and there passing a small, darkened cabin. The thought of families snuggled inside made me ache for home. Finally, ahead, the black silhouettes of taller buildings came into view. Pale smoke drifted from chimneys—either last night's embers or morning's first sparks, I didn't know which. I didn't know the hour. I did know we'd made it to the pretty town, the one just an hour's ride from Carson.

In minutes we were galloping past the outermost businesses, me peering down the street and trying to remember which building housed the Pony Express station. Outta the corner of my eye I saw a door open. A woman—I know that 'cause I remember the skirts—flailed her arms in distress. Something white was flung into my path. There was an orange flash of fire and my horse fell out from underneath me. Hooves and dirt and leather and bone tumbled over and over. I tasted blood. Heard distant hoofbeats. And then, nothing.

CHAPTER TWENTY-THREE

When I came to, the blurry faces of a couple of strangers were hovering over me, and I smelled like I'd drowned in whiskey. Somebody must've splashed out a whole bottle, trying to raise me to my senses. I found myself laid on a high bed in a room that was overwarm and stuffy. Scratchy white pillows cradled my throbbing head. I couldn't tell if it was night or day.

Blinking, I tried to bring the faces into focus. The nearer one belonged to a woman. It was round, smiling, and darker skinned than my ma's. Beside it, hanging back a mite, was a man's face. It was serious looking, worried even . . . with the white skin of my father. My heart exploded. In sudden rapture I shot straight up in bed and reached my arms out.

"Lord, he's seein' the angels." The woman—now I noticed how big she was—took hold of my arms and pressed me back against the pillows. Her deep laugh sounded free of worry, which would've been soothing on any other day, and the leathery palm she laid on my forehead left traces of butter and sugar and something else sweet I couldn't name. But that wasn't important. What was important was that she was blocking my view, blocking my view of my father.

Struggling to see, I craned my neck past her oxenlike shoulders. The place where he'd stood was empty. He was gone. The pictures on the wall started to waver and tremble; the dresser mirror gleamed silvery wet and ran. I sank into the pillows, giving up, giving in.

Next time I came to, the room was still shadowy. The shade was pulled tight over the lone window, but the thin strip of light edging it told me it was day. My head still pounded like thunder. The least little movement, I found, even turning my head to one side, sent a shock of zigzagging lightning bolts through my brain. Someone had left a pitcher of water and a glass by the bed, and that made my throat ache, but I was too shaky to reach for the handle.

I lay there, scarcely breathing, wondering if I'd imagined the faces. I wondered where I was. Guess I was kinda outta my mind, 'cause I thought for a while that maybe I was dead and gone to heaven. That's why my pa was with me again, and I suppose Ma had died too. I wondered who was looking after Althea and Jewel, poor orphans.

The bed under me was fluffy and white as a cloud, so I floated among the angels in and outta sleep. Wasn't as peaceable as I would've thought. Noises that didn't belong in heaven kept poking through my dreams. There was the rattling of pots and pans far below, for one thing. And the voices of people and the creak of wagons and the clip-clop of horses somewhere outside the window, for another. Where exactly was I?

Opening my eyes, I studied the room. It had a low, sloping ceiling, painted white, so I knew I was tight under the roof of some tall building. The bed, a four-poster, was pressed into one corner, and the chopped-off table beside it held the water pitcher. Next to a closed door at the foot of the bed was a small dresser and mirror, and on either side of them was a pair of faded pictures showing cattle standing in a gray pond or grazing in a chalky meadow.

Would've been a cheerless attic if not for the piles of white linens. There were layers upon layers of 'em: curtains and coverlets and tablecloths and doilies, all embroidered and dripping in lace. They made the room a soft white cocoon.

Drifting back into sleep, I remembered the day long ago that I'd found a cocoon hidden in the bushes behind our house. It had a small hole in it, so I knew the butterfly was getting near his time. In my eagerness to see him I broke the cocoon open. The wrinkled creature inside was beautiful, sure enough, but papery and frail looking too. He was struggling some, so I peeled the cocoon clean away, and his first tickly steps on my palm swelled me up with heart-skipping joy. That was short lived, though. I found myself watching in horror as the tiny creature spun recklessly, unable to unfold his too-new wings. In no more'n a few seconds he was crumpled in my palm, dead.

My eyes shot open. The shadowy room I was in was spinning, and my body felt funny, kinda prickly and cottony at once. Maybe I *was* dead, dead as that butterfly torn from its cocoon. I hurt bad enough to be dead. I hurt all over.

Floorboards squeaked outside the room. A mourner coming to pay his last respects. I watched the doorknob rattle, heard it whine as it was slowly turned.

The face that peeked round it belonged to the woman I'd woken to earlier, and she was still smiling big as all outdoors. "Well, look at you! You're awake again, and maybe now I can make my apologies."

My throat was too parched for talk.

"I'm sorry," she began, "so sorry to tell you, but I'm the one that tossed that burnin' apron in your path this morning, though I had no intention of spookin' your horse so. I just didn't see you comin'." She slapped her big hands on her starched apron, leaving damp imprints. "Honestly! You will never get me on the back of one of those skitterish creatures long as I live." She bent over me, still grinning and looking to share a smile, but I couldn't make my face move. Hers drooped. "I'm so sorry, puddin'. I didn't mean you no harm, understand?"

I moved my head against the pillow, attempting a nod. Lordy, that hurt!

She smiled afresh and wider than ever. "Good! 'cause I'm gonna fix you up good as new, too. Now then, my name's Charlotte Barber, but you can call me Aunt Charlotte. Most folks do."

I made another attempt at a smile, which made my scalp scream like someone was trying to lift it. "Where am I?" I whispered.

"In my house," Aunt Charlotte said. "Mine and my husband Ben's. In Genoa."

I tried to sit up, winced, and eased back onto the pillows. "I gotta get the mail to Carson," I croaked like a frog. "I'm the Pony rider."

"Oh, I know 'bout that, and don't you worry none 'bout the mail, young Mr.—say, what's your name, puddin'?"

"Colton Wescott."

"Don't you worry 'bout the mail, Mr. Colton Wescott. The station manager and I've sent my neighbor's boy, Farley, on with it. He's fifteen years old and just as responsible as the day is long, and my, won't he think he's important when he returns. Now, he's been given strict orders to explain to Mr. Roberts—that's your boss man's name, isn't it? Mr. Bolivar Roberts?—'bout your delay and to say it wasn't your fault. Not your fault at all."

I was having to concentrate on her words real hard 'cause her face kept coming in and outta focus. There was something familiar 'bout it. I'd seen it before today. Then I remembered. "I saw you," I said.

She crossed her arms and smiled down at me, like she was newly happy 'bout something.

Working to bring the words out one by one, I said, "When I rode through here . . . a few days ago." It was all coming back to me. "I saw you wave . . . it was you, wasn't it? You said something odd . . . something like 'Keep it together' or 'Keep us together,' I think."

"Did I?"

That gave me pause. *Had* she said it? How much of all that was happening was real and how much was I dreaming? "Is my pa here?"

"Your pa?"

"I saw him . . . earlier."

She shook her head, pursed and unpursed her lips a couple of times. "No, I don't 'spect you did, and I don't 'spect you ever will again." She laid her hand on my arm for comfort. "But maybe you mean my husband, Ben. He's white, like your pa was."

Was. She said it like he was dead for sure. I'd been saying it, but this was different. This made it real. Tears wet my eyes. I hated that.

And I hated her for talking 'bout him that way. How would she know, anyway?

And I hated my pa for running off and leaving us.

And I hated myself for blubbering over that same old thing again. Pa was gone; he wasn't coming back. But when was it gonna stop hurting?

"There, there," she soothed, and I turned my head away. I didn't need to be babied. I didn't need anyone.

Aunt Charlotte left me alone with my misery.

I must've dozed again, or maybe she'd never gone outta the room, but when I turned my head back, there she was again. Still smiling. That was starting to sandpaper me some 'cause I didn't see what there was to be so all-fired happy about.

"Why did you tell me to keep it together?" I asked, and it sounded gruff. "Why did you say that?"

She didn't ruffle a single feather. "I said it 'cause you, Colton Wescott, are gonna keep it together. You're gonna keep us all together. Can't say more'n that; can't even say how you're gonna do it. But I knew I had to tell you."

Her words gave me chicken skin. "Whaddya mean you knew you had to tell me?"

She was shaking her head. "Can't say. All I know is I've been having a lot of feelings lately, *lot* of feelings. *Strong* feelings. Folks round here say I'm a prophetess and that I've got a gift. Well, maybe I do, 'cause I get these feelings, and often enough to put the fear of God into a person, they come true. One of 'em I've been having of late is that folks like you and me ain't gonna have to worry too much longer 'bout slavery. Pretty soon there ain't gonna be any more slaves. They're all gonna rise up and walk away from their masters, just rise up and walk away. President Abraham Lincoln's gonna tell 'em to do so. 'Just rise up and walk away,' he's gonna say."

I looked at her like she'd been eating locoweed. *I get these feelings.* Huh. That was nonsense. And what did she mean by saying "folks like you and me"? My head throbbed harder and I heaved a sigh. This whole territory was full of crazy people. Aunt Charlotte was just another one, only she was maybe crazier than old Jeremiah McGahee. I guess that's what the territory's hard living did to a person: It made you talk crazy. *President* Lincoln? I decided to set her straight. "The election hasn't even happened yet, ma'am."

"Hasn't it?" She didn't appear any more ruffled than before. "I'm certain it's President Lincoln that's gonna free 'em."

"If Abraham Lincoln gets to be president, there's talk of war. Union's gonna split in two."

The expression that took hold of her was one I hadn't seen since sitting in church back in Missouri. Her face got shiny wet with a rapture of her own. She folded her hands together like she was praying. "That *must* be where you fit in, Colton. *You're* gonna have to keep us together."

"*I'm* gonna have to? The whole Union—all the states and territories?" Now she *was* talking crazy. "Just how would I do that, ma'am?"

"Don't know," she said, frowning while she pondered that. "Maybe with your riding."

"I'm not riding now."

"You will be, Colton." She patted my arm. "You will be. You're gonna change things."

Her nonsense was really starting to rasp me. "My ma says things are the way they are and you can't change 'em."

Aunt Charlotte's smile disappeared fast as the sun on a stormy day. "I guess I haven't met your ma, but . . . but I'm sure we'll be good friends when I do." She smoothed her apron and turned for the door. Before she left, though, she paused. "What *I* always say is, any person who don't like the way he's living— he can change that. He's gotta change that or he ain't half a man. And that I solemnly believe." She closed the door quietly.

Bed wasn't as comfortable after she left. Pillows felt smothering. Room was hotter than ever. I wanted outta there; I wanted to be on the back of a horse, galloping.

I was still wriggling round, fuming over her words and feeling sorry for myself, when Aunt Charlotte carried in a tray of food that smelled awful good. Part of me didn't want to eat it, just to spite her, but I was too hungry.

"Now," she said, after fluffing the pillows behind me and handing me a bowl of milky porridge, "I try to learn something from everyone who passes through my door, so you're gonna tell me where you've been and what you've seen." She pulled a chair over to the bed and settled herself.

I took a spoonful of porridge. It was salty and molassesy at the same time, and I ended up downing two more spoonfuls before answering her. "I haven't seen all that much."

"Where're you from?"

While hungrily swallowing the porridge, I told her 'bout my family's trip cross the territory, 'bout Pa running off and little Willie dying. I told her 'bout how my sisters and I'd been looking after things, with Ma being so sick. I didn't talk of color at all, and yet I sensed she knew the rest of our story anyway. Maybe the townsfolk were right 'bout her. Maybe she was a person who just knew things.

"My, you have had some trials." Her eyes glowed with interest when I'd finished. "What kinda people you met over the mountains? I ain't never been there myself."

"Aw, there isn't anything to the people up there," I said. I was still in a foul mood 'bout the way I'd left Sportsman's Hall: running and hiding from Jeremiah McGahee, nodding agreement with the slave chaser, of all people, and betraying Newt. Most of all, I guess, I was mad at myself. But instead I said, "They just look at you and decide, is all. Just look at you and decide. They don't treat you fair."

"How they not treat you fair?"

I told her 'bout Jeremiah McGahee's accusations and 'bout the slave chaser's speeches and how I felt that everyone in the dining hall had been staring at me. I told her 'bout sleeping in the barn. I didn't tell her 'bout Newt. "They don't look past your face," I said. "Not a one of 'em."

"What're you talking 'bout? I can't believe many'd linger on *your* face; you pass as white."

Maybe it was true, maybe it wasn't. I didn't seem to know who I was anymore or who I was supposed to be.

She frowned at my silence. "Well, what do you see when you look at their faces?"

I lowered the spoon from my mouth. "I see a whole bunch of white faces *expecting* me to go sleep in the barn."

She sat back, surprised. After thinking for a minute, she said, "Maybe you don't look past *their* faces. Did you ever consider that?"

I'm sure mine was showing itself blank, 'cause I had no idea what she was talking 'bout.

"Maybe all you see is the color of *their* skin instead of

a whole person." She was looking real serious, and her voice got deep as a church bell. Ma in her worst finger shakings had nothing on Aunt Charlotte. "And far as I'm concerned, your goin' and hidin' in the barn like you're an animal is askin' to be treated like an animal. I oughtta take you over my knee for a fool act like that."

The spoon was still in midair. I didn't know what to say. Been a long time since I'd had such a tongue-lashing.

"Colton Wescott," she said, and I knew she was nowhere near being done with me, "I'm gonna tell you something my ma told me, and you're gonna listen. People is people. We all breathe the same air, we all walk 'stead of crawl. A man puts on his pants one leg at a time just like you do, and a lady drinks her tea outta a cup just like I do. He wants respect, she wants a family, we all want to be loved. It's human." Her brown eyes glowed like embers. "We're more alike than different, Colton. You gotta remember that."

CHAPTER TWENTY-FOUR

Aunt Charlotte practically tied me to that four-poster bed of hers. Not that I would've got far anyway. My head felt like a china cup that'd been dropped on the floor. I imagined it spiderwebbed with fine gray cracks—just waiting to shatter if I moved too fast. But I was determined to finish my ride, mail or no mail.

She ignored my pleas. Smiling that rubbery smile of hers, she moved 'bout the room tidying this and fluffing that, humming to herself. "You're hurt," she told me, "hurt more than even you know." Soon she had a drippy poultice wrapped tight round my head, and soon after that she was balancing herself on the edge of the bed, so that the mattress spilled me near into her lap, and serving me up apple sauce and creamed rice. By that evening, when the lamp was turned low and a soft-boiled egg was sliding down my throat, I wondered glumly if I'd ever break outta her smothering cocoon, if I'd ever make it back to Carson. And if I did make it back, if I'd still have a job.

Next morning, with my head pounding less, I was able to walk a few steps to her satisfaction, and she decided to let me go. To my unending embarrassment, she walked me—like some half-pint, fresh-scrubbed schoolchild—all the way down Genoa's main street to the Pony Express stable. She asked 'em to saddle me "a gentle-minded horse" and "one that prefers amblin' to gallopin'." My face went hot. I fully expected 'em to laugh us into the dirt, but the station keeper tipped his hat and, polite as Sunday, said, "Right away, Aunt Charlotte." In no more'n a couple of minutes I was settled onto the back of a smallish dappled mare, the stirrups adjusted to suit my legs.

The station keeper still had ahold of the mare's bridle, but I could feel her swelling up with the itch to run. She was a Pony Express horse, after all. I grabbed a hank of mane just as a great snort shot outta her nostrils. She started prancing in place, and the saddle rocked side to side like a little boat on a stormy sea. The mare tossed her head, fighting the restraint. I tried to hold mine steady.

I don't know how it was done, couldn't even say, in fact, that it was done, by any human means. What I saw, though, was Aunt Charlotte walk up to that horse and tap her smart on the nose—once, twice—and murmur some sorta gibberish to her. And that mare settled right down, acting just as calm as a fat pony on a breezeless day. The station keeper let go of the bridle, and with a prickly feeling that I'd witnessed something that wasn't part of the natural world, I set off for Carson.

That morning, walking a rolling trail that was gentle on my cracked head, I had occasion to thank the Lord. I thanked him for the blessing of a smooth road. I thanked him for the sun that warmed my shoulders on a cool day, thanked him for the joys of a comfortable saddle and a good horse. I probably had him to thank too—or maybe it was Aunt Charlotte—for Mr. Roberts's welcome.

As I came into town a couple of hours later, I saw the hawkish man sitting on the bench outside his office. He was holding a newspaper but doing as much southward looking down the street as reading. When he saw me approach, he stood.

I expected him to be mad as a wet rooster, so I started spewing apologies as soon as I rode up. He stopped me with one hand.

"How are you feeling?" he asked.

"Fine, sir." I swung my leg neatly over the saddle and jumped free, proving my soundness. The instant my feet smacked the dirt, a rattling sounded in my head. Gritting my teeth, I smiled at Mr. Roberts's wavery silhouette. "I'm sorry 'bout the mail, sir. I—"

"Nothing to worry 'bout, son." He clapped me on the shoulder and I felt a couple of new cracks shoot through the cup. "Farley Danes rode it in all right. Had his horse galloping so fast, though, the two of 'em almost jumped through my window and laid the mail in my lap." He laughed with the memory, then stood back a ways and eyed me. His words came out kind, gentle even, but they tore through me like bullets. "I think I probably erred in hiring you, Colton. You're just too young for this job."

His silhouette came into sharp focus then. "No, I'm not." Even to my ears my voice sounded too shrill. "Honest, sir. I can do this. I can ride out again Saturday, if you'll let me. I'll even ride out again today."

He smiled the way you do when a puppy's jumping at your leg and yipping, and I knew he wasn't gonna let me. "You go on back to your ma and kin," he said, turning for his office. "I'll get your pay for this ride and we'll call it quits, okay?"

I felt like I'd been shot. The sharp blast was a whole lot worse than when I'd hit my head yesterday morning. Seemed like I kept getting pushed farther and farther away from where I needed to go.

Mr. Roberts returned, handing me some folded paper money, which I didn't look at. He held out his other hand and I reluctantly laid the Colt revolver in it. I felt like a child caught playing with grown-up things, brought out into public to be punished. The stableman came to take the reins to the gray mare, and then I was left standing alone in the street, just as ashamed as if I was naked.

I started walking blindly. Carson City was busy that fall morning. I numbly realized that, 'cause I kept bumping into people or getting shoved aside by them. They had work to do and places to go, unlike me. Into and outta stores they marched, loading up their arms and their wagons with goods. Laughing and talking like it was a bright, sunny day, when anyone with any sense could feel the coming winter's chill. I had no work and no place to go other than Chinatown. 'Bout all I had to my name was that sorry-looking black horse. Leastways I wouldn't have to walk.

Mr. Bucher brought him out for me, already tacked, and to pay for his care I handed over some of the money I'd just got. The horse looked even scrawnier than I remembered, like some kid's pony foundering neath a too-big saddle. His coat was dirty as a dog's, only rougher. The hairs swirled different ways and banged into each other in disagreement. His eyes were the same, though—small and brown and angry at the world. Well, today we were well matched. I stepped into the saddle.

Course he humped his back first thing and put his head

between his legs. With me pulling on the reins, he set to bucking and crow-hopping down the busy street. People stopped to watch and laugh, and I was so mad by then that they got themselves a real good show. Each time that imp of Satan leaped in the air, I thumped his sides before he came down, daring him to do it again. He spun and sunfished, and I hauled on the reins, yelling. He raced off a couple of strides, then pulled up short to buck again—one, two, three, each time harder, trying his best to get rid of me. I hollered at the top of my lungs. Never mind my cracked head; I couldn't feel a thing at that moment 'cept the burning in my veins.

Knowing a horse can't buck while he's galloping, leastways not for very long, I yanked his head round toward the north end of town, kicked him hard, and let him go. And that horse galloped. We tore outta town like a spinning dust devil. Kept galloping and galloping and galloping. I figured he wouldn't last more'n a mile or two, 'cause he wasn't fit, but his stubby legs kept pumping, like he thought he was a Pony Express horse or something. It was like riding the mail all over again—'cept for the fact that I'd been fired and we were headed in the wrong direction.

Before you knew it, we were alongside the Carson River, the yellow leaves of the cottonwood trees shivering in the stiff breeze. That horse wouldn't let go of his anger and just kept galloping, near flat out for close to an hour, though he was breathing mighty hard by the end. When Chinatown came into sight, I pulled him up, not so much outta kindness, but 'cause I didn't want to make a scene. I didn't want to come galloping into town like a hero. I was so far from that it was like I was in a whole nother territory. Here I'd spent 'most all my money on a miserable mount; I'd failed to deliver Ma's letter; and I'd been fired from the Pony Express—all this in one week to the day since I'd left. Only one week. So much had happened it seemed like a lifetime.

Even though the black horse was breathing hard, with his ribby sides sucking in and out like a bellows, he was still tugging on the bit and wanting to run some more. Stubborn fool. I guided him round and behind the row of buildings where my ma and sisters were staying, only half surprised to find Jewel there, playing house near the trash heap. Sure enough, Lucky was sitting beside her, his lips drawn back in a doggy smile. It was a mighty embarrassed smile 'cause a lady's string bonnet was tied round his head. Maybe he was feeling a little ornery, too, 'cause he rose to his feet, growling, when I jumped down from the saddle.

"Hey, now," I scolded. "I'm the one that rescued you, remember?"

He stopped his growling and Jewel looked up. "Colton!" she squealed, and came running into my arms, hitting me with a thud that reminded me, finally, that my head was still suffering. "Where'd you go?"

I pointed to the Sierra Nevada range, which edged the valley. "See those mountains? I've been up and over 'em and back again."

"Is this your horse?" She'd already lost interest in me and had walked over to where the blowing animal was nosing Lucky. She patted him on the head and he nibbled about her shoes. "He's nice."

"Yeah?" I chuckled. "Well, you won't say that after you get to know him better."

Althea came round the corner lugging a basket of wet laundry on her hip. I know she saw me, but she pretended she hadn't. "What're you doing?" she scolded Jewel. "I told you to hang those clothes on the line!" Pointing to a basket set by the back door, she said, "If they're dirty, I'm not the one who's gonna be washing 'em again."

Jewel dragged herself, limp limbed, toward the basket. She pulled a wet shirt off the top, carried it to a rope that'd been strung low between a fence post and the back of the building, and flopped it over. She took her own sweet time working a clothespin into place.

"Looks like you two are in business," I said to Althea.

"Somebody's gotta earn some money round here." She glared at me, finally, as she carried the second basket of laundry toward the line and began pinning up clothes.

"How's Ma?"

"If you'd stayed, you'd know."

That brought my heart to a stop. "Is she okay? Althea, tell me."

She spun, pleased with her secret knowledge but still angry. "She's some better. She's eating, and yesterday she sat outside awhile." She paused. "No thanks to you."

I deserved it. I'd run off to satisfy my own needs more'n a need to earn money. And what had I gained? Heaving a sigh and trying to make amends, I walked over and started pinning up clothes too. There was a large man's shirt with decorative stripes on it that I held up. "You two taken on a whole lot of beaus since I left?"

Jewel giggled. "They're not beaus, they're miners . . . and they're smelly," she whispered.

"We get paid thirty-five cents a shirt," Althea said, her face stone serious. "Others in town charge forty. I do the washing—got a tub and some lye down by the river—and Jewel, if she doesn't get herself distracted, does the pinning up."

I whistled. It was quite an operation.

"What've *you* been doing, Colton?"

My face flushed. "Well," I said, "I've been doing a lot of riding."

"He's been over the mountains," Jewel said. She, at least, was proud of me.

I dug the paper money outta my pocket and showed it to Althea as proof that I'd been working too. She looked it over, keeping sober.

"Mind if I go up and look in on Ma, then?"

"Suit yourself," she said. "We got work to do here."

"Will you look after my horse, Jewel?"

She nodded happily. "What's his name?"

"Can't say as I've thought of one that wouldn't make the both of you blush. Maybe you can."

"Okay."

I turned for the door, noticing for the first time that Ma's thorny, leafless rose canes had been stuck in the ground next to a stone wall. There was a little circle of mud round 'em. "What are these doing here?"

"We planted 'em," Althea answered. And like I was some half-wit, she added, "Roses prefer being planted in one place."

"Only if you're planning on staying with 'em," I shot back. "And we're not staying here, so you can just dig 'em up." Suddenly I was angry all over again—at her and at me and at us and our situation.

The thought that they were putting down roots in this little town so far from Sacramento addled me all through my talk with Ma. Course I was happy to see her; had to fight back tears when she put her thin arms round me and gave me a hug. She did look some better, not near as trembly. At the same time, though, she looked like she'd given up. She looked like a lantern that'd been trimmed and polished but left dark, with no flame lit. I wished I could've given her the uplifting news that I'd seen her sister and delivered the envelope into her hand. But I couldn't. I couldn't give her one bit of good news 'cause I hadn't done one bit of good. So when she said she felt like taking a nap, I scooted outta the room in shameful relief.

First thing I did was give all the money I had to the lady doctor who'd been taking care of Ma and Althea and Jewel. She handed two bills back to me. "Always keep some for seed," she instructed. "There's another spring coming." So I pocketed 'em, 'cept for a few pennies' worth, which I spent at the emporium on some molasses candy for Ma and my sisters. They each had a fearsome sweet tooth. Pa used to say bees swarmed round 'em in jealousy 'cause they had more sugar than the bees did. And as much as Althea liked the stuff, I knew she wouldn't part with any of her hard-earned coins for such a frill.

Sitting round Ma's bed after lunch, sucking on our candy, I said outta the blue, "We should all pick up and move over to Genoa." The three faces that looked at me already had their heels pushed into the ground. "At least for the winter," I coaxed. "You're mending, Ma, and it's a real pretty town and there's some nice people there. You'd like 'em."

As expected, it was Althea that began the arguing. "You can't just show up after a whole week and tell us what to do, Colton." Ma tried to hush her, but she would be heard. "You're the one who went running off. Besides, Jewel and I got our work here."

"I didn't go *running* off," I shot back. "I went to—"

"Looked like running off to me."

"Well, I didn't!"

"Did so!"

"Did not!" And just like that we were spatting like a couple of wildcats. Or like a couple of kids who hadn't been kids for a long time. Maybe it was the candy made us feel that way, maybe it was just being back together as a family. To tell truth, it felt kinda good. I knew Althea felt the same, 'cause she tried to hide a smile by rolling her eyes in exasperation. The way she was bobbing her leg cross her knee, though, showed she was excited. She wasn't ready to give up on our goal of getting to Sacramento, I knew. I could count her on my side.

CHAPTER TWENTY-FIVE

Ma and I sat up late that night. Althea wanted to stay up with us; I saw it in her eyes. But she knew Ma and I needed to talk, so she bundled Jewel up in her blankets and then cuddled next to her, reciting one of the Bible stories that Ma used to tell us. I think all of us—'cept little Jewel, maybe—knew there was something left unsaid between Ma and me. That something practically pulled up a chair in the middle of our room and sat down, just waiting for one of us to look over and say howdy.

Pretending like the two girls were sleeping and needed the quiet, I helped Ma out to the tiny balcony. I managed to wedge a rocker between the wall and railing, and Ma hunched in it, wrapped in a quilt. The night was cold and dry, and when I turned a certain way, I could see my breath in the moonlight. The wind clattered through the leaves clinging to the cottonwood trees. Talk and laughter rose up from the saloons below.

Ma pushed the rocker back and forth with the balls of her feet. The wooden joints made a slow, rhythmic keening in the night. It was a lonesome sorta noise, telling of things drying up and blowing away, of winter coming.

For a long while we sat like that, her in her chair and me on the balcony floor with my arms wrapped round my knees. Together we watched a gigantic silver moon push up past the pale hills. That sight chased away any human talk. Inside my coat, inside my skin, I could feel my heart thud against its ribbed cage, awed by the spectacle. Big as the sun, that moon was, and so bright it painted a latticework of black shadows cross the dirt street below. But so cold, too. It didn't give off any heat, didn't stir anything to life. Just left you watching it with a hollow feeling that there could've been something more.

As Ma and I sat I noticed a change not only in the air, but in the town itself. The moon was draining everything of its color. Cross the street the red letters on the sign went gray, and next door the yellow window trim turned white. I glanced at Ma. She'd 'most disappeared in shadow, and the blue and green patches on her quilt had gone inky and dull. With my heart thumping uneasily, I studied my own fingers clasping my knees. They were neither dark nor light now, but just another shade of gray. Did that change 'em?

Ma was shivering some, so I shook myself free of my woolgathering to tippy-toe back into the room and pull the second quilt off her bed. It was a thinner one, and as I wrapped it round her I said, "That's not much help, I suppose."

She smiled up at me. "Beggars can't be choosers."

That's when it happened. All that anger and unsettledness I'd been bottling up inside me came busting out. "I don't want to be a beggar, Ma. I don't want to live always running and hiding. I want to be a man."

She looked at me like she didn't know what I was saying. And how could she? I went rambling on 'bout animals in the shadows and putting on pants one leg at a time and cut-off ears and chases and hangings and changing things. I kept stumbling over words, stopping and starting sentences, until one thought made itself heard: "Why do you think Pa ran off?"

Her eyes slid away from me. She pressed her lips together and stuck out her small chin and rocked faster. "He's coming back," she said. And the way she said it, so determined, and staring into the distance like a rider was approaching at that very moment, made me turn. Guess a part of me still wanted to believe he was alive. But the sandy road wound outta town and disappeared into the hills, empty as a pale ribbon in the moonlight.

The hurt wasn't as sharp now. Pa was gone. Gone for good. He'd run, and it'd cost him his life, most likely. There was no way he could've survived out there by himself. I just couldn't tell Ma that. Not while she was still sick.

Turning away from the empty road, I gripped the railing and watched a couple of miners stumble down the street, in and outta the moon shadows. The light washed over 'em again and again, draining their colors, and I wondered if they even knew.

It wasn't fair, but when I realized Ma was looking up at me, just studying and staring at me, I demanded irritably, "What? What are you looking at?"

"My first baby," she answered smoothly, not taking any offense. "Already grown into a man."

"A man just like Pa?" I heard the bitterness in my voice, and I suppose she did too.

"You *look* an awful lot like your pa," she said kinda quiet and kinda sad, "but I reckon there's more to you. There's something in you that makes you stronger than him. You don't give up."

That's what I wanted to hear, wasn't it? She wasn't ashamed of me for not making it to Sacramento. She knew I'd try again. Her words should've filled me with pride. Problem was, ever since I'd run outta Sportsman's Hall and hid in the stable, I'd been feeling a whole lot more like Pa than I wanted.

She was still looking up at me, her face lit with motherly love, and I squirmed. "I told 'em I was white," I blurted out. "I lied." And like a swollen river that's broken through its dam, I rushed on to tell her how I'd woke up with a stranger in my face making accusations, and how the talk in the dining hall had turned ugly, and how I'd run scared to the barn and hid. And lied some more. Newt's hurt face still haunted me.

"Nothing so terrible wrong with that, Colton," she soothed. Reaching out her thin hand, which looked waxy and bony in the moonlight, she touched my sleeve. "To get by in this world, a man's gotta do what he's gotta do. Some things you just can't change."

"There's a woman over in Genoa," I answered, "the one who fixed me up, who said different. She said a person has to try and change things he doesn't like." I remembered her taking my arm too.

"Is that so? Well, what's her name?"

"She said to call her Aunt Charlotte." I paused, then plunged. "She said I was being like what those men said— nothing more'n an animal—the way I ran off and hid in the barn."

Ma rocked even faster and the keening reached a feverish pitch. "This Aunt Charlotte knows 'bout such things, does she?"

And that was all. I waited for her to say Aunt Charlotte

was wrong. I waited for her to say she was proud of me just the way I was, no matter what I did or didn't tell people, no matter where I slept.

Trouble was, *I* wasn't proud of me.

In pained silence we watched the moon climb higher and higher and pull away from us. The night got bitter cold and the town deathly still. I blew air cross my fingers to warm 'em. They were pale white in the moonlight. But what about the inside of me, my blood and my heart and my bones? Just how much of me was her and how much of me was Pa? What color, exactly, was I?

CHAPTER TWENTY-SIX

Round about the time we were making our way inside and to our beds, a swarm of clouds silently swallowed the moon. By morning a whistling wind was chasing tumbleweeds and snow dust along the street. That same fitfulness was running through me, and I couldn't sit still for breakfast. I had to finish what I'd set out to do. I had to get to Sacramento and deliver the freedom papers to Ma's sister before that slave chaser happened cross her. And to get there fast—at least most of the way—I was gonna need my job back with the Pony Express. Turning up my collar, I went out to saddle the black horse.

My sisters followed, shivering, rubbing at their dripping noses. The miners' shirts hung stiff as boards on the rope lines. "Where're you going now?" Althea demanded. "I thought you wanted us to pack up and move over to Genoa before winter."

"I do," I answered. My numbed fingers, clumsy as a fistful of thumbs, struggled with the cinch. "Soon as I get back. But I have to go to Sacramento first."

She stamped her foot and the ice-crusted mud crackled. "*Why*, Colton? Why is it always *you*? I know we were going there to live with Ma's sister, but why do *you* have to get there of a sudden without us?"

It was Ma's secret, trusted to me, so all I said was, "Ma asked me to."

"You're fibbing. Besides, you think you can just jump on this horse of yours and climb over those mountains? All by your lonesome?"

"Already been there and back once. And if I can ride the Pony Express horses, it's doable again. Otherwise"— I slapped the black horse on the neck, and he pinned his ears and shook his teeth at me—"otherwise I'm gonna ride him—all the way, if I have to. But I'm gonna get there."

"Badger," Jewel said.

"Huh?"

"You said I could name him, and it's Badger 'cause he looks like a badger."

"When did you ever see a badger?"

"I saw one one time. At night. He was mostly black, like your horse, and he showed me his teeth, like this." She lifted her chin, drew back her lips, and shook her head. "See? Just like him."

I had to laugh. "Well, that looks like a badger, all right. Okay, Badger it is." Giving the cinch a final tug and pounding the knot flat with my fist, I flopped down the stirrup and turned to Althea. She was angry through and through.

"You're just running out on us again."

Her words didn't ire me at all. "I'm not running out," I said, slipping the bridle over Badger's ears. There was a steady fire in my belly, but it was pushing me on, not tearing me apart. I had control of it. "I'll be careful and I'll come back," I said. "I promise."

Swinging up into the saddle, I waved good-bye. Jewel waved back, but Althea folded her arms and stared at the ground. I knew she was more scared than angry, scared that I might ride off and not come back—like Pa had. Realizing that very real possibility chilled my fire some.

I jiggled Badger's reins. I fully expected him to set to bucking and carrying on, but he didn't. He must've still been tired from yesterday. I hoped he wasn't too beat. If I couldn't persuade Mr. Roberts to hire me back, I was gonna have to try and ride Badger up into the mountains, and he'd sure need some brass in him for that. I didn't know if he had it.

I pressed my heel into him to hurry him along, and it was like that horse had heard me doubting. He quit his lollygagging and, just to prove me wrong, leaped into the air and landed in a dead run. In less than two minutes Chinatown was behind us and getting smaller.

The wind was so cold and we were going so fast that I could hardly breathe. I glanced at the sky once, looking for those two little hawks, but they were nowhere to be found. Probably holed up in their nest somewhere on a day such as this. Clouds, iron gray and heavy, hung low cross the entire valley. I shivered and tried to catch some warmth from Badger's steaming hide.

As we galloped, I also tried to think of what I was gonna say to Mr. Roberts. I was *not* too young. Maybe when I'd hired on I was, but a lot had happened since then. I was tougher now. And I knew—sure as if I was holding my hand to a Bible—that I was riding all the way to Sacramento.

A couple of jackrabbits zigzagged cross our path. Badger jumped sideways, I yanked him in line, and he set to bucking like I'd twisted his tail. Here I was, coming outta the saddle only five miles into my journey.

"Hey!" I shouted. "Whoa, there!" He bucked harder. I knew something was gonna happen and it wasn't gonna be pretty. Changing tactics fast, I lowered my voice. With the saddle slapping me hard, I soothed, "Easy, boy. Easy, now." I managed to scratch his withers, even with my hands clutching his mane. "Eea-sy. Eea-sy."

He stopped cold. Stood there stiff legged, chewing the bit, trying to figure me out. I 'most laughed out loud. Instead I petted his neck. "Good boy," I said. "Good boy. Now, let's you and me start getting along together, okay? You get me to Carson City in one piece, and when I ride back through, I'll return you to Jewel. She'll fuss over you and feed you sugar till you think you've died and gone to horse heaven."

That horse was smart, I tell you. He chomped on the bit awhile longer, his sides going in and out, and you could almost hear him thinking. Finally he lowered his head and pawed the ground. *Okay,* he seemed to be saying. I eased my grip on his mane and jiggled the reins. He picked up a nice, easy gallop. In less than an hour we were arriving in Carson City.

He wasn't completely baptized, though, 'cause when I went to pull him to a walk, he started shaking his head, fighting the bit and trying to run on. I guess he wanted to prove he was tough, that *he* could keep going. The fool.

For a mid morning the streets were mighty empty. 'bout the only sound was the sudden wind whistling round corners, which made you jump. Snow was beginning to pile into doorways and windowsills, icing the buildings in white. Outside one of the saloons a couple of horses waited, hunched against the icy gusts. Their tail hairs swirled round their legs like wind-torn ribbons.

I rode straight to the Pony Express office. After tying Badger outside, I opened the door and walked in. A little dusting of snow blew in with me. Mr. Roberts was at his desk, reading something from a newspaper to another man sitting in the room. They'd both glanced up when the door opened, but when Mr. Roberts chose to ignore me, the other man had no choice but to do the same.

"It says here," Mr. Roberts went on, "that Mr. Lincoln was in tears when he spoke."

"Read that last part over again, if you will." The other man sniffled and quickly cleared his throat, trying to disguise his emotion.

Mr. Roberts peered past his paper. "Henry, if you're going to start crying too, I'm not going to read it again."

The man took his pipe outta his mouth and wiped his sleeve cross his eyes. "The whole nation should be crying!" he exclaimed. "And with no shame! People ought to be down on their knees and bawling, because we're coming apart; and that doughface President Buchanan's sitting on his hands and doing nothing to stop it."

"He does talk outta both sides of his mouth, doesn't he?" Mr. Roberts didn't hide his scorn.

"I tell you, we need someone with backbone in Washington, someone who can put this country right. How long can we survive with states taking up guns and aiming them at their own neighbors? Why, folks down at Jack's Saloon are saying that California's going to secede too and side with the South. They're saying the state's shipping out gold at this very minute to finance Southern interests."

Mr. Roberts rolled his eyes at that. "Come, now. The folks down at Jack's Saloon wouldn't know a war chest from a washbasin. Unless, of course, one of them was packed full of whiskey."

"Be that as it may," Henry replied, brandishing his pipe like a weapon, "if the South gets California—what with all its gold and ships and soldiers—why, it won't be a fair fight. Or a long one." He wiped some ash from his knee. "I fear the very worst if it's Mr. Lincoln who is elected president. It's certainly not a job I would want. But I hope he makes it. I truly do. Now please, read that last part again."

Mr. Roberts sighed. "'I have said before,'" he recited, "'that a house divided against itself cannot stand. Slavery is wrong, plain and true. I know that my opponent does not care about the men and women in chains, but God cares and I care, and with his help I shall not fail to right this wrong. I may not see the end of the battle, but I shall take a stand and begin it. Because I know in my heart that I will be proven right, and that one day men of all colors will rise up to build this house greater than it has ever been before.'"

I was awestruck.

Mr. Roberts snapped the newspaper closed. "Yes?" he barked at me.

I stood tall as I could. "I came to tell you, sir, that I'm ready to carry the mail tomorrow."

"I believe I fired you," he replied, just as cold as the icy wind outside. Henry hastily put his pipe in his mouth and looked away.

"You did, but I want my job back."

Mr. Roberts leaned across his desk. "This isn't a job for children," he began, and my jaws clenched at that. "Didn't you listen just now? Our nation's coming apart at the seams, and it needs the Pony mail more than ever. Newspapers can't be delivered over the telegraph wires." He slapped the paper with the back of his hand. "We are the only way that misguided folks in the West are going to hear the brave words of such men as Mr. Lincoln here." Shooting a look straight at me, he said, "I can't have my riders falling off and abandoning the mail."

I narrowed my eyes to match his. "I won't fall off. Sir."

"No."

"I'm gonna ride to Sacramento," I kept on, holding my temper in the face of his. "I might as well carry the mail with me."

"You're not riding there on one of *my* horses."

"I can take my own horse."

He looked out the window. His lips curled and he laughed, just once. "That piece of buzzard meat? He won't last you another two miles. Looks like he's already been ridden into the ground."

I didn't follow his gaze. I knew what Badger looked like on the outside. I expected he was tougher on the inside. Like me.

Before I could add to my argument, though, a horse and rider came racing up to the post where Badger was tied. He startled, then pinned his ears at the newcomer. The rider jumped off and came charging into the office, dropping the mochila on Mr. Roberts's desk. I recognized him right off as the one who'd ridden against me last week, the one with the handsome grullo horse. He was working the Pony route east of here.

Concern jolted Mr. Roberts upright. "What are you doing here? I didn't expect you until tomorrow."

The older rider tapped the mochila. "Something important coming from back East, sir—from a senator in Washington, I think. Don't know for sure—it's just a rumor—but I heard it's a letter for the authorities in Sacramento, alerting 'em to a plot to blow up some forts and steal government ammunition."

"I told you California was planning to side with the South," Henry said. He leaned forward in his chair and listened intently.

"There's something else, too, I think." The rider stared kinda wide eyed at the mochila, like it was set to explode as part of the plot. "They say there's information 'bout another plot, planned by the same folks, to shoot Mr. Lincoln if he gets elected and take over the government for themselves." He opened his hands to show his uncertainty. "Could all be rumor, I suppose, but there's gotta be something important in there, 'cause soon as that senator's letter reached the fort, they turned me round and sent me back early with it. I've been chewing through horses getting here."

Mr. Roberts pulled out his key and hurriedly worked the lock on one of the pouches. "This weather's none too friendly to fast-flying mail," he grumbled, "and I'm a rider short." Looking up, he asked, "But if what you say is true, think you can ride on—carry it over the mountains, once you get some food in you?"

"Well . . . sure," the rider said with more'n a little hesitation. He slid a cheap glance in my direction. "But there's a helluva storm brewing up there. Might be better to wait just a couple of hours and see if it eases up."

The fearfulness he'd let into the room made us all twitch. I knew he was thinking 'bout his friend that'd been lost in the wicked mountain weather, the one they'd never found. Only the horse had made it through.

Mr. Roberts clutched several letters in his hands and looked out the window. A sudden clattering of hooves sounded as a riderless horse galloped down the street, reins flopping and stirrups dangling—spooked by who knows what.

I saw my chance. "I'll head out now, sir."

Mr. Roberts turned his cold blue eyes past me to the other rider. "Go get something to eat at the hotel," he said, "and stay ready. I want to see if there's any potatoes on this vine of yours before I go risking people's lives."

Nodding, the rider spun on his heel and left. Mr. Roberts sorted through the few envelopes. He pulled out a long, important-looking one sealed with wax. The other man scooched forward in his chair, and I inched closer.

"I don't know, Henry. With this weather, do I risk sending the mail on? I worry I may lose it and a rider."

"Can you telegraph ahead, ask for advice?"

He shook his head, sighing heavily. "In times such as these I don't know who to trust. What if I telegraph even a hint of what we've just heard and end up tipping off the wrong person?" A gust of wind rattled the door. "The only way I can justify sending it into this storm is knowing it really is a war plot."

"And a murder plot," Henry added. "Which the boy said it was."

"He said it was a *rumor*. I've had banks and businessmen create such rumors just to hurry their mail along. They can never wait."

"Well," Henry replied, "if you do wait, it could be another two weeks before there's a trail cleared through the snow. This storm's apt to pile it ten feet deep in the elevations. The forts could be blown up by then and the ammunition stolen. And those murdering heathens could be headed east."

I spoke up again. "I'll take it. I'll ride on with it right now."

Mr. Roberts finally loosed his temper. "What's wrong with you, son? You have more sand than sense? The best mountain men in the West wouldn't willingly ride into a Sierra snowstorm the likes of this one. If the wind doesn't blow you off the face of the mountain, the snow will drown you in drifts as heavy as Mississippi mud. Hell, you ever stop to think why we ask for orphans in our advertisements? It's because we don't want to put more kinfolk than necessary into mourning when our riders die."

"I'm not planning on dying."

"Good, because I'm not planning on letting you ride." He stuffed the letters back in the pouch, dragged the mochila off his desk and into the big safe beside it, and kicked the door closed. "Come on, Henry," he said, pushing his chair back, "let's get us a cup of coffee and think this thing through. One hour won't hurt." They rose together, and Mr. Roberts leveled his gaze at me. "And I'd advise you to get back on that scrubby mount of yours and ride home before this storm really hits." He waited. In the uncomfortable silence I heard the relentless ticking of a wall clock. Under his stare I had no choice but to turn and leave the office.

I climbed on Badger and pointed him toward Chinatown, but kept him reined to a walk. I wasn't done in yet.

The wind was whistling so loud I couldn't hear when the

two men left the office, so after I passed a couple more buildings, I looked over my shoulder. There they were, hurrying down the boardwalk. The fire was blazing hot inside me now. All I could think 'bout was Mr. Lincoln, how he'd said in his speech that slavery was wrong, "plain and true," and how Aunt Charlotte had had a vision 'bout *President* Lincoln setting all the slaves free. Maybe the ammunition plot was more urgent, maybe both plots were just rumors; but if there was a kernel of truth in the senator's letter, I wasn't gonna let the mail sit. I wasn't gonna risk Mr. Lincoln's being killed.

Inside my head I heard the pounding boots of that slave chaser searching through Sacramento. It was my job to give Ma's sister her freedom papers. But President Abraham Lincoln was gonna see to it that all the other men and women lived free too. We each had our role to play, and I was going through with mine.

As soon as the men ducked into the hotel, I spun Badger round and trotted him back to the Pony Express office. I jumped off and ran inside. I didn't know how I was gonna get the mochila outta the safe if it was truly locked. I was banking on something I hadn't seen. After he'd hastily slammed its door, Mr. Roberts hadn't bent down to spin the dial on the combination lock. So maybe, just maybe . . .

Luck was on my side. The mochila was so bulky it'd kept the door from latching securely. All I had to do was tug on the cold metal handle, and the safe sprang open. With blood rushing through my veins in a torrent, I grabbed the mochila, ran outside, and threw it over my saddle. It didn't fit as well as it did over the specially made Pony Express saddles, but it was secure enough. Badger stood stone still, like he knew this was important. I climbed onto his back and turned his head toward the south end of town, toward the road that led west. With only one nervous glance up toward the mountains and the lead sky round 'em, I leaned over his neck and loosed the reins. And we were gone.

CHAPTER TWENTY-SEVEN

My heart was thundering so loud in my ears then, it beat out Badger's thundering hooves. I was feverish with excitement, thrilled with my bravery. Sure, there was a small nagging voice that warned I'd overstepped my boundaries, that said I didn't know the dangers I was taking on, but I wasn't listening. I was galloping *toward* something now, not running from it.

But just how far could I keep galloping on the same horse? By the time we got to Genoa, Badger would've covered close to thirty miles. I'd need a fresh mount. Yet, girlish as it was, I didn't want to leave him behind. He'd got to me somehow. I glanced down at the mochila. Long as I was carrying the Pony mail—and looking official—I could probably light out on a fresh Pony Express horse and keep leading Badger. And that became my plan.

The station keeper in Genoa seemed surprised to find me back in the saddle so soon, specially a strange saddle. Giving Badger a skeptical once-over, he said, "Don't remember seein' him before."

"He's mine," I said, leaping down. "And I'll be leading him on, so he can stay saddled. It's mine too."

Telling him those things was a mistake, 'cause I saw the doubt rise up sudden in his eyes. "That so?" he said, greatly slowing his steps toward the stable. "How come you're using your own horse and saddle to carry the mail?"

My heart thudded an alarm. Words tumbled round in my head. "Mr. Roberts is worried about the storm," I explained, nodding toward the sky. "But I told him Badger and I could make it over the mountains." Calming myself, I gave the man my best smile. "Just need a fresh horse to spell him a mite."

That seemed to work, 'cause he got a thick-bodied chestnut horse outta its stall and saddled it in record time. He still seemed grouchy 'bout something, and I was nervously expecting more questions. But when I heard him muttering 'bout a stable hand taking too long to eat lunch with his lady friend, I was glad it was that that was occupying his mind.

Soon as he was finished, I transferred the mochila to the chestnut, said my thank-yous, and climbed on. The station keeper didn't let go of the reins.

"How's your head?" Maybe he thought it was the fall that was making me act unusual.

"Got it on straight now," I answered. I gave him another big smile.

He kept squinting at me, trying to figure things out. There was a moment there, I could tell, where he was still wondering if he should let me go. I forced myself to sit calm in the saddle, to chuckle, even, at my own joke.

He finally grunted and released the reins. "Well, see that you hold on to it this time." A blustery wind chased him back inside the stable entry.

The chestnut lunged forward instantly. But I was near

yanked backward outta the saddle 'cause stubborn Badger had set his feet. He looked awful angry. I could tell he wasn't gonna cotton to another horse going ahead of him. To make matters worse, he charged forward and sank his teeth into the chestnut's neck. There was an answering squeal, then a frenzy of muscled bodies shoving and hooves striking.

I started yelling. Reaching out with my heel, I kicked Badger in the shoulder. "Git back!" I ordered, snapping his reins, too. "Git back! I'm just trying to give you a rest, is all."

He fell back, all right—too far back—and proceeded to sulk at the very end of his reins. He was hardly budging. The chestnut, on the other hand, was all balled up with fire. He was practically bucking in place, he wanted to gallop so bad, and it was all I could do to stay in the saddle and drag Badger forward an inch at a time. Maybe my plan wasn't gonna work. Maybe I'd *have* to leave him behind.

Feeling my face burn, and not just from the whipping wind, I yelled again. "Will you come along, you pigheaded fool!"

We were making our way through town in fits and starts, and just passing the door to Aunt Charlotte's house when I remembered what she'd hollered the first time we rode through: "You keep it together." I hadn't understood then, but now I did. I had to keep our family together, including Ma's sister. And in some small way, perhaps, I had to help keep our nation together, by delivering the senator's letter to Sacramento.

Badger lunged at the chestnut horse again, and I kicked at him just in time. "Listen, you dad-blamed imp of Satan," I yelled. "This is important. I need your help."

Maybe it had something to do with passing Aunt

Charlotte's house—maybe her spirit had reached out and tapped Badger on the nose like she'd done with the gray mare—or maybe he just got tired finally. Whatever the reason, the way that black horse settled down of a sudden sent a shiver shinnying up my spine. He put his nose beside my knee and came along sweet and easy as a lamb. You couldn't have surprised me more if you'd had me shake hands with a ghost.

I took advantage of the horses' getting along by leaning forward and urging them into a gallop. With the flakes coming down faster, the three of us swept outta Genoa.

Hard on our right and curving round ahead of us, the Sierra Nevada loomed large. I searched the cloud-covered peaks for the horseshoe print, the one made by the giant sky horse leaping over, but it wasn't there. The mountains looked so very different today; the slopes were completely white, and there certainly weren't any prints to follow. That gave me a kinda uncomfortable feeling.

In no time at all we were making the sharp turn and beginning the climb. The horses slowed from a gallop to a trot to a determined straining. The higher we went, the harder the wind blew, and I snugged the horses close to the hill side of the trail. I didn't want a gust tumbling us over the edge, 'cause it sure felt strong enough to lift a couple of horses and one rider high into the air. Icy bullets of snow pelted our heads. The pills settled in the horses' manes and stuck to my pants and coat sleeves. Some of 'em worked their way down the back of my neck, and I fumbled with my collar while trying not to drop the reins.

I was keeping an ear cocked too for anyone coming down the trail above us. The snow-slickened grade would make trying to pass each other a dangerous venture. Heck, just trying to climb this steep trail on a day like this was a dangerous venture.

The chestnut stopped to shake, and I balanced atop the jerking and jolting, holding the saddle horn as well as my breath. A cloud of flakes exploded round him and melded with the storm. We trudged on.

Seemed like we climbed and climbed through that snowstorm and never could reach the top. We angled round the switchbacks, marked our progress against the trees holding up the telegraph wires, and always we were facing another steep stretch. Badger stumbled once, nearly pulling the reins outta my hand and stopping my heart. Having doubts that we were gonna be able to do this, I decided to let both horses catch their breath. They huddled against the mountain wall, the lashes of their half-closed eyes heavy with snow, looking miserable. Feeling 'bout the same, I hunched my shoulders and tried to warm my hands in the cold caves of my pockets. Thoughts of the warm, stuffy room in Aunt Charlotte's attic not far below tempted me strongly to turn round. A downhill ride would go faster, and we could be there in no time. The horses would be safe inside a stable and I'd be snuggled deep in that soft bed. My frozen hands tightened on the reins. It would be so easy.

Heaving a long sigh and holding to my promise, though, I shook the snow off my coat and urged the horses on and up.

We finally did get to the top of that first mountain, and when we staggered into the pine forest there, it was like we'd stepped into a storybook world. Absolutely everything was quiet, so quiet you could hear the snow piling up on the branches. And everything was painted white: the trees, the rocks, the shrubs, the frozen stream, the ground. It lifted me up a little and I started believing we were gonna make it to the next station. It wasn't far, I knew. The chestnut horse knew it too, 'cause he started tugging on the reins and wanting to move along faster. I let him go at a trot, and we covered some ground then.

We found that first mountaintop station, the lone cabin and shed, nestled in its clearing among the pine trees. A gray plume of smoke drifted from its chimney. I was so cold and it was such a welcoming sight that I think I got a little teary eyed, so it was a good thing Althea wasn't round.

When the chestnut whinnied loudly, the cabin's door banged open and the keeper peered through the snowflakes.

"Well, I'll be!" he exclaimed. Pulling on his coat, he hurried out to take the reins of the two horses. "Whaddya doin' just sittin' there like that—makin' yourself into an icicle?"

"Delivering some important mail." My teeth chattered the words.

He laughed. "Not by my eyes, you're not. Well, get inside." He motioned me toward the door.

I kicked my frozen feet outta the stirrups, managed to twist my back and bend my legs enough to climb outta the saddle. My clothes crackled. Hot, stabbing pain shot through both legs the instant they touched ground. Groaning under my breath, I tugged the mochila off before the horses were led away.

"There's some beans warmin' in the pot. I'll tend to the horses, then see if T. J. can rustle ya up somethin' more rib stickin'. Say, how come you got two horses?"

"The black one's mine," I said, and that seemed like enough of an explanation for him, 'cause he just said, "Oh," and trudged off toward the small three-sided shelter beside the cabin.

The inside of the cabin was smoky and warm and greasy smelling, and I could've stumbled straight over to a bed and fallen asleep for hours, maybe days. Fighting that urge, I set the mochila on the table and plopped into the nearest chair.

Beside the fire was a man working leather. I assumed he was T. J. He looked up slowly and said, "Howdy."

"Howdy," I answered.

When he noticed the mochila, he straightened. Right away he laid aside his tools and came over. "You got some mail for us?"

I shrugged. "Don't know."

Curious as a raccoon, he tugged on each of the three locked pouches before inspecting the unlocked one. His long fingers pulled out some envelopes and painted cards one at a time, and he examined each carefully. "Say, here's one from all the way back in Chicago."

"For you?" I asked.

"Nah. For someone named R. R. DeWalt, in San Francisco. But it's come a mighty long ways, hasn't it?" He stood staring at the postmark, and I got a strong sense of how far this little cabin was, not just from Chicago, but from the whole rest of the world.

The keeper came in, stamping the snow off his shoes and shaking it from his beard. "Say, we gotta get this boy somethin' to eat. He's skinny as a fence post."

T. J. held up the letter. "Come all the way from Chicago."

"For us?"

"No, for someone over in San Francisco."

"Then, whaddya holdin' on to it for? Come on, now.

Get this boy some of those beans and cut him off a slab of ham." He pulled out a chair and sat down at the table, thumbing through the mail while trying to hide his own black-eyed curiosity. When there wasn't anything worth reading, even a gossipy note scribbled on a card, he stuffed the letters and such back in the pouch.

I was handed a bowl of beans with a strip of ham floating on top. "You want some coffee?" I nodded, and the man set a cup beside me before returning to his leatherworking.

The keeper, who'd been watching me eat, like that alone was a thing of interest, pushed his chair away from the table. He stretched his legs out and moaned. "Oh, this storm's gonna pile one on us for sure. My knees've been barkin' at me for two days now."

I shoveled a few more spoonfuls of beans into my mouth and stood up. "I gotta get back on the trail, then."

Neither of 'em moved. "Son, you'll never find the trail."

I shouldered the mochila. "Horse'll know the way, won't he?"

They looked at each other. "I expect Freckles would," the keeper said. "He's been at it the longest, ever since the Pony mail started back in April. But why risk it? Besides, I just got 'em unsaddled."

"Sit tight for a day," T. J. agreed. "See what this storm brings. Maybe it'll blow past us."

"It's not gonna blow past us," the keeper argued. "I told you, my knees've been barkin'—"

"Well," I interrupted, "I promised I'd keep riding through it. Got some mighty important mail to deliver."

They looked at each other and shrugged in unison, then the keeper rose. "Suit yourself," he said, putting on his coat again and heading for the door. "Maybe you'll come across that other feller that rode on when we told him not to. Who knows what trail he took?"

It was meant to scare me, but I wasn't gonna let it. "And if you'll keep my saddle on the black horse," I said, "I'll be leading him."

He shook his head. "More fools the merrier."

T. J. was absorbed in his leatherwork and I was left standing. I spooned some more of the beans into my mouth. Couldn't taste 'em going down 'cause I was thinking 'bout the storm, worrying. Pretty soon I heard the crunch of footsteps outside. I double-checked the mochila's pouches and walked out.

Freckles was a horse that was rightly named, 'cause he was a dirty white with dollar-size brown spots sprinkled cross his whole body. Standing there in the snowfall, he looked excited at the prospect of traveling with another horse. I thanked the man for saddling the horses, put the mochila cross Freckles's back, and climbed on. His fuzzy ears pointed toward the heart of the dense pine forest, and with a tight hold of Badger's reins, I let him lead the way.

We trotted for a while, going kinda easy and getting used to the weather again. Then, since the needle-covered forest floor had good footing, I urged Freckles and Badger into a controlled gallop. We climbed and dipped and scrambled over some rocky areas, and then, all of a sudden, we were out in the storm once more.

The snow was coming down even harder and thicker. The way the wind was swirling it round, spraying it this way and that, made me dizzy; so I hunched my shoulders and kept my eyes on the ground, following the heads of dried weeds.

There was already about a foot of the white stuff. You couldn't see the gullies or stones or frozen creeks until the horses grunted and stumbled, until the saddle went dropping out from underneath you in a gasping second. I had a death grip on the saddle horn. The creeks, especially, were tricky. Near the edge the ice supported the horses' weight. But after a couple of steps it always broke with a splintering crash and a splash, and we had to hurry through icy shards and rushing water to climb onto solid ground on the other side.

It seemed like we rode for hours, but I blamed that on the dizzying snow. I just kept thinking 'bout the next station, remembering it as a nice one, with several large barns and a two-story lodging house. I was more'n ready to be there. The cold had seeped right through my clothes and my skin, and now it was starting to chill my bones. I felt myself stiffening.

We entered another pine forest, which gave us a break from the wind and provided some soft footing. I hurried the horses on. They galloped eagerly, their huffing breaths coming in unison. Round a bend in the trail we raced, and there before us was a familiar-looking cabin, a little one, nestled among the trees, with smoke drifting from the chimney.

My heart plummeted like a stone dropped down a well. Freckles had led us in a huge circle! We were back where we'd started.

The horse whinnied happily and the cabin door opened. Two heads poked out this time; the men were smiling.

I was so angry! I jumped off Freckles right then and there, yanking the mochila after me. Dropping the reins—

which sent the spotted horse trotting quickly toward his shelter—I threw the mochila over Badger's saddle. The men started hollering, but I wouldn't listen. I climbed onto Badger, spun him round, and headed back into the snowy forest.

CHAPTER TWENTY-EIGHT

It was a foolish thing to do, heading out like that, not knowing the way. With a hateful knot in my stomach I realized it was exactly what my pa'd done—just jumped on his horse and ridden off into the territory. Not knowing the way. And what had happened to him?

That kinda thinking was like carrying stones in your pockets, though, so I shook myself free of 'em. What I had to do now was find the right trail. That's where I had an edge over my pa. At least I'd traveled this way once before.

The next station was higher up still—Friday's, I think it was called—so I peered through the snowfall, searching. That made the wind howl with scornful laughter. It smacked me with a bucketful of snow, then sent the flakes whirling round me in frenzied confusion. I tucked my chin inside my collar, but not before glimpsing the jagged outline of a near mountain. I pointed Badger in that direction and he shouldered into the storm.

The wind kept blowing and blowing, and for the longest time it seemed we were at a standstill in an endless, swirling sea of white. There was no sense of it being night or day.

You couldn't see the sun, though there was a blinding glare that made my head ache. I clutched Badger's mane and let him pull me along. His blackness was the only thing that felt solid—until the snow began building up on his thick fur and he began melding into the white madness too.

Step after step we trudged. The wind kept swirling and swooshing round us, taunting and tiring us. And ever so slowly it wrapped me in its whiteness—its sheet of whiteness. Just like the thin white sheet we'd wrapped Willie in. Or the one the little German boy had been laid to rest in so, so long ago.

Laid to rest. That sounded good. I was getting awful tired. The saddle's steady swaying—back and forth, back and forth—was soothing as a rocker. I was so sleepy. Maybe it'd be okay to stop awhile and rest.

Badger quit moving at once, as if he knew my thoughts. I pulled his head round and it was completely white, like some bald-faced cow's. Only, a cow wouldn't be struggling so hard for me. A cow was just grub on the hoof. Seemed it took a horse to understand a person's needs. Maybe that kinda thinking was proving I was light headed, but I didn't care. Right then I was happy to count Badger as a friend.

Getting off was gonna be hard 'cause there was no feeling in my legs. I ordered the crusted limb clamped to the right side of the saddle to move. Might as well've been ordering a tree stump to get up and walk, for all the response I got. Straining to bend over, feeling like I was splintering and cracking—ow!—I managed to shake my foot free of the stirrup. Badger never budged.

With my teeth chattering uncontrollably, I dragged my

leg over Badger's snow-covered rump—and lost my balance. Like a block of ice, I plunked deep into a snowdrift. The white stuff rose past my ears, cocooning me with an unexpected warmth. It felt good.

Sitting there like that, sheltered from the wind at last, made me feel safe. It was like taking a long swallow of tonic from Ma's spoon and feeling the warm fire ooze through your veins and pull you toward sleep. Just a little sleep, a little rest, was all I needed, and then we'd move on.

Deep within my snow cocoon I was dully aware of my breathing getting slower and heavier, of my tingling chin drooping over my chest. It felt good, so good to be resting, so good to just be quiet and still.

Next thing I knew, something cold and whiskery was bumping me in the face. I turned away 'cause I wanted to sleep more, but the bumping got harder and a jangling joined it. It was so loud in my ears. I struggled to think what it was.

First thing I saw when I opened my eyes was the snow-plastered face of a horse. It was hairy and wet, and the cold metal shank of the bit banged cross my lips, drawing blood, I think. That woke me more. Badger nickered, low and worrying. He bumped my cheek again and I reached up to shield myself.

"All right, all right," I mumbled. I couldn't hardly make my mouth work. In struggling to move my frozen limbs, I began to remember where I was. A cold horror shook me as I realized what had almost happened. In my sleep I'd been slipping toward the arms of death—a peaceful, frozen death. I shivered all over, couldn't stop. If Badger hadn't wakened me, I would've never wakened. A particularly violent chill grabbed me by the neck and yanked me to my feet.

Badger nickered again, louder this time, satisfied I was up. I collapsed into the curve of his shoulder, petting him and thanking him over and over. I owed my life to this ornery little black horse, and I thanked the Lord that I'd decided to keep him with me. He was something special, all right.

It must've been the fear of dying that got my stiff body up and into the saddle so fast, 'cause I couldn't feel my legs or my arms, my feet or my hands. There was a buzzing in my head. To my surprise, the snow had stopped falling and the sky was clear and blue as a jay. Lordy, how long had I slept? Sucking in a deep breath and wincing as the icy air stabbed my lungs, I squinted into the blinding light. There was a faint plume of smoke coming from higher up the mountain. I didn't know if it was the next station or not, but it was life and warmth, and we needed to get there. Nudging Badger in that direction, I gave him his head and he began floundering gamely through the chest-deep drifts. I balanced rigid on his back, with all the grace of a wooden clothespin.

I don't know how we did it, but somehow we found our way to Friday's Station. That two-story building was an even more welcome sight than the cabin. And its smoky smell made me long to spread myself in front of the blazing fire. But instead I rode straight to the barn. Badger deserved attention first.

It was empty 'cept for the horses and mules. I guess on a blizzardy day like this no one would be expecting the Pony mail. Everyone in his right mind would've found an excuse to cozy up to the fireplace and swap stories.

Don't know what that said 'bout me. I hunted up a bag of oats for Badger and scooped out a double measure. While he ate, I stamped up and down, trying to kindle some sorta warmth inside me. I wasn't hungry; I was more worried 'bout how long this ride was taking. We'd lost time, I knew—a lot of time—and I was anxious to make it up. That was assuming, of course, that we could even follow the trail outta here. I considered borrowing another Pony Express horse but right away decided to keep my money on Badger. He'd proved himself, and if he was willing, so was I.

Outside the snow and the cold and the vast wilderness ahead did scare me some, but I knew I was gonna keep going. I had to. A whole lot of people, my ma included, needed me to.

Thinking 'bout the mail I was carrying reminded me to check through the unlocked pouch. I found only one card addressed to the care of Friday's Station. It was from Smiths Creek, and its inked scrawl announced the birth of a son—Ephraim Sikes—and related how Uncle Stanley was recovering from his illness, and how the neighbors had sold their land at a cheap price and returned to Illinois. Nothing that would affect anyone's freedom, but I set it on the bag of oats. Someone would find it in the afternoon when they came out to feed, and someone else, later, would cherish the news, scanty as it was.

Badger was done eating. The snow had melted off his black coat and he was watching me with those little brown eyes of his. He should've been tired, but his ears were pricked.

"What do you think, fella?" I asked. "Can we do this?" And wouldn't you know it, he answered with a nicker.

I smiled. Since I could feel my fingers again, I gave him a pat, gathered up my courage, and climbed into the stiff saddle. Together we headed out into the snow.

It was mostly downhill going now. Even with the drifts the trail was easier to follow 'cause it had been hacked through a thick forest, but it was a whole lot colder, too, riding in the shadows. Now and again that huge mountain lake came into view between the trees, its waters choppy and gray. It stretched so far across the horizon I didn't think an ocean could look much bigger. That set me to wondering if I'd see an ocean when we got settled in California. If I ever got my family to California.

Badger and I finally made it to some flat ground and the forest thinned. The snow wasn't as deep here, so we were able to take up a steady trot and hold to it. I just knew he'd make an awful good Pony Express horse if they could see past his size.

Sometime late in the afternoon we arrived at the station run by Mr. Clement, who everyone called Yank. Again there was no horse saddled and waiting, so I knew they weren't expecting me. I pulled Badger up just long enough to check the unlocked pouch, but there wasn't any mail to be delivered, and we rode on.

A lot of the forest round here had been cleared, and I could look cross the thousands of pale stumps to see where the trail ahead of us climbed through the hills. The setting sun was lingering behind those lavender peaks, flooding the sky with a cold pink and a molten orange. It fired the lengths of the few standing trees—one side briefly burning bright while the other stayed chiseled in shadow.

As the light dimmed, the pine branches became black paper cutouts against a blue gray sky. And then, before you could pinpoint the moment, the fire was gone and everything round us was dark as a cave and oh so quiet.

I missed the Colt pistol.

Badger slowed to a walk, and only his crunching steps through the snow broke the silence of the wilderness. I was growing more and more jumpy in the darkness, until a big silver moon rose to light our way. I watched with awe as it swelled, realizing it was the very same moon I'd been looking at with Ma—when was that, just last night? And here I was, so far away from her.

The world seemed upside down then, the ground light and the sky dark. Washed in a silvery glow, the mountain came alive. Deer tiptoed out from the trees, quiet as shadows, only the white undersides of their nervous tails giving them away. They tugged on branches and showered themselves with snow as they nibbled. Rabbits scampered and skidded cross the crusted ground, seeming to enjoy their newly white world. A huge owl floated past our heads. He threaded his way in and out along the edge of the forest, flapping his broad wings without making a sound.

The trail got rockier as we climbed. Luckily the moon shone off the sheer granite cliffs like a beacon and kept us from plunging into the darkened river gorge below. We picked our way up and down the mountainside, splashing cross the ice-edged river at least once. Not one of the three stations we passed by had a horse waiting. The doors were all shut up tight, and only the smoke from the chimneys showed there were people inside. I dutifully checked the pouch at each stop, but there was no mail to be delivered, and so I rode on, not even bothering to let anyone know that I'd passed through. We might have missed one station, or maybe I nodded off for a bit, but Badger just kept on going, steady as a little black locomotive.

Somehow we found our way to Sportsman's Hall. The snow-covered yard there was hardly disturbed, so I knew not many people had ventured out during the storm. My stomach grumbled at the memories of the wonderful food in the dining hall, and Badger hesitated. He shook his head and pawed the ground. I worried 'bout pushing him too hard, but there were other memories here that kept me from stopping. There was a letter to be delivered, though, so climbing stiffly outta the saddle, I jammed it in the crack between the main door and its frame. I wanted to glance through the windows—just to see if Jeremiah or the slave chaser or even the pretty girl from the dining hall was there—but the glass panes were frosted over. "C'mon, boy," I said, pulling myself back into the saddle and giving Badger an encouraging pat on the neck. "It's not much farther. We'll be in Sacramento by sunup."

We had to dive into strange territory then, so of course the forest got thicker and darker. Enormous trees clasped their branches over our heads and blocked out the moon. My heart thumped uneasily. I'd only seen harmless animals so far—deer and rabbits and owls—but I had a feeling if there were any bears out and about, this would be the kinda place where they'd roam. Cocking my ears for any unusual sounds made the forest come alive with 'em.

Time after time I had to calm my heart by dismissing the sounds as ordinary ones: a bush rustling, a clump of snow falling. Till I heard something big—really big—crashing through the trees. I was sure it was making straight for us. I pulled Badger to a stop. Surely there was no reason to panic. But the branches kept snapping. Common sense screamed at me to run—but which way? What if there were more of 'em? What if I was surrounded?

Oddly, Badger's ears were pricked forward. He seemed to be interested in what was coming—cautious, but not afraid. Not me. I was 'bout ready to soak my pants when a big mule, saddled but riderless, came stumbling into the clearing. He blew a whistling sound of exhaustion and touched noses with Badger, happy, I guess, to find us. There was something light colored balancing on his saddle. I thought it was a snowball at first, till it sat up and mewed. It was the ginger kitten. That's when I knew whose mule this was: Jeremiah McGahee's. Something bad must've happened to him; he'd been killed maybe or got himself lost in the blizzard. *Good riddance,* I thought blackly, though I didn't ride off.

The kitten looked straight at me and mewed again, louder. He was holding up one paw in such a pitiful posture that I nudged Badger over and lifted the creature into my lap. He was shivering something fierce. With hesitation—'cause I remembered how ornery he was—I let him crawl inside my coat. He didn't even think 'bout fighting. I felt him nose round a bit, then ball himself up tight. He got heavy real fast, so I knew he was sleeping.

That's when the mule turned and plodded off the trail and back into the forest. I didn't want to follow him. I had my own business to attend to. And Jeremiah McGahee, be he dead or injured or neither, had done me no favors. Besides, I'd lost enough time. I wasn't going.

Badger must've been arguing the other side, 'cause with a hard tug on the reins he carried us off the trail. Just like that, we were plunging through the dark, following a mule.

CHAPTER TWENTY-NINE

O ver here."
The voice, raspy with cold, came outta the black emptiness ahead. I couldn't tell if it was Jeremiah. I sure as heck couldn't see him. What should I do? I worried I was being coaxed into some sorta trap, a thought that set my heart to pounding and my mind to galloping. Maybe I'd be smarter to turn round. I was so close to Sacramento now; this was really no time to stop.

"I'm over *here*," the voice called again, a notch higher. And even though I still wasn't sure it was Jeremiah, still didn't know if it was a trap, I did know this was someone who sounded just as scared as I was. The mule began carefully picking his way down the rock-strewn bank toward the creek, and I put Badger close on his tail.

When we got to the bottom, even though we were half standing in the gurgling waters, I still couldn't see anything. And now I couldn't hear anything either. Where had the voice gone? It had to be a trap. A strip of moonlight on the opposite bank showed the snow there had been heavily trampled. There'd been quite a commotion, a fight maybe. I started hauling back on the reins.

Cross the wide stream a huge, heavy-boughed pine tree quivered. It rustled and sighed and showered a ring of snow round itself. "Under *here*."

The mule flicked one of his big ears in recognition and calmly sloshed through the water. I wasn't so easily convinced. Glancing over my shoulder to mark a lightning retreat, I reluctantly let Badger follow. I was riding so stiff in the saddle that one little "Boo" right then would've shot me straight up to the stars.

After clambering up the bank, the mule stopped beside the mysterious tree, and Badger did too. There, mostly hidden under its lower boughs, was Jeremiah McGahee. He was lying on his back, obviously needing help—but still acting mean: "What took you so long?"

He didn't know who I was, I was pretty sure of that, and I came 'bout this close to wheeling Badger round and skedaddling outta there. Except for Ma's "do unto others" preaching, I would've.

"Well," Jeremiah said, "hop down here and help me. Can't you see my leg's broke?"

Steaming mad, I climbed outta the saddle. Badger sidled off a ways, cocked a hip, and set to dozing. When Jeremiah pulled back one of the boughs, I saw how he was a whole lot more'n right: The lower half of one of his legs was bent at right angles from where it should've been. White bone, snapped like a broomstick, shot up through the ripped and bloodied trousers. My stomach flipped, but I couldn't stop staring. I'd never seen anything like it.

"It ain't gonna jump up and bite you," he grumbled. "It's just broke." He craned his neck, trying to get a better look at my shadowed face. "Oh," he said in surprise, realizing for the first time who I was. "It's you. What're you doing all the way out here?"

"Carrying the mail," I answered. I was still staring. "I'm the Pony rider, remember?"

"Got anything for me?"

Now, that was an odd question. The old man had to be crazy. "I don't think so."

"Be nice to get some mail now and again. Just one letter'd do."

"Who'd be sending you mail?" The words came out fast, though I didn't intend 'em to sound so hard.

He got real quiet and let the pine bough fall into place. I thought he was pouting, till he started talking again. "I don't rightly know anymore," he said. "Used to have a sister in St. Louis, but I ain't heard from her in so long I don't know if she's still alive. Always reckoned she was too tough to die. She buried three husbands, you know."

There was a pause. The stars flickered and the stream gurgled, and I began to feel ridiculous for standing in the middle of the mountains talking to a man hiding under a pine tree. Besides, I had places to be.

"Still," Jeremiah mused, "it'd be nice to get some mail."

I pulled the bough aside. Maybe it was too fast, 'cause he flinched like I was gonna attack him. Nodding toward his leg, I asked, "How'd this happen?"

"Bunch of snot-nosed jaspers is how! Claim-jumping jaspers—chased us outta our own mine!" His hands made little flailing movements and his eyes blinked fast, though in the pale moonlight I saw that his face stayed frozen. He reminded me of a turtle flipped onto its back, helpless but anxious. "There were four or five of 'em," he went on, his voice getting louder. "Came busting in holding guns in our faces and telling us they had papers to our claim. Put us out with nothing but the clothes on our back, gol-dang pack of saloon rats." He looked up at me, his old eyes filmy with worry. "I don't know what happened to the others, just don't know. I thought we were all gonna stick together, but maybe they run off and hid. I was hurrying over to Hangtown to find me a lawyer or a judge to make things right, when this happened. Guess I was going kinda fast, leastways my mule was. He went slipping and sliding down this hill like he was ice-skating or something and dumped me but good." Picking up a handful of snow, he tossed it in the general direction of the mule. "Save your act for the circus," he croaked, "'cause that's where I'm selling you when I see one."

I glanced over at the mule. He'd just saved the man's life and seemed not to care that he wasn't getting thanked for it. If it were me, I'd be happy to own an animal like that.

Jeremiah fell back, wheezing. "I tried crawling out, but my leg hurt so bad I couldn't get but from there to here." He pointed to the snow-trampled place near the creek. "Been laying here since yesterday. Figured that snowfall was gonna bury me a-fore a shovel could. Figured the animals knew it too 'cause they lit out 'bout an hour ago. Even my cat left me." The crack in his voice was painful enough that I looked away. "Ungrateful critter!" he muttered. "And to think I fed him off my own plate."

The years piled on him of a sudden, heavier than any

snow, and he wasn't the crazy old coot whispering in my ear anymore. He was just a beaten old man who'd been run outta his own home and found himself hurt and alone in the world. Didn't have his friends. Didn't have any family, it seemed. Didn't have so much as one person in his life that'd take the time to send him a letter.

Gave me a lot of pleasure then to reach inside my jacket and pull out the ginger-colored ball of fur. The kitten hung limp in sleepy warmth. Jeremiah's thin lips made a round O, and he reached up his shaky hands and pulled the animal to his face and kissed it just like a girl would. I rolled my eyes some, but I knew I couldn't be mad at him anymore. With people chasing after him and being so mean to him, we were more alike than different.

Soon as I thought it, I heard Aunt Charlotte saying those very same words to me. Gave me a chill 'cause she seemed to know an awful lot—a whole lot more'n was natural.

"How're you gonna get outta here?" I asked. I was itching to get moving.

Jeremiah, hugging the kitten to his chest and stroking it to the point the animal risked baldness, appeared humbled. "Well, I can do the talking if you can do the walking."

I rolled my eyes again but smiled in resigned agreement. "Tell me what to do."

There was a small hatchet hanging from his mule's saddle. Under Jeremiah's direction, I cut down two young pine trees and cleaned their trunks of branches. With some rope I fastened one springy pole on each side of his mule, tying the ends together in front of the saddle. The branches I'd cut off I lashed crosswise behind the mule, making a sorta hammock that stretched between the two poles down to where they dragged on the ground. "It's a travvy," he explained. "Paiutes use 'em to drag their laundry round. Reckon that's what I'm reduced to now: laundry."

I glanced at the icy stream. How was I gonna get him and his cat and his mule and the travvy safely over?

"You're gonna have to lay me cross the saddle," he said, following my gaze, "at least till we get to the other side."

I'd rather've swum across the creek naked than do what I had to do next. I'd never laid my hands on a grown person before, and it made me redden to grab him so close to his privates. "C'mon, son," he scolded, "just think of me as a sack of oats; I probably weigh less. But mind my leg—it's hurt bad." Careful as I could, I lifted him to standing on his one good foot, my heart shooting through my chest each time he yelped in pain. Wrapping my arms round that same thigh, I did my best to lift him into the saddle while he struggled to pull himself over it. The leather creaked and the mule staggered, but the two of us kept at it until he was hanging cross on his belly. Back in Kansas I'd seen a dead person carried that way once. Noticing the way Jeremiah's face had turned fish-belly white made me think of that. "C'mon, now," he gasped, "I can't stay this way too long."

I scooped up the kitten and tucked him inside my coat again, climbed on Badger, and grabbed hold of the mule's reins to lead him. We inched our way down the bank and out into the rushing waters. The travvy rose up with the current but got a good soaking anyway. Jeremiah groaned and wheezed cross the saddle, then he stopped making any sounds at all. I figured for certain I'd be dragging a corpse into Hangtown.

Soon as his mule cleared the icy waters, Jeremiah let himself drop outta the saddle to crumple on the rocky bank. He clawed at his broken leg and cried out like a child. I didn't know what to do for him. I climbed down slowly, stood there like a goose. Problem was, I knew the worst of it wasn't over, 'cause we still had the steep bank ahead of us.

After a spell, when he'd stopped rocking back and forth, I helped Jeremiah lay himself down on the travvy. He grabbed hold of one pole with each hand, gritted his teeth, and stared at the night sky, ready as he could be. I piled some more pine boughs on top of him and over that exposed stick of bone. I couldn't stand looking at it. Don't know if they added any warmth, but we didn't have any blankets. Sending Badger on up the hill ahead of us, I wrapped the mule's reins round my fist and, shoulder-to-shoulder with him so he wouldn't go too fast, began climbing. Clambering and slipping, and feeling every one of Jeremiah's anguished moans in my own bones, we made our way outta the gorge.

We took a breather at the top. The forest was dark and still, the sky coming gray with first light. I could just make out Jeremiah's face, which was beaded with sweat. His watery eyes were closed now, and he looked like he might've stopped breathing. I wasn't gonna check.

Deciding it'd be better to go at a walk so I could keep a close eye on him, I held on to the mule's reins and took up Badger's as well. The snow made it a slow march, but it kept the travvy going smooth. In the quiet morning I settled into a steady crunch-crunching step, matched by a rhythmic in-and-out huffing. Clouds of breath, horse and human and mule, measured our progress. It was mind numbing and kinda peaceful, till the one-two beat reminded me of the slave chaser. He was tromping along too, somewhere ahead of us probably. Tromping after a runaway. I hoped I'd make it to Sacramento in time.

We'd covered two or three miles when I realized Jeremiah was staring up at the sky and blinking. He wasn't dead after all. Reaching inside my coat, I lifted the kitten out and set him on the man's chest again. The animal stretched and yawned, then curled up next to Jeremiah's neck, making a nest between his beard and his collar. Jeremiah sorta smiled at me. His eyes did, anyway.

I felt like I should say something. "How're you doing?"

"Still breathing," he rasped.

"You know if we're headed the right way?"

"Trail follows the creek, creek goes to Hangtown," he replied.

I figured that was gonna be the extent of our conversation, but he seemed to be feeling enough better to start telling me 'bout his life. He rattled on and off 'bout the places he'd been and the things he'd done and seen. No particular order. He was friendly with a Paiute chief in the territory, and he'd sailed on a ship all the way round South America. He described San Francisco, told me how big it was and how rich everyone was there. Said he'd fought off a grizzly once with none other'n Kit Carson.

All the time we walked, that kitten of his slept curled up tight next to his neck. I had to ask. "Why do you carry that cat with you everywhere?"

With a trembling hand he stroked the animal's fur. "So someone doesn't go and steal him, that's why. You know how much a cat's worth in a miner's camp? With all the varmints that gnaw through our food and run cross our beds? Why, this little critter here's worth his weight in gold—no fooling 'bout that." The kitten lifted his head and chirruped, looking pleased. Then he buried his face and was instantly asleep again. "Besides," Jeremiah said, "he can keep a secret better'n anybody."

He made a sputtering sound, something that could've been either a wheeze or a chuckle, or both. I wondered what kinda secrets the two of 'em had. I remembered him boasting back at Sportsman's Hall that no one could keep a secret from him. Well, I guess I had one or two that he didn't know 'bout.

And one of 'em was making it awful hard to walk when I needed to gallop.

Maybe some of those same thoughts were weighing on his mind, 'cause after we'd gone a ways more, he said, "Listen, boy, I'm sorry I rode you so hard back at the hall. I don't expect you can help being who you are any more than I can help being who I am. And you're all right, far as I'm concerned. I'll be owing you."

I nodded, not knowing what to say. Should've appeared more grateful, I suppose, but I never was one to show my feelings much. Besides, I was thinking 'bout the slave chaser and how he'd shown Newt and me the dried ears on his watch chain. That was a sight that stuck with a person. I reached up to tug on my own ears, making sure they were both there, which was kinda silly. They were right where I'd left 'em, hanging under my hair like little icicles.

"Almost to Hangtown," Jeremiah said.

CHAPTER THIRTY

The solemn *bong . . . bong . . . bong* of a church bell vibrated in the crisp morning air. That had to be Hangtown and that had to mean it was Sunday.

No, it couldn't be. I'd left Carson yesterday morning, which was Friday, so this was Saturday. Maybe the church was calling people for another reason, a funeral maybe. Whatever the occasion, I was more'n ready to find a doctor and leave Jeremiah with him and be on my way. Time was ticking away with each chime of the bell.

A smoky haze drifted through the trees ahead. The trail dropped through it and we found ourselves near the creek, traveling between the high walls of a canyon. Tunnels riddled the dirt on both sides, the snow-crusted tailings from mining efforts spilling down the banks. Prosperity seemed to hang in the air just as thick as the smoke. Roofs appeared and we dropped past 'em, and then we were trudging along the muddy main street of Placerville. Or Hangtown.

The streets were crowded. People stared at us curiously, though no one offered help. Jeremiah had his arm slung over his eyes, trying to block out the sun. Or maybe he was sleeping again. Squinting into the light, I searched for a doctor's sign. There was none to be seen, but there was a tall brick hotel ahead that shouted authority with its gilt lettering and fancy iron balcony. A couple of nice-looking people were going in, so figuring someone there could call for a doctor, I tied up Badger and the mule.

In all my life I'd never stepped inside a room so fancy. I half expected the governor himself to be sitting in one of the red velvet chairs, smoking a pipe and gazing at the crackling flames in the marble fireplace. Almost too late I remembered to swipe my feet cross the mat. Feeling rough as a bear outta the woods, I practically tiptoed toward the front desk. The man behind it stiffened. He peered over his spectacles at me.

"Can I help you?" he asked in a hollow voice that said he'd rather not.

That's when I noticed the sign. Beside his drumming fingers was a small, hand-lettered placard that read: NO COLOREDS. Was he guessing 'bout me? Or was he just wishing I'd remove my muddy self from his royal parlor? I pressed for help anyway. "Got a man with a broken leg outside," I said. "It's real bad."

"This is a hostelry not a hospital."

Huh. Maybe he did know. Or maybe rudeness ran in his blood. Stretching myself to stand tall as I could, I asked, "Well, do you know where I can find a doctor?"

With an impatient whisking of his hands he motioned me toward the doorway. "Wait outside," he ordered. "I'll see what I can do."

Having some doubts that he'd do anything at all, I returned to the street. After being inside the dark lobby, I was near knocked to my knees by the glare of the wintry sun. I wavered on the boardwalk a minute, trying to get my bearings. I had enough sense to step aside as some people in their Sunday best, a man and his wife with their two daughters, came parading by. They stared with shock and interest at Jeremiah lying on his crude travvy. Glancing at me, the woman whispered to her older daughter. They made a point of gathering their skirts tight round 'em as they passed by.

I stepped down into the mud. Antsy as all get-out, I checked the locks on the mochila. I could practically feel the heat of that letter sitting inside its pouch. And the one lying next to my skin. I needed to get to Sacramento.

Jeremiah moaned, and I slogged over to stand beside him. "They're fetching a doctor," I told him. "Shouldn't be long now."

He nodded slightly, leaving his head to loll at a sickly angle. "That over there's the hanging tree," he said.

I wished he hadn't brought it up again. Gave me a sick feeling to even think 'bout it. I'd already seen it, of course, 'cause how could you miss a giant oak with an empty noose hanging still and cold from it? Against my will, I looked. The tree stood in a small yard not far from the hotel. With its gnarled arms outstretched, harsh and naked in the wintry light, it seemed like Death itself, waiting to grab another life and squeeze it dry. I began to think it really was a funeral taking place at the church, and with a queasy feeling I wondered how the person had died.

"I've seen a couple of fellers doing their air dancing there," Jeremiah said. "Ain't a pretty sight." He let his head flop toward me. I must've been looking real scared, 'cause he said, "You got nothing to worry about, son." Then he paused, and I guessed he was still wanting to know my secret. "'Less you done something wrong."

His watery blue eyes made me shift uneasily. *Had* I done anything wrong? The letter in the mochila was to be delivered as soon as possible, and that's all I was doing. I hadn't really stolen the mail. Still, I suddenly felt like everyone was watching me, judging me, and reaching for that rope. I wanted to run.

The man from the hotel peeked out the window. Another man's face appeared beside his, but he didn't look like a doctor. We waited longer. Other people passed, looking us over and hurrying on. I checked the mochila again, growing more and more nervous, though I couldn't lay a finger on why exactly.

The sun poked through the haze, hot for a snowy morning, and it was like that circle of white had its fire aimed directly at me. No matter which way I ducked, or how low I pulled my hat, I couldn't escape its insistence. More people in fine clothes took to the street, streaming toward the painted white church at its bottom like bees to a hive. Even as stragglers kept arriving the tinny notes of a piano began wavering on the morning air. Earnest voices joined the melody, searching for a hold and gradually coming together in shaky harmony: "Just as I am, Lord, take me just as I am."

Still we waited. My head ached.

The kitten woke up, stretched, and bounded off to investigate a rustling under the steps to the next building. Jeremiah had his arm over his eyes again, blocking out the unforgiving sun, so he couldn't notice the man leaning over the balcony. I did.

Still as a buzzard, the man was, dressed all in black, clutching the railing with stubby fingers and watching us. Just watching us. Or me, more likely, 'cause I recognized him right off. I tugged on my collar and folded my arms and stamped my feet. *Where* was that doctor? It was all I could do to keep from jumping onto Badger and galloping away. Putting some distance between me and that man who was watching me over the railing, that thick-chested man with the limp brown hair and the oversize ears—the slave chaser.

"Nice morning."

His words pelted my shoulders like hot lead. I didn't answer.

"I said, *nice morning*."

Like a fish yanked outta the water by a hook, I felt my face lifting skyward. The snow-bright sun like to blinded me. "Yes, sir," I said into the glare.

He held out a glinting, silvery flask of liquor. "Take a smile?"

I shook my head. "No . . . thank you."

"Warms your ears."

His oily voice came straight outta the preacher's sermons. I heard the devil in it for sure, and I knew his pointy tail was swishing somewhere under his long coat.

"Didn't we cross paths a few days ago?" he persisted. "Now, just where was that?"

Still squinting into the sun, I lied. "I don't know. Sir." Growing frantic, I pulled my eyes away and searched the street. *Where* was the doctor? Maybe I was gonna have to leave Jeremiah.

"Hmm." I heard a gurgling sound above me, then smacking lips. "Ahh! A very nice morning indeed."

A few buildings up the street a door opened, and a man came striding toward us with evident purpose. He was trailed closely by another man. I sure hoped one of 'em was the doctor. My heart sank as they both walked straight up to me. "You the Pony rider?" the first man asked.

The sun was so bright I couldn't hardly see into his face. Something star-shaped glinted on the vest under his coat, so I knew he was the sheriff. "Yes, sir," I answered.

"He's hiding somethin'!" came the slurred voice from the railing above.

The sheriff looked up only briefly before taking to studying me hard. It was like he was trying to see right through my skin, and I stood stone still beneath his gaze and the sun's glare and felt my breath going in and outta my chest. I noticed that Jeremiah was peeking out from under his arm and watching the goings-on. A couple of other people stopped to watch and listen. "What's your name, boy?" the sheriff asked.

"Colton Wescott."

"That your horse over there?" He nodded toward Badger, waiting with the Pony Express's mochila—big as daylight—draped cross the saddle.

"Yes, sir."

"I got a telegram here from Carson City saying you stole the Pony mail."

"Sportsman's Hall!" the slave chaser called out. "That's where it was. He was real friendly with a colored boy there. I betcha they cooked up the plot together."

"Maybe they killed the real Pony rider," somebody said.

The sheriff held up his hand for quiet. "This telegram says I'm to hold you over till the mochila can be inspected and the mail accounted for."

"If'n he stole it, let's hang 'im!" a man shouted. "One less thief in California'll only improve the population."

My blood was pounding in my ears. Suddenly I couldn't swallow. It was like the noose was already tightening round my neck.

Jeremiah let out a grievous moan, and all the faces in the swelling crowd swung toward him. With one feeble hand he motioned for the sheriff to come over. The man seemed uncertain, but with a warning look to me to stay put, he bent over Jeremiah.

Quick as a cat the old miner grabbed the sheriff's collar with one hand. From under his coat he pulled a long-barreled revolver and buried the metal in the man's belly. The sheriff got a bulging-eyed expression on his face and I saw his arms stiffen, but he didn't resist. "Hold steady," Jeremiah said. "Everyone just hold steady. 'Cause if anyone moves, anyone at all, my finger's liable to slip." He glanced at me, once, real quick. "Run," he said.

And I did. Beneath that blinding white sun I bolted through the crowd, unlashed Badger's reins, and jumped into the saddle. I drummed his sides for all I was worth, and in a grunting leap we were running away from the sheriff and the noose and the crowd and the man behind the desk and the NO COLOREDS sign and the church and the song, "Just as I am, Lord, take me just as I am." In a dozen more leaps we were round the bend and outta sight, galloping through the thick brush and scrubby pines that lined the road toward Sacramento. For the time being we were safe. We could keep running.

And I pulled Badger to a stop.

My heart was pounding and my head was spinning, and Lordy, how I wanted to keep galloping. But I saw that if I ran now, I'd spend my whole life running. I didn't want to do that. It wasn't human.

Badger shook his head and chomped the bit and pranced. *Which way?* he was asking.

That muddy spot on the trail got all churned up as I reined him first one way and then the other, trying to think what I should do. I had two important pieces of mail to deliver. I had to get 'em to Sacramento. And . . . I had to get myself safely back to Chinatown. I'd promised Althea and Jewel that.

Badger whinnied: *Which way?*

I looked down the sun-speckled path through the chaparral. All my promises pointed that way. But, taking a deep breath, I spun Badger round and I squirted him back toward Hangtown.

Jeremiah was still lying on his travvy. His long-barreled gun had been wrestled away and was pointing hard at his nose now. The people all looked surprised to see me. Heck, I was surprised to see me there.

I rode Badger right up to the sheriff. "I'm not running," I said. My throat was so dry the words came out in a choked whisper. I said 'em again, louder. "I'm not running. Not anymore." I said it to Jeremiah. And I said it to the slave chaser. And I said it to the sheriff. And I said it to myself.

The sheriff lifted the gun away from Jeremiah and pointed it straight at me. My heart tried to come through my shirt. Leveling my gaze at him, I swallowed. If he was gonna kill me, then amen. Someone else would have to deliver the letters. But I wasn't spending the rest of my life running. I wasn't gonna be a slave to fear. "I *am* Colton Wescott," I said. "And I *am* a rider for the Pony Express." My voice cracked. Inside I was praying for the bullet and not the noose. The bullet would be quicker.

"I'm delivering an important letter to Sacramento," I went on. "I didn't steal it. The other rider didn't want to ride into the storm, so I did. The letter's 'bout a plot to blow up forts and steal ammunition, and it's trying to stop that. That's all I know." I caught my breath. "Soon as I deliver it into the safety of the Pony Express office in Sacramento, I plan on delivering a personal letter from my mother to her sister, also in Sacramento. I've made those promises and I intend to keep 'em."

I stared into the round black eye of the gun and, just above it, into the two narrowed eyes of the sheriff. Swallowing again, and with my hands shaking so hard they rattled the bit, I reined Badger round.

I waited for the bullet to tear into my back. It didn't. Nudging Badger's sides, I urged him into a trot. The crowd parted. Still no bullet. I kicked his sides and Badger started galloping. In seconds we were outta town again and flying down the road. Faster and faster we went, the reds and yellows of the brush blurring as we sped past. I let out a holler 'cause it seemed we were flying up through the sky. Maybe I *had* been shot in the back and we were dead, 'cause I felt light as an angel, freer'n I'd ever felt before. I didn't have to run anymore, and was that ever a breath of fresh air. It was like I'd delivered a letter of freedom, a letter of freedom to myself.

CHAPTER THIRTY-ONE

We kept galloping so blazingly fast the frozen snow beneath Badger's hooves probably melted away to nothing behind us. That was fine with me. After all the waiting with Jeremiah, it was like springtime to be moving again. I put my mind to finishing the job I'd started.

I knew we still had a few more hours to Sacramento—'bout five, I figured, if we made good time. That was gonna be hard to do 'cause the road still had some hills to it and Badger was getting awful tired. He was doing his best, giving me all he had, but his breath was coming in labored chugs. He sounded like a locomotive straining to move a load that was just too heavy. Before the road leveled, his hoofbeats slowed and his breathing climbed a pitch. It took on a raw, wounded sound, one that ended in a plaintive whistle over and over again.

"Come on, boy," I urged. "You can make it." Halfheartedly I shook the reins at him. He dug down for some more speed, wheezing harder. I'd heard the term *broken-winded* used round liveries and wondered if that's what was happening to him. Could a horse die from that? I didn't remember. Holding on to the saddle horn, I leaned way over to look into his face. His brown eyes were dark with determination. But his mouth was gaping, and foam was falling away from it in bubbly gobs. Was that blood tingeing it red? I pictured Badger busting a hole in his windpipe and collapsing like he'd been shot, and just as I did that he stumbled. My heart got left in the air.

"Whoa, there," I said, easing him up. He shook his head and fought the bit. I hauled on the reins. "*Whoa.*" He humped his back and stiffened his neck and fell to a trot—gradually— but he wouldn't stop. Like the horizon was his magnet, he kept surging toward it. His gait became rambly and slack jointed, but he still covered ground. I didn't know what to do. I near chewed my lip off wondering whether I should stop him or let him choose his own speed and hope we made it.

With Badger's ragged breathing ripping right through me, I gave in and loosed the reins. I knew there'd be more Pony Express stations between Placerville and Sacramento. I could sure use a fresh horse, but I didn't want to risk stopping—who knew how many more telegrams Mr. Roberts had sent out?—and Badger did seem unwilling to call it quits.

Bracing one hand on the saddle horn, I stood in the stirrups. Even though the seat rose up to slap me in the backside, I stayed there. Maybe it'd ease his load a little.

The minutes and quarter hours and hours trickled by, and the land flattened. The air warmed. Great expanses of golden-colored grasses shimmered under the afternoon sun. It would've been a pretty sight, 'cept the odor of horse sweat clung to us like a swamp fog. Most days the sweat of a horse was a clean, sweet smell. But Badger's was full-out sickly. It smelled of overuse and cramped muscles and sunburnt hide and blood. It smelled of dying. I tried to lift myself outta the saddle some more.

The sun shone brighter than ever, but we traveled in a rapidly darkening nightmare. Badger's sides heaved in and out so strenuously that I knew he wasn't getting enough air, and I'd pretty much decided we weren't gonna make it, at least as a team. I was even trying to choose a nice tree to leave him under while I walked the rest of the way in. So when a sprawling city that could've been Sacramento finally showed itself on the horizon, I figured it was my imagination. I looked away, down at his black mane, then up again. Wiping the tears outta my eyes, I blinked. Yep, it was still there and it had to be Sacramento. We'd made it! We'd actually, matter-of-fact made it! I slapped Badger on the neck. "We did it!" I yelled loud enough for 'em to hear us coming. "You did it!" And I slapped that tough ol' horse on the neck again and again and again.

In no time at all then, we were stumbling through the bustling city, both of us panting, me looking left and right for the Pony Express office. I figured we'd find it on one of the main streets, and sure enough, that's where it was, at the corner of J and Second. Weighted down with tiredness but floating on joy, I climbed off Badger for the last time. I tugged the mochila after me and staggered into the office.

The man behind the desk looked up. A storm of expressions raced across his face—surprise first, then hesitance, followed by wonderment, and maybe some anger—so I knew he'd already heard 'bout me. He probably had the telegram in front of him.

I introduced myself anyway. "I'm Colton Wescott," I said, flopping the mochila onto his desk and trying to keep from laughing out loud at his thunderstruck expression. I was feeling mighty full of myself and all I'd done. "The Pony rider outta Carson. And you don't have to send for the sheriff, 'cause the mail's all here, safe and sound. I've delivered it, just like I told Mr. Roberts I would. You can wire him and tell him so."

The man still eyed me like I was some kinda criminal. I smothered another laugh. It didn't matter anymore what he thought, or what anyone thought. I knew who I was, what I could do. And I'd done good. Can't arrest a person for that.

"There's a letter from Washington in there," I told him, "an urgent one that needs to get delivered right away."

That sent him scrambling. While he dug for his key to the mochila, I glanced round the office and out the window. Badger waited stiff legged, his head drooped past his knees. I couldn't rest yet. "Can you point me toward the stables?" I asked. "I need to bed down my horse. He's had a long go of it."

The man looked round behind him, like he needed to ask someone's permission to tell me where the Pony Express stables were. But the other two desks were empty. Clearing his throat, he waggled his finger at the bustling intersection. "Rightmire's, over on K," is all he managed to get out.

I nodded. "Thank you. And just one more thing. Could you tell me how I might go 'bout finding a Luzenia Tullis?" That was the name written on Ma's envelope.

He shook his head and shrugged, looking fearful, like I might pull a gun on him. "You could try the *Daily Union*," he near squeaked. When he searched over his shoulder again, the wicked part of me rose up and made me tap the mochila.

"Don't forget," I warned in my deepest voice. "Important letter." And I returned to Badger.

There was no more climbing into the saddle. I'd done enough riding and he'd done enough carrying. Gathering up the reins and dodging the wagon traffic, I led Badger cross the muddy street, and we slogged our way past a few more buildings to the huge livery that stabled the Pony Express horses.

It was a good-size barn, cold inside, but quiet and clean smelling. Instantly I got a hankering to dive into one of the straw-filled stalls myself and just hibernate till next year. I was that tired. But I needed to take care of Badger.

A man who'd been cleaning stalls, a wide-shouldered man with coffee-colored skin and close-cropped white hair, set his fork down and hurried over. 'Cept he walked right past me to Badger.

Taking hold of the bridle, he looked into the horse's eyes and crooned, "Well, well, now. You've been rode pretty hard, haven't you?"

I sidled closer, patting Badger on the neck. "He sure has. We just rode all the way from Carson City. Actually, we rode from Chinatown, other side of Carson."

The man looked at me with the same wide-eyed expression as the man in the Pony Express office. "But it blizzarded last night in the mountains, or so I heard. When did you head out?"

My mouth opened. And closed. When *had* I started out? Seemed like I'd been in the saddle for days. But as I started to think back I surprised even myself by saying, "Yesterday morning."

"Yesterday morning! Why, that's more'n a hundred miles!

Well over a hundred miles! What's so blessed important you gotta wear a poor horse down to his belly by goin' more'n a hundred miles in only a day?"

"Being free," I answered, thinking that had a nice sound to it. And I started pumping out the news along with my excitement. "There's some people that want to blow up the forts round here and steal a lot of ammunition to help the South so they'll win the war if it comes to that. And they're planning to kill Mr. Abraham Lincoln, too, if he's elected president. But Badger and I, we just delivered a letter in record time that'll put a stop to that. And when he gets elected—Mr. Lincoln, that is—he's gonna free all the slaves. Everyone'll be free." I was giddy with light-headedness.

The man smiled from ear to ear. "You don't say! And this horse done that?"

I nodded and slapped Badger's neck again. "Yep. And he saved my life and together we saved another man's life and . . . and well . . ." I was stammering with fatigue and emotion and a choking helping of pride.

"Well enough," he said, taking the reins. "You just come along with me. I got a special stall for special horses. What did you say his name was?"

"Badger," I answered.

"Badger, huh? Well, he's tough as a badger, I can see that. Riding more'n a hundred miles in a day!" The man led the exhausted black horse deeper into the livery, past the rows of narrow tie stalls displaying the varied rumps of other horses and mules, and down to the end, where there were a couple of large box stalls. After unfastening the rope to an empty one, he led him in, explaining over his shoulder, "Man who keeps his horse here is outta town for a few days on business. I guarantee he won't mind letting it out to a horse like Badger."

He quickly removed the saddle and bridle, and turned Badger loose in fluffy yellow straw so deep it rose past the horse's knees. We watched as he nosed round and through it, then buckled his legs and collapsed. I expected him to roll once or twice, scratching his back, then get up; but he just lay there, real still of a sudden. Too still. We were both tired, I knew, but the way his lips were drawn back and his teeth were showing gave me the allovers. Suddenly all the joy went outta the afternoon. I looked at the man and he looked at me, and we hurried in to kneel on each side of the gelding.

I laid my hand on his neck. His thick fur was wet and matted with cold sweat, and he was still breathing hard—too hard for lying down.

"I'll get some rags," the livery man said, and almost before he could finish saying it, he was back at my side with an armful. We set to rubbing the horse all over, trying to stir some warmth and life back into him. Badger didn't move. He just lay stretched out full, with his eyes closed and his nostrils fluttering. When he took a deep breath and blew out a long, whistling groan—now, that was the oddest thing, and maybe it was 'cause I was so flat-out exhausted myself that I wasn't thinking straight—all at once it was *me* stretched out on the ground, knocked flat by my father's gun and groaning. A crushing sense of loss came back fresh as ever, and all of a sudden I couldn't bear to lose this horse. I couldn't shoulder another loss. Rubbing harder and harder, I whispered encouragement in his ear.

"What he needs is a hot bran mash," the man said. "That'll fix him up good." And he left to make one.

I sat back on my heels and stared at the rough-hewn black body. Mud from a hundred miles was caked in his feet, pine needles from rescuing Jeremiah were still caught up in his tail, a hairless half-moon showed on his neck where he'd picked a fight with the chestnut horse way back in Genoa— all 'cause he wanted to be the one to go first. He was some kinda horse. I saw that now more'n I ever had.

It wasn't supposed to turn out this way. I was supposed to ride to Sacramento, deliver the mochila and Ma's letter, and ride home. On Badger. I couldn't go home without him. Not now. He'd saved my life. He was the reason I'd made it at all.

"Badger," I scolded, doing my darnedest not to cry. "You'd better not die on me."

He flicked an ear and let out a long, rattly breath. I held mine, waiting to hear him inhale. Nothing.

"Come on," I begged. "You're too tough to die."

There was no response. I couldn't take watching him go. Scrambling to my feet, I lunged under the rope. I felt like I was gonna be sick, and sucked in the cold air in big gulps, trying to steady myself. Angrily I kicked at the stall's wooden planks over and over. This couldn't be happening; it just couldn't.

I was so crazy full of fury that I stomped back into Badger's stall and ordered him to get up. "You can't die," I said, standing over his wet black body. "You just can't . . . because I need you." Tears blurred his motionless outline and I shakily sank into the straw, hugging his neck. "I need you, Badger. Please get up. Please."

He was still breathing; I could feel it under my own chest. The breaths were shallow, but they were coming quicker, like he was trying to gather himself. Sure enough, after a couple more he stirred. He folded one knee under himself and waited.

I gave him some room. "Come on, Badger," I pleaded.

He took a few more breaths. Grunting, and with an all-out effort, he lurched upright, so that he was resting on his belly. He looked beat. He turned his head toward me, those little brown eyes of his burning with fire, and managed a nicker. Clear as day it said, *You do need me.*

I threw my arms round his neck again. Burying my face in his mane, I whispered, "Thank you. Thank you, you ornery ol' horse. I don't know what I'd do without you, so don't you ever, ever leave me."

The livery man returned with a steaming bucket. When he saw Badger resting upright, he faltered a step, shook as if he'd seen a ghost.

"Tough as a badger," I said proudly.

"Well, I'll be," is all he could say, again and again. "Well, I'll be." He set the bucket under Badger's nose. After first startling at the warm vapor, the horse began licking up the mash. "He'll be all right now," the man said. "He's just done in. I'll look after him. You better go on over to the hotel and rest yourself."

I rose stiffly, swaying on my feet. The ride was catching up to me. "Got one more thing to do first."

"Just one, huh?" The man looked weary, like he had a whole pile of things always waiting on him. "Well, you can be thankful for that."

I smiled. "Yes, I can." Nodding toward Badger, I said, "Promise to take good care of him? I'll be back soon as I can."

"You can bet on it."

As I walked outta the livery, more tired than I'd ever been in my life and just as relieved, I counted out my thanks. I was thankful that Badger and I were both still breathing. He'd survived the hard journey and I'd come through it without being frozen to death . . . or shot . . . or hung. I was thankful I'd made it to Sacramento at all; but what was even better was I'd made it ahead of the slave chaser. I didn't have to worry 'bout him finding Ma's sister before I did. And I was thankful I was gonna be the one to deliver her freedom papers to her.

CHAPTER THIRTY-TWO

The *Sacramento Daily Union* newspaper was housed in a building on the main street, just blocks from the Pony Express office. As I opened its varnished door and stepped into the small entry, I was near knocked over by ink fumes. The noxious cloud was drifting from a larger room behind, where men seated in rows of desks were setting pages of type. At the counter in front of me a man in a vest and rolled shirtsleeves looked up from his work. "Yes?" he asked quickly.

"Do you know where I could find a woman named Luzenia Tullis?"

He scratched his head. "Miss or Mrs.?"

I shrugged. "I'm not sure."

He hollered into the back room. "Anyone heard of a Luzenia Tullis, marital status unknown?" The name jumped from desk to desk. After it'd made the rounds, the general agreement was that while no one knew of a Luzenia Tullis, there was a woman named Lucille living over on Montgomery Street, and a colored woman named Luzie, or some such, living over on Alder Street. I was pointed in two different directions and nodded my thanks.

Assuming the second woman was more likely to be Ma's sister, I headed toward Alder Street. That sent me downhill toward the river. The closer I got, the danker and colder the air became. The buildings aged too. They were mostly made of wood here, unlike the fancier brick and stone buildings facing Sacramento's main streets. As I turned onto Alder I saw right off that this was the area of town where most of the colored people lived. Dozens of faces like Ma's paused to look at me—this one holding a baby, that one sweeping a porch, another one pinning up laundry—and I got a salty-sweet pang. Salty 'cause I missed Ma and my sisters something awful; but sweet, too, 'cause these were my people. I hadn't seen so many welcome-looking faces since we'd left Missouri.

Only thing was, while their faces looked the same as family to me, I got the feeling that mine was drawing attention. It took a few steps before I remembered how easily I'd been passing as white. Huh. I shook my head and smiled. Here I'd been trying to hide the colored part of me for weeks, and now I was feeling like I needed to prove it. The world sure was funny.

Curious though they were, people were friendly enough. When I stopped to ask a man standing beside a shoe display if he'd heard of Luzenia Tullis, he bent an ear and pondered my question. Nodding agreeably, he pointed toward a door at the top of a stairway attached to the side of a building. I trotted cross the street and started climbing.

By then I was tired through to the bone, but it was like my feet had springs in 'em. My heart kicked up and the envelope shifted against my skin, like it, too, knew the moment was near. In seconds I was gonna hand Ma's sister her legal freedom. She wouldn't have to run and hide anymore. I took the last two stairs in one leap.

Taking a deep breath and trying to calm my heart, I knocked.

No one came to open the door. There was no sound inside at all. Oh, no. Ma's sister was already dead or captured or she'd run off again. Or maybe the man below was wrong.

I knocked louder. This time I heard shuffling footsteps. The door opened a crack. "Yes?"

The woman didn't look anything like Ma, which surprised me. She was darker skinned and a full head taller. She was edgier, too, with that same kinda nervous manner I'd seen in the miners round Sportsman's Hall. I guess that's what happened to people when they got treated bad as a matter of habit.

"Are you Miss Luzenia Tullis?"

I thought for a second she was gonna pull back and close the door. She looked that worried. But then she nodded hesitantly.

"I'm Colton Wescott," I said, talking soft, like I would to a skittish horse. "My ma's your sister." I expected her to light up with joy or squeal with surprise, but nothing on her face changed. I pulled the envelope outta my shirt and handed it to her. "She sent me to give you this." Serious as a preacher, she took it and studied the writing on the outside. Still nothing changed on her face.

It was like she didn't understand me. Or couldn't read her own name. "There's a paper inside that says you're free,"

I explained. "It's all legal. My ma—your sister—bought your freedom. You don't have to hide anymore." At that she glanced up, quick as a bird, and shot me a look that warned me not to be funning her. Lordy, didn't I know that one. "It's true," I insisted. "I can read it for you, or you can have someone else read it for you. But the fact is, you're free."

She stopped looking so scared then. She sorta smiled, then snuffed it out, not wanting to risk disappointment, I suppose. Her hands were fairly shaking. Holding the envelope close to her bosom, she opened the door wider and motioned for me to come in.

It was a tiny room, dark with no window. On the floor was a mattress and a couple of blankets pulled smooth. A shelf was nailed to the wall. There were two stools and an upside-down crate that served for a table. She motioned for me to sit.

"You're my sister's boy?"

She had a rich, smooth voice, sweet as molasses, and I warmed to her right off. Nodding, I answered, "She and my two sisters are staying in Chinatown right now, over the mountains. Ma's been sick ever since her baby died—we named him Willie—but now she's getting better."

"Where's your pa?"

I looked at my feet, feeling my face flush hot with shame. "I don't know. He just took off one morning, after . . . after an accident."

She reached out and laid her hand on my knee, and I 'most crawled into her arms like I was some little kid needing a hug. It was just 'cause I was so tired, I told myself. And I straightened my back to sit tall.

She carefully opened the envelope, then pulled out and unfolded the heavy sheet of paper. She looked at it with wonderment, and that smile crept back and spread across her whole face like sunrise. "Will you read it for me?"

"Sure." I took the paper and began from the very top. There were some *hear ye*s and *know that*s and a complete physical description of the woman sitting across from me before I got to the good part. "'Now, therefore,'" I continued, "'I, William Tiberius Brown, clerk of the Circuit Court of Washington County, State of Missouri, certify that said Luzenia Tullis is a free person of color and entitled to be respected accordingly, in person and property, at all times and places.'" It was dated and witnessed and signed, and stamped with a large, round seal.

I handed it back to her. She spread it flat on the crate, ironed it with her hands, and bent over it, studying where her name had been written in and just smiling the toothiest smile. "A free person of color," she repeated. "A *free* person." Looking up, she spoke full of awe. "And my sister done this for me? She paid for my freedom, then sent her own son all this way to deliver me this paper?" Shaking her head in disbelief, she said, "I don't know what to say other than thank you, though that hardly seems enough."

I returned her smile, happy for her, happy for me. "It's enough," I replied, and stood up.

"You're not going so soon? Why, we've only just met, and outside your ma and sisters, you're my only kin west of the Mississippi. There's so much I'd like to talk 'bout, so much more I'd like to know 'bout your ma."

"Well, right now there's a horse I gotta see to. But I could come back tomorrow maybe."

She nodded, pressing the paper to her heart. "That'd be fine."

"And besides," I told her, "Ma's aiming for all of us to move here to Sacramento. That's why we started west in the first place. I figure we can come soon as she's back on her feet and the snow's melted. Next spring probably."

She clapped her hands together. "Really? That *would* be fine! And won't that thought alone keep me warm all this winter."

Promising to return tomorrow, I walked down the stairs and back up the street. Without Ma's envelope stuck to my chest, I felt kinda lost. It'd been my compass, constantly needling me west. Now what was I gonna do with myself?

Thinking my future looked awful hazy, I hurried back to the stable. Badger, bless his heart, was still lying comfortable in his straw, his legs tucked under him. His coat was badly matted from the rubbing we'd given him—it looked like a roiling black river full of whirlpools—so I hunted up a brush and began smoothing him. Didn't take long before the brush got too heavy and the stall got too warm and I allowed myself to collapse in the straw, one arm thrown over his neck. Together we slept like a couple of hibernating bears.

I didn't know when it was that a hand clapped hold of my shoulder and shook it. An excited voice shouted in my ear. "Say, whaddya doing here in a horse stall? Come on over to the hotel and get yourself a real bed. You're a hero tonight."

CHAPTER THIRTY-THREE

It was a full month and a half later—mid November—before I was riding homeward. I'd had to wait for a series of storms to blow through and for a track to be cleared through the mountains, and after that I'd had to wait for Badger to get well enough to climb 'em. There was never any question of me leaving him behind. After all, he hadn't left me.

I spent part of my waiting time getting to know Ma's sister, my aunt. She was so tickled to have blood kin in Sacramento she wouldn't hardly let me outta her sight, or so it seemed. Instead of cards she kept a set of wood playing pieces called dominoes for entertainment. We'd spread 'em out on the floor 'most every evening, and she showed me how to play games like Chicken Foot and Black Train Coming and Four Down. As we took turns adding dominoes onto the chain, she pulled from me every last story 'bout my family, piecing together her own chain of understanding. When the last domino was laid down, or when her husband was due home, she'd walk me ever so slowly to the corner of Alder, clutching my hand tight as if I was her own son, and make me promise to return the following day. There was a hunger in her eyes such that I wasn't sure any one person could ever fill, but I did my best to visit with her evenings, after my work in the stables was finished.

That's what I did with the rest of my waiting time: worked in Rightmire's Stables. There wasn't as pressing a need for riders on this end of the Pony Express route, I learned. A steamboat took the mail westward to San Francisco, and sometimes, even, the eastbound mail was sent out by train a ways before a Pony rider slapped the mochila over his saddle and headed into the Sierra Nevada. I didn't officially have a job as a rider anyway, so I was grateful for the position of stable boy, though it paid only a quarter of the wages I'd been making.

Now as Badger and I steadily made our way up the steep grade toward Sportsman's Hall, slicing through bands of frosty sun and damp shadow, I was thinking 'bout those meager wages. They certainly wouldn't go far in paying for Ma's care. I'd have to find another job as soon as I got to Chinatown—'less I could convince Mr. Roberts to hire me back. I pictured his flinty blue eyes shooting sparks, and it wasn't the cold that made me shiver then.

At least I'd done what I'd promised: I'd delivered the mail through the storm. And I'd made certain that he knew it. Come that first Monday morning after I rode into Sacramento, I'd hurried back down the street to the Pony Express office. I'd remembered it shared space with a couple of different telegraph companies, and I'd figured one of 'em had a wire run to Carson City.

A different man was sitting behind the front desk. He

had a neatly trimmed mustache and gold spectacles, and smelled faintly of peppermint. When I started to introduce myself, he near sprang over his desk to shake my hand, which certainly took me by surprise. "What can I do for you, Mr. Wescott?" he asked, and I began to explain how I'd come to carry the mochila outta Carson City. He stopped me. "I know all about that, and Mr. Roberts has been notified that the mail was delivered safely. No one on this end is going to arrest you." I was still of the belief that word needed to come from me, too, so he helped me write out a telegram. That belief proved expensive: cost me two whole dollars to send only ten words to Mr. Roberts. The wire read, "MAIL DELIVERED PLEASE TELL MA IN CHINATOWN AM OK COLTON."

After I handed over my money, I asked 'bout sending a second wire. Only, this one required more of his assistance. I explained how Jeremiah had helped me keep the mail moving through Hangtown—er, Placerville—and I offered to pay for another dispatch to the sheriff there, if only he would write it. So the message that was tapped out was: "W HOLMSBY SACRAMENTO MGR AUTHORIZES YOU TO FREE JEREMIAH MCGAHEE." I hoped that was enough to point the gun away from Jeremiah.

But that wasn't all the communicating I'd done. Remembering how Jeremiah had wished he could get some mail, I bought some writing paper and a fancy envelope with a colorful picture of Sacramento painted on it, and hunkered down in Badger's stall to write him a letter. In it I assured him that Badger and I had made it to Sacramento safely, and I thanked him for his "assistance." I asked him 'bout his cat and if he'd got his broken leg set straight, and just before signing my name, I wrote, "You were right." I addressed it to him care of Placerville and sent it by Wells Fargo and Company's overland stage. So if he'd received it, he knew my secret.

An hour ago, though, when I'd ridden through Placerville, I hadn't seen hide nor hair of him. That wicked noose was still hanging stiff and empty from its oak tree, so I didn't want to linger long. I'd reined Badger over to ask a man hauling lumber if he knew anything 'bout the cranky old miner. He thought he remembered seeing him last month in the mercantile—several times, in fact—resting his splinted leg on a barrel and talking with some of the other men. Always had a cat on his lap, as he recalled. He didn't know more'n that, so I tipped my hat and rode on. Those three'd do just fine wherever they settled, I was thinking. Yes, Jeremiah and his cat and his mule would do just fine.

A pair of horses were coming down the slope above us, picking their way real slow 'cause it was icy in patches. The two riders, with hats pulled down past their ears, were bundled to a bearlike bulk. Only when we were carefully edging past each other did I realize it was more'n two riders; it was a whole family. The father, I saw, was riding the first horse, carefully balancing his young son on the saddle in front of him. The mother and a daughter, it looked like, were wrapped in the same shawl and sharing the second horse. The sight of 'em made me miss my own family all the more, and I had to swallow hard to keep that lump in my throat from choking me. I sure did hope that Ma had got news of my whereabouts.

After I'd sent those two telegrams from Sacramento,

I'd got to thinking 'bout Mr. Roberts. I figured there was a good chance he was still so angry with me that he might just wad up my telegram and toss it in the wastebasket. So I bought some writing paper and an envelope for Ma, too, and neatly printed a letter telling her I was okay and promising to make my way home as soon as I could. It'd gone off by overland stage too, but with all the storms there was no telling how many days had passed before it was delivered. *If* it had been delivered. Accidents were always occurring with the mail. Meanwhile, she would've been worrying herself sicker than she already was. I nudged Badger's sides to hurry him along. He lifted his shoulders and lengthened his steps.

I wasn't pushing him much this trip. He seemed fit enough, eager as I was to get home, but he was too special to me to risk damaging. So we were walking and trotting mostly. I was even planning on spending the night at Sportsman's Hall and traveling on the next day, weather permitting. That'd give him a good rest and me a chance to talk to Newt.

I'd tried writing a letter to him, too—which would've been more letters in one day than I'd ever written in my life. I'd even addressed the envelope: "Newt Perkins, care of Sportsman's Hall." Only, the sheet of paper stayed blank. I couldn't get the words to come. I just stared at it and stared at it, feeling the shame all over again of betraying him, and hating myself for my cowardice. I chewed on a stalk of straw and combed Badger's mane and paced up and down outside his stall, and still I couldn't find the words. In the end I'd just pocketed the empty envelope till I could make my apologies in person.

That *till* was coming up soon, 'cause I could smell steaks

frying and a wood fire burning and lye boiling, so it had to be Sportsman's Hall ahead. It'd been a long time since breakfast, and my stomach gurgled a hearty hello when we trotted into the yard. First things first, though. I had to see to Badger, and I had to apologize to Newt—and tell him the good news, if he hadn't already heard it.

It was just two days ago now that I'd heard Mr. Lincoln had been elected president, just as Aunt Charlotte had prophesied. And it was Pony Express riders that had galloped the news from back in the States all the way cross the territory and delivered it to the telegraph in Carson City in only six days. Six days! People were calling 'em heroes. Even the *Daily Union* claimed it was the Pony Express alone that was keeping the nation together, though talk of war was threatening to tear it apart. I wished I could've been a part of that ride. Guess I had to be satisfied with the small role Badger and I'd played in keeping ammunition outta the hands of the war-bent Southern states, and Mr. Lincoln—I mean, President Lincoln—alive.

The yard in front of Sportsman's Hall was churned to a muddy mess. There were pack mules and saddle horses by the dozen, and even a beat-up old sleigh hitched to a shaggy pony. I bypassed 'em all to head down the slippery path to the stable.

Newt recognized me right off. Looking pointedly at my empty saddle, he asked, "What're you doing here?"

"Passing through on my way home."

"You quit, didn't you?" There was more'n a little smugness in his voice. "'Cause I see they keep putting new riders on this route—two in the last month alone. Nobody lasts. Told you the same."

I hid a smile. I could brag to him 'bout how I'd "lasted" on my all-out ride through the blizzard. Only, I hadn't done it for the glory. Shrugging instead, I explained, "My horse got sick, so we've been holing up in Sacramento awhile. We're both better now."

Giving me kind of a funny look, he reached for Badger's reins. "You staying the night?" He nodded toward Sportsman's Hall.

"If I can afford it. Don't have the Pony Express paying my way now."

"Well, you want me to give him oats, then, or just straw?"

"Oats," I answered quick, "the best you got. And give him a whole can. I'll go without eating if I have to, but he gets fed."

Looking at me like I'd lost my mind, Newt led Badger down the aisle. I followed, watching him unsaddle and unbridle him. He measured out a heaping can of oats and held it up for my approval before spilling it in front of Badger.

I couldn't put it off any longer. "Say," I began, glancing round uncomfortably and feeling my face grow hot, "last time I was here . . . well, there was that slave chaser, remember? The man with the big ears?"

He froze, like he was waiting to be struck.

This was awful. "And well, he made me say some things, or at least nod to 'em, that . . . that I wish I hadn't. I'm sorry."

"What're you sorry for?" He was simmering with anger. "What's it matter to you what anyone says to me?"

"It wasn't right. And it wasn't true."

"That don't mean a thing."

"I'm still sorry."

He shrugged. From cross a chasm he stared at me. Those words back then had been hurtful enough to put that chasm between us, and there was no crossing over it now.

Leaving the election news unsaid, I slogged up the hill and into the dining hall and made my way to the very same table by the window where I'd sat before. I sat up straight and looked round the room. No one stared, no one whispered. Had I changed that much—or not changed at all? Had I been foolish to run and hide in the first place?

I did have enough money in my pocket to sleep in a real bed, and I rode on the next morning rested, yet sobered and thoughtful. Even had enough to spend a second night at one of the small hostelries that served as a Pony Express relay station. Without the mochila, I wasn't recognized as anything other'n a youthful traveler and was fed moderately well. That was the very last of my money, though, so I was happy when Badger and I finally descended onto the flatlands of Carson Valley. Both of us were so eager to get home that we even galloped a ways. We sped right through Genoa—I didn't see Aunt Charlotte, though I expected I would again—and by the middle of that afternoon we were back in Carson City.

The streets were bustling as usual with wagons and horses and people and mules. As Badger meandered through the traffic I spotted Mr. Roberts in his office, bent over his papers. I wanted to stop; I wanted to explain things to him face-to-face, but I was worried, even after all these weeks, that he might still have me arrested—or worse. Right when I was thinking that, of course, he looked up and saw me. Swallowing hard, I got off Badger and walked into the office.

The air inside was brittle as tinder. You wouldn't have wanted to strike a match. Crossing his arms, Mr. Roberts, division superintendent, leaned back in his chair and aimed those hard blue eyes of his like a gun. He waited for me to speak first.

My tongue got thick. My mind scrambled. "I delivered that mail," is all I could come up with.

"I received the telegrams," he replied. "And I heard later that you almost got yourself killed doing it."

His eyes were shooting bullets. I turned to go.

"Think you can ride out again Saturday?"

"This Saturday?"

"Yes, this Saturday."

"I . . . I can have my job back?"

"Colton Wescott, I've gone through two riders since you run off with the mail. Neither lasted. The second one quit on me yesterday. Said it was harder than he'd counted on, the Nellie. While I still say you're too young, at least you get the mail through. Now"—he looked out the window—"what do you want for that horse of yours?"

I followed his gaze. I was fair to busting with having my job back, so I certainly didn't want to make him mad, but I wasn't selling Badger. Not for any amount of money. "Sir, he's not for sale."

"The company's offering two hundred dollars. That's four times the price of an average horse."

I shook my head. "I realize that, sir, and thank you. But no."

He leaned his weight onto his desk. "Don't you want to ride for the Pony Express?"

My heart thudded to a stop. He was gonna take the job away. Fast as he'd given it, he was gonna take it away. "Yes, sir, I do. Really."

"And don't you want to keep riding him?" He nodded toward Badger.

"Yes, but I can't sell him. Couldn't I have my job back and keep riding him without selling him?"

"It's not done that way," he grumbled. He shuffled some papers and closed his ledger and looked through a drawer, and I stood there cooling my heels, wondering if I should be leaving. "How about if the COC & PP leases the horse from you?" he said of a sudden. "We could stable him in our barn, feed him like he was ours, and pay you something on top of that for his use. How does that sound?"

"Sounds royal," I agreed. "To both of us."

"There's just one more thing."

Was that a smile tugging at his mouth?

"Could you tie him up in front of somebody else's office from now on? It pains me to look at the pitiful creature." He pressed his lips together hard, like he was serious, but his eyes were laughing.

"Well," I answered, feeling bold, "I reckon you won't have to look at him, 'cause we'll be galloping by so fast all you'll see is black lightning."

He let out a laugh and handed me some advance money and told me to take my room in the hotel by Friday night. I promised I would and walked outta his office on air.

My heart was pounding with excitement as we rode outta Carson. I had my job back and I was gonna be riding Badger, and now I was so close to seeing Ma.

The air was cool and misty, and as we were coming up on Chinatown, Badger and I found ourselves wading through a pogonip, a sorta icy fog that filled the air with sparkling white. Here and there sunlight glinted through the cloud, setting fire to the ice crystals, so that silent explosions of orange and red and blue surrounded us. Everything was muffled. You couldn't even hear Badger's hooves touch the ground. It was so quiet it was like we were the only two creatures in the world. The colors came and went. The damp air washed over us and through us. But we were unchanged. We were still blood and bone and heart and muscle, and it didn't matter what the world saw when it looked at us. Long as we knew who we were and what we could do.

Somewhere ahead a horse heard us coming and whinnied. It sounded like Ned, and my heart jumped instinctively, as it always did. I was still scanning faces in every town I passed through, looking for Pa. Didn't know as I'd ever stop. I did know now there were a lot of things could make a man run, and I'd forgiven him. Every night I asked God to watch over my pa if he's still on this earth.

Riding up behind the doctor's office, I let myself outta the saddle. Badger begged for his head to be scratched, and while I was doing that, Lucky came wiggling and whining and beating me round the shins with his welcome.

Stepping inside the back door, I happened upon a newspaper left folded on the stair. A small heading caught my eye: SLAVERY IS A MUST FOR THE ECONOMY. I didn't read on. Didn't have to 'cause I was pretty certain this was all gonna end in a war. My small part in freeing people was nothing compared with what others were gonna have to do.

It did seem like strange times we were living in. People were getting ready to kill one another so they could go on holding whips over one another. As I climbed the stairs I remembered Aunt Charlotte saying we were all more alike than different. I wanted to believe her. But then I'd read something like that and I'd think God must be funning us.

There was one thing I believed in, though. And that was, looking at just the outside of a man is no way to measure his inside. Oh, and one other thing. You can't run from who you are.

Turning the handle, I opened the door. "I'm home."

"In the years before the Civil War, the Pony Express held the nation together."

When I came across those words, I knew I had the foundation of a story. Teenage riders, on the fastest horses available, had held a nation together by galloping important news between the East and the West. Most importantly, I soon learned, they had helped keep the wealthy state of California—which at the time had pro-South leanings—aligned with the Union.

As I read the diaries of pioneers, I realized that many people had headed to California to begin new lives, even to forge new identities. But California was no utopia. For blacks it was a free state in name only. Slave owners could bring slaves into the state; the free blacks living there had no legal rights, even to defend themselves in court; and almost any black person could be accused of being a runaway and reclaimed on the spot. Although the Pony Express route was nearly two thousand miles long, I knew then that my story had to take place along its western end, in the tempting but treacherous state of California.

I began my physical research by visiting the Pony Express Museum in St. Joseph, Missouri. Housed within the original stables, the museum gave me a chance to heft a mochila from one saddle to another, to sit inside a crudely built relay station, and to stare into the faces of those young riders who had risked their lives to deliver the mail across desolate territory. I learned that Bolivar Roberts had been the division superintendent for the westernmost part of the route and that his office was in Carson City, Nevada. That became my next stop.

In northern California I drove the historic Pony Express route from Sacramento across the Sierra Nevada to Carson City, Nevada (and slightly beyond, to Dayton), and back. The trail was steep and the scenery spectacular. By the time I'd logged more than three hundred miles, I'd experienced the trail much as the riders had. I'd been awed by the giant horseshoe high on the sheer mountain face ahead; I'd raced through endless shadowy forests, feeling their dampness chill my skin; I'd begun to anticipate the appearance of each successive relay station, or at least the marker dedicated to it. Whew.

Along the way I stopped at museums and bookstores, picking up details of life in the 1860s. I learned about Jack Slade, a man who tortured and killed as many as twenty-three men, and who reportedly cut off a man's ears and made a watch fob out of them. Gruesome, but too interesting to pass up, so I loosely modeled the slave chaser after him. I'd already decided that my main character was a mixed-race boy, even though I didn't know how mixed marriages were accepted at that time. I made a happy discovery at a museum in Carson City that inspired another character in my story. Rounding a corner, I came upon a temporary exhibit on black pioneers. One panel featured a black woman named Charlotte Barber (1825-1887), who had been married to a white man and lived in nearby Genoa, a Pony Express stop. Her obituary described her as "a rancher and a prophet" and went on to say that she "never let anyone pass through her door without interviewing them and learning from them."

In libraries and used bookstores I found journals and letters that provided such wonderful details as "The telegraph wires are attached to the trees." I learned that a miner "would steal a good kitten" if he could, and that nothing tasted better on a cold day than a cup of hot coffee "thick enough to float a horseshoe."

And then I set Colton Wescott loose. He is a boy with a foot in each of two worlds—the black and the white, the slave and the free, the East and the West. As he gallops back and forth, helping to hold the nation together, he is deciding for himself where he stands.